# Whispers of Dead Girls

"Haunting, propulsive, and chillingly atmospheric with claustrophobic small-town vibes, I was completely gripped by Marlee Bush's *Whispers of Dead Girls*, which I devoured in one sitting! Fans of Lisa Jewell and Mary Kubica will be OBSESSED with this riveting thriller that will keep you guessing, but trust me—you'll be wrong!"

—May Cobb, author of *The Hunting Wives*

"*Whispers of Dead Girls*, Marlee Bush's propulsive new thriller, forces readers to wonder if a damaged person can truly heal. In the case of Bush's exquisitely crafted protagonist, Ren Taylor, the jury is decidedly out…much to our pleasure. Ren is the most morally gray of all heroes, a characterization that not only rings true but allows us to see ourselves in her. Could we let our fractured pasts go, or would we forever chase absolution, only to realize that doing so serves only to keep us imprisoned? There is no clear answer, and there shouldn't be, but the chase itself makes for one hell of story. I devoured this powerful, gutsy book, and you will, too."

—Carter Wilson, *USA Today* bestselling
author of *Tell Me What You Did*

"A dark, twisted, and gripping thriller with a main character who is as complicated and compelling as any heroine you've ever wondered if you can really trust."

—Stacie Grey, author of *She Left*

"Emotions run deep in this tension-filled and expertly plotted thriller about grief, sisterhood, the hurts that won't heal, and the haunting memories we can't leave behind. *Whispers of Dead Girls* is a gripping exploration of damaged girls and the things that break them."

—Anne-Sophie Jouhanneau, author of *The French Honeymoon*

"Puzzle pieces change shape as the fierce female characters shift in the shadows, and the author keeps us twisting and tumbling until the whispers become roars. Unforgettable."

—KD Aldyn, author of *Sister, Butcher, Sister*

"Propulsive, creepy, and oh-so-satisfying! Marlee Bush's *Whispers of Dead Girls* grabbed me and wouldn't let go."

—Stacy Johns, author of *What Remains of Teague House*

# Praise for *When She Was Me*

"A searing, blistering thriller that grabs you and doesn't let go until its final, dizzying twist. Beautifully written and as tender as it is terrifying, Marlee Bush is a breakout new voice to watch."

—Jenny Hollander, author of *Everyone Who Can Forgive Me Is Dead*

"A nail-biting story of sisterhood, suspicion, and suspense. *When She Was Me* weaves together past and present seamlessly to create a twist you won't see coming. I couldn't put it down!"

—Tracy Sierra, author of *Nightwatching*

"I tore through *When She Was Me* with my heart in my throat—the prose was cunning and beautiful, the atmosphere was claustrophobic and unsettling, the imagery was dark and vibrant, and the strange dynamic between the sisters was hard to look away from. In short, Marlee Bush has crafted one of the most mesmerizing psychological thrillers I have ever read."

—Ashley Tate, author of *Twenty-Seven Minutes*

"*When She Was Me* is eerie, captivating, and full of twists. I gasped out loud multiple times."

—Darcy Coates, *USA Today* bestselling author of *Dead of Winter*

"*When She Was Me* is a powerfully gripping debut. Atmospheric and richly described, it reads like a tense, vivid dream. The serpentine twists and nuanced character relationships will haunt you long after you turn the last page."

—RJ Jacobs, author of *This Is How We End Things*

"A mesmerizing, addictive thriller that will keep readers guessing from start to its jaw-dropping finish. Told in vibrant, hypnotic prose with complex relationships and haunting secrets at its core, *When She Was Me* is a standout debut from a wildly talented new author. Marlee Bush is one to watch."

—Laurie Elizabeth Flynn, author of *The Girls Are All So Nice Here*

# Also by Marlee Bush

*When She Was Me*

# WHISPERS

# OF

# DEAD

# GIRLS

**A NOVEL**

# MARLEE BUSH

Poisoned Pen
PRESS

Published by Poisoned Pen Press, an imprint of Sourcebooks
P.O. Box 4410, Naperville, Illinois 60567–4410
(630) 961-3900
sourcebooks.com

Cataloging-in-Publication Data is on file with the Library of Congress.

Printed and bound in the United States of America.
PAH 10 9 8 7 6 5 4 3 2 1

*This one is for Bow, Miles, and Shiloh. Of all the tiny humans in the universe who have ever been born or will be, I am infinitely grateful itis you three that get to raise me.*

# 1

*In Loving Memory of Margo Glass*

The rust-colored memorial bench is new. Though I guess it could have been here the last ten years. It's new to me. The bench sits under the awning, out of place and covered in cobwebs. Forgotten. I look away and press the buzzer that belongs on a spaceship or in a doomsday movie. Along with the bench, it's also an upgrade. I guess there's nothing like a dead student to make a school invest in safety.

The school itself, a redbrick monstrosity that could be confused with a prison at first glance, has no fencing and sits directly on the main road. When I drove up, the sign welcoming visitors was faded from age and missing letters—*Welco to Benton Hi.*

It was close enough but not quite right. Which is an apt description for much of this town.

"Can I help you?" asks a voice through the speaker.

"I'm here for the faculty meeting."

There's another buzzing and the sound of a latch hissing, like it's releasing the breath that's been caught in my own throat since I stepped out of my car. It's all as anticlimactic as the last glimpse I catch of the courtyard behind me. With its peeling paint and wobbly picnic tables, it's one thing, at least, that hasn't changed. Those are probably the same tables I sat on ten years ago.

Walking in, the memories hit me with a brutal intensity before I'm even fully inside. The smell of the building—a mixture of antiseptic, crayons, and sawdust—is as strong as my sense of foreboding as I walk through a definitely new metal detector and wait behind plexiglass.

Another barrier before reaching the hallway. Security was ultratight at the last school I taught at. But here, in Benton, a town with one traffic light, one diner, a pizza place, two gas stations, and a Dollar General, it feels like too much. Like the real world finally slithered in and obliterated the nostalgia.

And maybe the obliteration began with me that very first day of my freshman year. I remember the feel of her hand on my wrist, my sister, as she pulled me through the doors.

I remember the buzz of student's voices like cicadas in the deepest of woods, electric and alive. "You're going to love it here," she'd promised, her face alight with excitement and encouragement. All for me.

A woman pops up from the other side of the glass behind a desk, a pencil in her hand. I recognize her instantly. Mrs. Caldwell. The attendance supervisor and secretary. I blink and see more memories of my sister and I attempting to sneak past her. Making up an excuse about traffic to get an excused tardy pass. My sister complimenting her hair so genuinely that it made Caldwell blush.

My sister usually got what she wanted, and she usually wanted good things.

Caldwell is plumper now and grayer. But the essence of the woman I knew remains in her smile. The same smile that always, to me, bordered on condescending.

"Sorry about all that. Principal Smart wanted me manning the doors. Told him we could leave them unlocked this once, but he wouldn't hear of it. You see how the world is these days. These kids shooting each other and whatnot." Her eyes narrow behind her glasses. "You're new, aren't you? Taylor, right? Ren Taylor?" Recognition sparks in her eye, but it doesn't quite ignite. I'm an unidentifiable flavor on the back of her tongue as she flicks through years of students, trying to figure out just who I am and why I am so familiar to her.

Faculty like Caldwell usually don't remember. They don't want to.

It should be enough that she doesn't know right away. Should give me relief. But the spark is there, and my mouth is a desert wasteland. I blink past the dryness in my eyes. Past the smell of parchment and decay and too bright fluorescents. "That's me."

"I'm sorry, you look very familiar."

"I just moved here from teaching at a private school in Atlanta," I say, carefully leaving off a crucial word. *Back*. I just moved *back*. I avert my face, scrunching my nose in the process. I've been told I look more like my father when I do this and less like my mother and sister. *Something about the bridge of your nose*, Dad used to say, back when getting words out of him wasn't like pulling teeth.

"Private school, huh? Wow. Well, I'm Martha Caldwell. Office manager. Nice to meet you. Taylor is your last name, correct?" She asks again as if she doesn't believe me. Guess that assumption on her part isn't wrong. I'm only half telling the truth. My last name hasn't always been Taylor.

"Yes. Do you know where the meeting is being held?" I don't mind her analyzing my last name. It won't lead anywhere. That's the only good thing that came from my failed marriage. Sometimes I think it's the only reason I wanted to get married at all.

"Oh, of course. I'll just show you. Easier that way. It's in the conference room through here." Another door buzzes, and she leads me through a dimly lit hallway to the front office.

A custodian is scrubbing the glass trophy case with earbuds in. He's my age, maybe a little older, and must see us out of the corner of his eye because he turns to give us a look, his eyes going wide when they land on me. I recognize him. Billy something. He was in my sister's grade.

A dribble of sweat makes its way down the small of my back.

I knew I'd see people I recognized but knowing it and experiencing it are two different feelings. And this feeling, the one churning inside me now, feels wrong.

Billy and Caldwell belong in the deepest recesses of my memories. I want to pluck them from the room and shove them back inside my head.

Maybe coming back here was a mistake.

Mrs. Caldwell doesn't notice my inner struggle as she bustles past me and pulls open a door at the end of the corridor. "In there, the door to the left. I think you're the last to arrive."

I glance behind me. Billy is back to scrubbing away, a bright orange key ring jingling aggressively on his hip. Clearly, he isn't unaffected by my presence either. We shared a class the year everything happened. He always used to tell everyone he was going to be a rapper.

Guess life rarely goes as planned for any of us.

"Thank you," I force out, following Mrs. Caldwell's instructions. The office hallway is bordering on too dark, and it takes a moment for my eyes to adjust enough to reach for the doorknob. To work up enough willpower to turn it.

But I do, mostly because I know Caldwell is still watching with that contemplative look on her face. Several staff and faculty members are sitting around a long conference table. Some are in folding chairs packed against the walls. They're in clusters with their heads pushed together. Talking. Whispering. Laughing.

The sound lowers exponentially when I enter. I hate every moment of this. I never liked attention. Even as a child.

But unlike my sister, I usually don't get what I want.

Avoiding their eyes, I scan the room, recognizing Principal Smart instantly. A wide-shouldered man with a booming voice and clean-shaven skin who'd interviewed me on Zoom mere weeks ago. He's the only one in a suit and stands in front of a PowerPoint display, fiddling with his computer. The look of concentration on his face is broken only when he spots me. "Ms. Taylor, glad you found us."

"Thank you."

My face warms, and I know my neck is a spiderweb of red as I attempt to find a seat. It's freshman year again except my sister isn't here to hold my hand. I slide into the first empty seat I touch, a folding chair shoved between a bored-looking man and a very pregnant woman.

The woman turns sideways in her seat. "Hi."

"Hey."

"You're new."

Principal Smart saves me from responding as he clears his throat. "I think that's everyone." He claps his hands, and I'm the only one who jumps. "Welcome or welcome back to Benton High School. Thank you all for being here, and good morning. I don't know about you all, but I'm ready to have a spectacular year." He's young, for a principal, with an air of optimism that the public school system hasn't yet snuffed out. That's a rare combination. He turns that exuberant gaze directly to me. "Before we get into the nitty-gritty, why don't we take a quick second and introduce ourselves to our newest faculty member. Ren?" He motions for me to stand. "Would you mind?"

I hate this part. It's all the same, whether you're a student or teacher. The new kid must always introduce themselves.

I stiffly move to my feet, clutching my notebook in my hands. "Sure. I'm Ren Taylor. I teach biology. I've spent the past five years teaching at a private school in Atlanta. And…" I fumble for words, any words. "I like…to read."

Their gazes linger unabashedly, if not a little disappointingly. I fidget beneath the weight of those stares, especially considering I know several teachers in this room. Many of them taught me, and I can see the recognition on their faces. I wonder if they're like Mrs. Caldwell, flipping through students faces like file folders in a drawer, desperately trying to place me. Or if they know exactly who I am with a single glance.

Exactly what I did.

It's the not knowing that makes me so uncomfortable. Like everything might be easier if someone would just stand up and demand, *What's* she *doing here?*

My eyes roam and catch the gaze of someone in the back.

A man sitting with his chair against the back wall.

I didn't notice him before.

*How* did I not notice him?

The room shrinks and narrows like some kind of fun house illusion, and the sounds in the room are consumed with white noise, violent as a storm. I sit heavily, feeling so aware of every move I make. Every expression on my face.

He leans back in his folding chair, his hands behind his head. The only person in the room still looking at me. *Been there, done that*, his eyes say. Teasing me. Twinkling with good humor and mischief.

I'm transported back in time. Back to the hallway with my sister. First day of freshman year. And if I had to go back and label this day, I would call it the day of cumulative effect. The day the first domino fell. My sister's hair slapped my chin as she whipped her head to the side too sharply, more excited than me. "You'll love him! He's the best. Trust me."

I'd heard all about my first-period teacher before this moment. In whispers coming from the bedroom while she and her friends gossiped. Anytime she looked at my schedule and felt the need to remind me how lucky I was to have his class.

Admittedly, I was curious to see him. He couldn't be *that* great.

"There he is." She'd nudged me with an elbow, a bright laugh slipping past her lips.

The man who had been leaning against the door of his classroom laughed at something another student said.

He looked young. The type of handsome I'd only ever seen on TV.

I stumbled over my feet, nearly bringing my sister down with me.

She took it in stride, bearing my weight, pulling me to my feet. Still smiling. "You're nervous, aren't you?"

But I couldn't answer because he was looking at me. And no one had ever looked at me like that.

Like they saw me.

His eyes landed on me the same way snow falls. Delicately. Like it's what they were meant to do. Like he didn't have a choice. There was no ominous feeling. No voice in my head telling me to run. There was only his eyes, and the dip in my stomach that made me want something I'd not wanted before.

"Wonderful, Ren." Principal Smart's booming voice draws me back. "Why don't we start to your left and go around the room."

The introductions begin. Some names I know. Some I won't remember. Only a couple stick out. My pregnant neighbor, Emma. With long brown hair and rain-cloud-gray eyes, she must be several years younger than me and fresh out of college. Beside her a man with the same last name as her introduces himself. A married couple at the same school.

Cute. Didn't work when it happened to me, but to each their own.

Finally, the man in the back of the room. My age, give or take a few years, with a thick head of black hair and a smirk. "I'm Bryson Lewis. Physics and chem."

My stomach squeezes.

And through the door, I swear I hear voices in the hallway. My sister's and my own. She'd snuck up behind me, poking a finger into my side. "So what's the verdict? You like him, right?"

"What?"

She motioned to the brown-eyed man at the end of the hall, a knowing smile on her face.

"Oh, right. Yeah. He's great." I'd mumbled, but the answer hadn't felt honest, and my breath caught with the weight of a secret.

"Great. Let's get started then." Principal Smart booms, clapping his hands together again. The room goes back into motion.

Throughout the presentation, my gaze returns to Bryson often. He doesn't take notes like everyone else. Doesn't appear interested in Principal Smart at all. I do the math in my head when I should be listening to the presentation. Smart's going over lunch schedules. Hard to pay attention when I'm trying to figure out how *he* is here. How they let him come back after—

It's not him.

I force my eyes away from Bryson. Make myself focus on Principal Smart, who is doing the absolute most with this PowerPoint. Anyway, I can't go back down that road. Can't see *that man* in every man. Not here.

Especially not here.

It only takes a little over an hour for Smart to go over important schedules, policies, and procedures. When he dismisses us, I gather my things and wait to file out like I'm deboarding an airplane. The pregnant woman taps my shoulder. "I know you most likely forgot my name. It's Emma. Where's your class?"

"I remembered. And 202."

"You must have a better memory than me." She rubs her belly. "Pregnancy brain, hubby calls it. Anyway, I'll show you to your class if you want?"

The word *hubby* makes me inwardly cringe. Even when I was married, I didn't use it. Allen's name in my phone was Allen Taylor. I bet Emma's husband's name in hers is a bunch of heart-eye emojis.

Maybe if I was more like her, I'd still be married.

And I absolutely would not be here.

"Thank you," I say even though I'm confident I could find it on my own, even if I wasn't already familiar with the place. The school is two horseshoes stacked on top of each other and an annex hall connecting to the back. A later addition that was brand-new when I attended Benton.

Emma leads me from the office and into the hall. Billy is no longer at his spot cleaning the trophy case. It makes me wonder what happened. How he got here. The vivacious boy with a crush on my sister—everyone had crushes on her—who dreamt of being a celebrity. What happened to that kid?

That's when I see it. Her photo.

There are other pictures too. I try to look at each of them first. The basketball team holding a trophy, grinning wildly. The cheerleaders, their pointer fingers aimed at the sky, paw prints painted on their cheeks. Art projects and students of the year and FFA club sign-ups.

They all pale in comparison to the photo in the middle.

A few other teachers trail in front and behind, talking casually. A man laughs loudly from somewhere I can't see. A door slams.

I am frozen in place.

Emma glances back, following my gaze to the freshly dusted photo proudly displayed in the trophy case. "Poor thing. Homecoming queen and prom queen her senior year. Didn't make it to graduation. Think they've had her picture up since she passed nearly fourteen years ago. Hey, you all right?"

"I'm fine."

She gives me one more long look before turning toward the stairs. "You're on the second floor. Next to the copy room, lucky lady. It's brand-new. Probably the newest item in the whole building. Even the air here is old. David makes this joke that we use recycled air to save money."

"What do you teach again?"

"American history. Different floor and wing. Hopefully I'll see you around though. Here you are." She points to a room just off the stairs. "That's you. Maybe there won't be a mess. Jenny retired after thirty-five years. She never was one for organization or…cleanliness."

"Mrs. Gats?"

Emma glances at me curiously. "You know her?"

I think of how much I want to reveal. How much I want to lie. But I know some of the people in that room recognized me. It won't be long before the rumors start. Might as well get in front of them. "I had her. Actually, I graduated from here ten years ago."

"No kidding. Wait, ten years ago." Her head tilts back a little too quickly like she's piecing something together. "Did you know Margo Glass?"

Behind my eyes and inside my head is the worst memory of all. Worse than forgotten memorial benches and faded photographs. There is the lurch of the boat, the black stillness of the waters, and the quiet that came after. "She was my sister."

"Wow. Seriously? I'm sorry," she says sincerely. "I didn't

think—I mean, I wouldn't have asked had I known. Your last name is different."

"It's OK. It's been so long." Like that helps. Grief is desperately trying to get to the peak of a mountain. People like me will climb their whole lives, never able to reach the top.

"I went to North Ridge, so like an hour from here. I was in elementary school when it happened. It was all anyone talked about. They still talk about it. No one is forgetting about Margo any time soon." She must mean for the sentence to be comforting, but something about her words do the opposite. They threaten.

No one will forget what I did.

She rocks back, rubbing her swollen stomach uneasily. "I should get back to my room and let you work, but let me know if you need anything or if I can help you, OK?"

"How far along are you?"

She looks at her belly and smiles. "Thirty weeks. A little girl."

"Congratulations."

"You have any? Children?"

"Had one. Ended up divorcing him."

It's a joke that takes a smidge too long to land. "Oh." Emma, bless her, laughs anyway. "I'm sorry."

"No, actually congratulations are more apt." The platitudes are meant to set people at ease. A way to make light of a situation that's not easy at all. I never considered Allen a child. Maybe I never loved him, but I always respected him.

If congratulations are in order, they should all go to him for getting the hell away from me.

This time her laugh is genuine as she backs away. "See you around, Ren. Let me know if I can help you with anything."

I wave, and right before she disappears down the hall, she glances back over her shoulder. "It couldn't have been easy coming back here. Why did you? Take this job, I mean? Why come back?"

There are a million words left unsaid. A million accusations. A million wonderings.

There is Allen, grasping my shoulders, tears on his face: *Who are you, Ren? Why are you doing this to us?*

"I guess I like making things difficult for myself."

"For the record, I was never one to feed into rumors," she says before turning around and walking down the stairs.

The line between truth and rumor glows effervescent in my head. And maybe I'll never make it to the top of grief mountain because I'm constantly teetering on the edge. Have been since I returned my sophomore year without Margo. Since I sunk inside myself at every pointed glance and whispered word.

Rumors intermingled with truth until I couldn't tell them apart.

Our teacher wasn't the only one who killed my sister.

It wasn't just his fault.

He couldn't have done it without my help.

"There you go again," the voice says from behind me. "Making everything about you. Even my own death."

I turn around to see her.

Margo.

"Hey, Renny," she says, flashing teeth that were always just a little whiter than mine. "Don't act so surprised. You know I never really left."

# 2

I don't breathe until the door is closed behind me. I want privacy. An empty room. Well, almost empty.

"You had enough already? It's only the first day."

Light flows in from the cracked window behind the desk, highlighting dust mites floating above the covered microscopes. Emma was right. Mrs. Gats wasn't one for cleaning. Margo sits on a black lab table with her feet propped up and crossed, oblivious to the disorganization that spawns around her.

People like Margo make others oblivious to it too.

They're too busy looking at her.

Her perfectly curled hair, the style she preferred most days, the same style as the picture in the trophy case, lies immaculately over one shoulder. "Who knew you'd end up teaching bio? Remember our biology teacher, Mrs. Gats? Actually"—her grin grows wicked—"this was her class, wasn't it? She always smelled like those beef sticks Mom used to buy. Gats caught Gordon trying to touch my thigh under the table once. I had to bend his fingers back. Gats never said anything. I think she thought he deserved it too."

Margo's swings her long legs off the table, white wedges landing on the dirty tile floor, and I feel as if I'm in a fever dream. How I feel every time I see her.

"They do that, don't they?" she says. "The teachers? Live vicariously through us?"

"What are you doing here?"

There it is. The spark of curiosity in her wide brown eyes. Mom used to say nothing good happened when Margo's eyes started shining. How many times had the sheriff brought her to the door after ding-dong-ditching or rolling someone's house? How many times had our mother tsked and tutted and then laughed when the officer finally left?

*Margo will be Margo*, she'd say.

And she was. At least until Margo wasn't anything at all anymore except for dirt beneath our feet.

"You thought I'd miss this?" Margo walks around the table, her finger sliding across the dusty surface. "Walking these halls were the best years of my life. I heard Emma ask, but I already know. That's why you came back, isn't it? You knew I like it here most."

Even though she isn't real, and despite knowing what I did to her, seeing her still feels euphoric. How can the pain and pleasure exist together so assuredly? How can she be right there but not really anywhere?

How can I look at her with the smallest degree of allowance when I know what her lifeless body feels like? When I'd laid my head on her icy, still chest and cried until my father pulled me off her?

I know those things happened.

But Margo is here, and when she's here, those memories seem so far away.

"I'm not real, Ren. Not real and not really here." She laughs, and the permanent knot in my chest loosens. "I'm dead. I'm only here because—actually, why am I here? Or better yet, why are you here, Ren?"

*Why did you? Take this job, I mean? Why come back?*

Emma's words and a flash of a face. A new face. The man in the faculty room.

"You're thinking of him, aren't you? Bryson. He was hot. Bet the girls love him. Could even make a girl like me enjoy physics."

I close my eyes and breathe out slowly. Like I can breathe the life back into the world that was stolen over a decade ago. One more breath before opening my eyes. The desk is empty, and I am impaired by a panic so severe my lungs constrict behind my bones.

I look at the desk she'd touched. See the dust completely undisturbed.

*It's OK*, I tell myself. *She'll be back.*

Margo always comes back.

———

My dead sister came back for the first time eight days after her death. At her funeral, in fact. My mother's sobs drowned out the preacher's sermon. He was a real nice guy, our preacher. A genuinely good man. But nothing about this sermon was comforting. Not hearing how she would be lifted in a rapture. Not hearing about Margo dancing and singing with angels like it was way better than breathing our gray air and hanging with her friends. With me.

"She gained her wings," he said reverently. "It's what we all really want."

I'd almost laughed. I remember fighting the feeling. Those words. We all want to *die*? Even though we spend our wholes lives avoiding death until our inevitable endings? Then suddenly it's a great reward?

I remember closing my eyes. Drowning him out.

But it was worse in the dark behind my eyelids. A place that ebbed and flowed with water. A place where there was no sense of time or peace, only a moving boat, angry streaks of red in the sky, the slap of the water, and a gurgle. I opened my eyes, gasping for the breath I'd been trying to take for eight days.

My mother had looked at me, briefly. I think this was the last time she'd look me in the face or look at anything with lucidity. When Margo died, something inside her broke and chipped away. She stood before me, breathing, blinking. But it wasn't her anymore. Not really. Our eyes met and held, and the thought came to me: *I can't fix this.*

But maybe she could. She was still my mother regardless of what I did. She would love me no matter what. I leaned toward her, hoping, needing. She held me for a second, her face contorting into despair. Then came the shutdown. The shuttering of herself, like even this emotion, loving her living daughter, was too hard now. She heaved herself onto my father. Away from me until I couldn't even feel her body heat.

I watched them.

My wailing mother.

My dry-eyed father.

He caught my eye, gave me a small sad smile. A visual pat on the head. His eyes told me not to take it personally. *Mom will get better soon.*

The people in the crowded chapel watched like reptiles curled around the carcass of a dead rabbit. Doesn't matter if they felt bad for the creature, they still planned to eat it.

I remember wanting out. Wanting the pit in my stomach out. The monster in my heart out. Out of this pew. Out of this family. I couldn't take it a second longer.

Then I looked sideways and saw her. Just there across the walkway. She sat in the pew beside one of our neighbors, mimicking being asleep. Bored out of her mind at her own funeral. Margo being Margo. I clenched my eyes shut, fearing perhaps I was dead too. Maybe I died on that boat with her, and this was my hell.

But when I opened them again, she was still there, watching me with that playful expression, like she understood every thought passing through my head.

She'd returned nearly every day since.

A coping mechanism, my therapist had said back when I used to see one. But she didn't know how real Margo was when I saw her. The freckles on her cheeks, the gap between her bottom teeth, her laughter, a burst of sound that seems to radiate from deep inside her, the smooth skin of her hands—never to fade or wrinkle, seventeen forever. It's her all the way down to her sarcastic musings.

My time-capsule sister.

I spend the rest of the day unpacking my things—walking back and forth from my car, up the stairs, and into the class. A cycle that does little to clear my head. Because the worm in my mind is digging and feeding. Margo's words are there. The accusation.

She's right. She's always right. I was thinking of him.

Bryson Lewis.

I clean out the closet. Fend off the endless stream of visiting teachers. Some recognize me. Some don't. The ones that do offer me condolences for my long-dead sister. Tell me they're glad to see I'm doing all right. Ask about my parents, but don't really listen to my answer. That's not the story they're really after anyway.

I'm unpacking a particularly messy box from the closet—apparently Mrs. Gats was a hoarder—when there's a knock on the door.

Bryson is standing there with a couple textbooks in his arms.

"Bryson." The feeling hits me again but even harder now that we're alone. It's a mixture of panic and nostalgia. Like I've met this man before. Like he ruined my life. The anger courses through me, and I bite it back.

Because I haven't, and he didn't.

"Hi, Ren. I wanted to drop in so I could reintroduce myself, but I guess that isn't necessary. You have a good memory." He fills the doorway entirely. Wide shoulders, big hands, a toothy grin. Probably played football in high school as well as he played with girls. A mammoth of a presence, and the smell of spice is overwhelming. It would take one step and pull and lunge, and we'd be alone in a dark storage room. Two animals battling in the dark.

My nostrils burn and fingers twitch at my sides.

I rock to my feet and inch toward him, hoping he gets the

hint to step back. "Some people just stick out to me, I guess. You mind?" For an entirely too long second, I think he won't move. Think he has me right where he wants me, and he isn't going anywhere. And he knows my secrets and fears and thoughts.

But then he moves—of course he moves—and laughs.

"I really had other motives for walking over." He raises a brow, pursing his lips to the side in a way that most women might consider charming. "I wanted to get another look at you. The talk of the school. You're not near as interesting as they're saying." He means it as a joke. That much is clear. But the joke falls a little flat because there is so much truth embedded in it. I work very hard to be as nondescript as possible. The kind of person your eyes skim over in public. Even though you just looked them in the face, you wouldn't be able to recall their hair color if you tried. It was easy to pull this off as a kid. After all, everyone was always looking at Margo.

"Sorry to disappoint."

"You look like her." His eyes darken, his face contorting into an expression I haven't seen before. Bone deep sadness. Surprise. Curiosity.

"Lucky me, I guess."

"I'm sorry. That was—" He cuts himself off with a quick shake of his head, his cheeks darkening with genuine embarrassment. "I shouldn't have said that. I didn't mean to say that."

"It's fine."

"I've seen her picture so many times, and seeing you…" He swallows, eyes holding mine so steady. "It's like seeing a ghost."

"I know the feeling," I whisper, but I'm already in another classroom. Another man's hands brushing my shoulder. A secret smile just for me. Then it's Bryson again, rocking nervously on his feet. Not quite in the past. Not quite in the present. Somewhere in between. "I'm used to being compared to Margo. Though not many people tell me we look alike."

"I'm sorry for your loss, and I'm sorry for bringing it up," he says sincerely. "I'm rather good at putting my foot in my mouth."

"It was a long time ago."

"That doesn't always matter. Can I ask you something?"

"I don't know. Where's your foot?"

He almost smiles. "Firmly on the ground."

"Then go for it."

"Why did you want to teach here? If it were me, I couldn't imagine ever returning to the place where something…like that happened."

*Something like that.* Is that how people describe what happened to Margo?

"I saw the job opportunity and figured it was about time to be closer to my parents." This is the truest answer I've given anyone all day. Maybe the endless stares and questioning glances have finally beat me down until the raw beating heart beneath my exterior was exposed.

And with Bryson of all people. I shiver.

"Your parents, how are they? They must be excited to have you back."

"You don't have to ask."

"Pardon?"

"You think you have to ask to be polite, but you really don't." I don't mean for the words to come out so sharply, but I'm having trouble focusing on anything other than putting a bullet in this conversation.

I think of my mother. The last memories I have of her before I left. My graduation night, when I'd returned home in my unbuttoned gown, feet aching from the walk, and seeing the television through the curtains. Home videos of Margo. My father sat on the front porch, stubbing out a cigarette like I hadn't seen the orange flicker from the bottom of the driveway. He stood up, waving his hands around with a too soft voice. *You made it. You know how it is. Mom couldn't go back. Had to stay with her. We're proud of you.*

Excuses. He was always so good at those.

Bryson straightens and steps away, and at first I think I've offended him. Then he grins bashfully. "I told you I was good at the whole foot-in-mouth thing. I did mention that right?" The tension in the room eases. "Anyway, I won't hold you up. I know you're busy. Just wanted to say I'm right across the hall. If you need anything, I'm your guy." He hooks his thumbs inward and smiles.

Charming.

Then his words register. "You're in the classroom across the hall?"

"Yes, and I've got to say, you're a lot easier on the eyes than Mrs. Gats." Another joke that doesn't work. Like the sign out front, crude and missing letters, I get it, but there's something wrong about it that I can't put my finger on.

"Funny," I say offhandedly, but the silence had been too long, and we both shift nervously.

"This is why you were never invited to parties, Ren," Margo says with a bark of laughter from somewhere in the front of my classroom.

I don't know when she got here, but I don't look in her direction.

Bryson clears his throat awkwardly while I grab a box from a nearby table. I brush past and wait for him to join me at the door, so I can lock it behind us both. "You're new here too, aren't you?"

"I transferred in last spring. What gave me away?" He steps into the hall.

"I could just tell. Middle of the year?" I say, balancing the box on my hip while I lock up.

"It was an opportunity I couldn't pass up."

He echoes the same sentiment I had, and I wonder if it had sounded as empty and careless on my lips. When I turn around, there's a tight expression on his face. He's leaning against his classroom doorway casually, but it doesn't quite match the anxiety in his eyes.

"So what's the verdict?" he asks. "Glad to be back?"

"I think the jury's still out on that one. Goodbye, Bryson."

"See you around, Ren." He dips inside his own classroom, leaving me alone with Margo.

She stares in his direction. "He's going to be a problem."

"No."

She snickers. "You always were a good liar."

━━━━━━━

I'm winding through a familiar dirt road. Crossing a barely visible wooden bridge. Staring at the gravel driveway all the way to where my parents' house peeks out from beneath a canopy of trees. A rustic white farmhouse with a massive porch. The whites are faded and flaked with black. The shutters, a minty blue, peel like skin in the sun too long.

The house itself is plagued by weather and age. But it's neat. Clean. The hedges are trimmed. Grass is cut. Well-cared-for plants swing from hanging planters. It's a place where people care just enough to survive.

This is where I stop.

"You won't do it," Margo says. She's stretched out on the passenger seat, heels on my dashboard, eyes closed. Always so casual. Always so confident. "You won't go in."

"I'm tired," I explain, my knuckles white on the wheel. Besides, it's getting late. It's nearly five. Mom will be watching some game show rerun. Dad will be on the porch though, staring into the thickening darkness and listening to the frogs and crickets. He'd told me once it's the only sound that can drown out his mind.

Wonder if he heard my tires.

If he's wondering who is waiting at the end of his driveway.

"You're scared." She sits up, leaning close to me, a wisdom in her eyes that far exceeds her seventeen years of life. "What are they going to do when they hear you're back? You didn't even tell them."

"I'm here for them." The words are meant to sound sure, but vulnerability creeps in. I remember the day I left for college. I walked into the kitchen to something bubbling over on the stove. Mom sat at the kitchen table scrubbing mindlessly at a spot I couldn't see. *Right here*, she'd said when I walked in. *You can see them moving, the dust mites.* When she'd looked at me, there'd been very little on her face that I recognized. *This is why I tell you and your sister to keep things tidy. To wash your hands. Germs are alive you know.*

Pathetically, I'd twiddled my thumbs by the door. I couldn't even bring myself to move to the stove and turn it off. Finally, when I heard the slam of the trunk outside and knew my father had finished loading my suitcase, I'd called out to her. She kept scrubbing without looking up. In the three years since my sister's death, I could number every word she'd said to me on two hands, but I'd thought this would be different.

I'd thought my leaving would be a wake-up call for her.

*Yes, Margo is dead, but I'm here. I'm still your daughter.*

Sometimes I have dreams of that night. My mother running to the door, pulling me into her arms. Telling me she loved me the same way she had all my life. But that was the last time I spoke to her. I'd tried to call that semester, but Dad always said she was busy. At an appointment. In the shower. And when I told Dad I wouldn't be able to make it back for Thanksgiving, he'd said he understood. He and Mom would miss me. But I could have sworn I heard relief in his voice.

"The prodigal daughter returns." Margo relaxes in her seat once again. Getting comfortable. We're not going anywhere, and she knows it. "Just not tonight."

I shift the car into reverse and back out, leaving the memories like stains on a sheet. I don't want to look at them.

Not yet.

They'll still be here another day.

# 3

The girls huddle near my door.

Two are my students, and three are Bryson's. They've lingered in the hall between our classrooms before the tardy bell the entire first month of school. Each day the girls stand shoulder to shoulder with their cell phones out and someone's name on their lips. Usually, their hushed whispers are accompanied by laughter or sly glances at Bryson, manning his own door and acting oblivious to their interested stares.

Today is different though.

I sense the shift. The intensity with which they're honed in on a single girl's phone. "Is that her?"

"I watched the press conference in first. They still haven't found her."

"What do you think happened?"

"Took off. Had to have taken off. Hell, I would after graduation."

"I met her once at volleyball camp."

The bell rings, and they dash apart, scattering to their respective classrooms like little mice.

That was weird.

"Maybe we should have given them a late slip for that. They cut it kind of close." Bryson's hands are in his pockets as he rocks back on his heels. Today his shirt and khakis are pressed. He's wearing a tie, floral patterned, and carefully styled hair.

We've gotten comfortable with one another over the past month. I've gotten used to his constant jokes and ribbing while he's gotten acclimated to my stoic demeanor and all-around rigidity. I wouldn't call us friends, but I've gotten over those feelings from the first day. Mostly. Bryson is not the man who killed my sister.

Though there is one thing about them that's the same. The kids love him. He identifies with his pupils by telling them all about his teenage years and his proclivity for pranking his parents and breaking bones. He'll walk around his class, pencil tucked behind his ear, laughing through every anecdote while his students watch him completely enraptured. He has TikTok and Snapchat—or so I've heard—and knows all the current lingo, the latest music trends, and the celebrities they're all going crazy over. The kids eat him up, and I still only want to spit him out.

With those similarities, the dark thoughts sometimes creep in, but I'm quick to push them away.

As a science teacher, I know better than anyone there are several ways to use the scientific method. Right now, I've formed a hypothesis about him in my head, one based on shadowed memories and feelings and not on any actual data or facts. It's all just speculation.

"It was close, but they made it," I finally answer him, trying to force the warring thoughts from my head.

"You know, you surprise me." His eyes are alight with amusement, but there's a softness in his voice that isn't very common for him.

I glance sideways and try to sound relaxed. "Because I'm the only one who assigned homework the first day?"

He chokes on a laugh. "You didn't."

"Just some reading." I watch him while he wipes under his eyes, his smile transforming his entire face. He really is handsome, even if I hate to admit it. Just another similarity to add to the list. A coincidence. I look at my feet quickly. "If it wasn't that, then what was it? Why do I surprise you?"

"You just don't…treat me like everyone else does."

"What does that mean?" I look up and catch his gaze. Aimed right at me. I want to ask how he does that, how he looks at people like they're all he sees, but I'm afraid of the answer. I'm afraid to think about the last time a man looked at me so thoroughly.

He lowers his voice, steps closer. The hallways are empty now and mostly silent. Our classrooms, full of children, are just background noise humming behind us. "I don't know. You're just completely yourself. I like that. I like you, I guess."

My stomach flips, and I want to blush, to step closer to him, to ask him to tell me more. Tell me the other ways I'm different.

It all feels so familiar.

So right in its wrongness.

"Sorry I'm late, Mr. Lewis." A girl hurriedly sprints the stairs, going straight for Bryson's class, interrupting the intensity between us. I take a step back, take a deep breath. Shit. *What was that?*

The girl is still explaining, looking close to tears. "I had to come all the way from the annex hall, and my locker kept sticking."

"Take a breath. It's OK. I'll let you slide this once," Bryson says with a casual shrug. "Though if it happens again, you'll need a pass. Got it?"

"Yes, sir." She blushes and smiles gratefully before ducking into his class.

I watch him. The way his eyes follow her. Pleased with himself. The earlier feeling inside dissipates.

And I'm still here, anchored to this hallway, but it's also fourteen years ago, and he isn't Bryson anymore. He's another too charming man. I guess they're all interchangeable, really.

I turn back to my own class, which has gone silent as the students are getting curious about what I'm still doing out here. His voice stops me.

"Ren?"

"Yes?" My door is halfway closed, but I'm aware of the heated stares on my back and what every single one of my students must be thinking. The rumors about Bryson and me started the first day. That's what we get for teaching on the same end of the hall and being about the same age. According to teenagers, we're as good as married.

Bryson's gaze stays firmly on me, something flashing within the pits of his eyes. "You don't quite like me yet, do you, Ren?"

I edge into the hallway a little more and lower my voice.

"Excuse me?"

"You say things that seem like you're joking around, but your eyes are always so serious. It's almost like you tell jokes to placate people, but you're above them. Like you're bored. Am I wrong?"

"How does any of that mean I don't like you?" He's spot-on though, and it makes me shift uneasily.

"You bristle." His mouth twists. "Sometimes I say something and you just…tense. It's OK, you know. That you don't like me. Though my mother might disagree with your opinion."

"The polite practice would be keeping that observation to yourself." Doesn't he know the key to Southern manners is staying shallow, skin-deep? Never saying something so honest to someone. Not to their face at least.

"Only you could turn it back around on me."

"But that's what you like about me, isn't it, Bryson? I tell you exactly what I'm thinking."

He sobers, something in his eyes flashing. "The thing is, Ren, I don't think that's what you're really doing."

Suddenly, Margo's at my side, her lips near my ear. Cold breath on my cheek. "What are you thinking, Ren? You like him? You hate him? What are you feeling? Why does it feel like you've felt all this before?" Margo asks. "Or maybe the real question should be, what are you going to do about it?"

I close my door without saying anything.

———

The lunch bell rings, but two students linger at my desk to lay out the reasons they should be excused from our lab next week. Pig dissection. Apparently, they're both two-week-old vegans, and the mere thought is unfathomable.

I sit back in my desk, looking between them. Nineties grunge-style clothing. Designer. Definitely not vintage. Phones clasped in their hands like service animals. Like they have to be touching them to stay calm. "We're not eating the pig, girls."

"Gross. No, we know." Delilah runs a hand through her chemically straightened hair. "But it's the principle for me. I can't take part in something that goes against my core beliefs."

"Against your core beliefs of learning about an animal?"

"Of handling a dead animal that was probably murdered just for this purpose."

"You're mostly right."

Their eyes widen. One nudges the other. "See. The slaughterhouses. I told you."

I can't imagine ever having these concerns. I've never batted an eye at being handed a scalpel in school and in college. Even when, in my more advanced courses, we were dissecting human cadavers. It all seemed so scientific, so necessary. Just another part of life.

Sometimes death is best for some living creatures.

Only once in my life can I remember shrinking away from the thought of cold flesh and unseeing eyes.

My sister.

From my peripheral, I see movement at Bryson's door. Force myself to focus on the girls. "I'm not opposed to you sitting out the lab. I respect you standing up for your beliefs. But you still have to learn the material. Let me think of what I can have you do to make us both happy and keep things fair to everyone else."

They both release breaths like they hadn't suspected it to be so easy. "Thank you."

"Yeah, thanks."

"Hey, could you close the door on your way—" But they're outside, voices already a whisper down the hall.

Teenagers. From private schools to public, they're all the same. That's one thing, amidst the uncertainty of returning to Benton, that's been a comfort. When I've avoided the main hall, that trophy case, nearly every day, or got swept into memories that left me breathless, it's been the monotony of my job that's pulled me through. Kept me going. Made me not regret this decision.

And I'm handling it.

Sure, I haven't actually made contact with my parents yet, but there's been a lot of unpacking, a lot of adjusting.

I'll do it. I'm going to do it.

I sigh and stand to go close the door myself just as a girl quickly walks out of Bryson's room. Her hands are tucked under the strap of her backpack and eyes are downcast. But her shoulders shake. A mewling sound comes from her mouth, and she attempts to stifle it with the back of her hand. She's crying.

No, sobbing.

I freeze, my hands still braced on my desk.

The girl stops, her head shooting up. Our eyes touch just for a moment before she turns away and rushes out of sight. I stand there, staring at the now empty hallway, unable to move just yet. The scene is still processing in my mind. The girl isn't familiar, but that's not so shocking. Most of my students are freshmen and sophomores, and Bryson teaches upperclassmen.

It's not uncommon to see a student crying, either. Things come up at home. Breakups. Bad grades. Bullies. Could be anything.

The door swings open, and Bryson distractedly walks out of his room. He catches me watching, still frozen at my desk. "Oh, Ren. What are you doing?"

"Is she OK?" No need to explain who.

He shrugs casually but can't seem to shake off the red snaking up his neck. "There's some stuff going on at home. You know how kids can be. She'll be OK."

Something is off about the way he says it. "She seemed really upset."

"Kids are resilient. Anyway, I'll see you."

He doesn't really wait for a response before he's off, his shoes squeaking along the tile. No jokes or sly smiles. He couldn't get away from me fast enough. It's not until he's gone that I think of what bothered me the most about his appearance.

Bryson was no longer wearing his tie.

# 4

The cafeteria smells like grease and soured milk, and the multitude of concentrated voices and laughter makes my pulse kick up. The scent, the sounds, the memories are all things I like to avoid, and none of it is enough to get the girl out of my mind. Bryson's rumpled demeanor. The way he wouldn't quite meet my eyes.

What would make a man act like that?

Where was his confidence? His charm? I've not seen him without it. He was practically disarmed.

I weave through the tables and warm bodies, bringing my sandwich to the faculty table. It sits in the front of the cafeteria, nearest the cashiers. Same place it's always been. Emma spots me and waves me over to an empty seat beside her, as she's done every day this month. Like she needs to remind me every time that I'm welcome.

Emma's stomach is so swollen, she sits back from the table,

legs spread apart, constant discomfort on her face. Just a few more weeks until her maternity leave, and you can see it in her eyes, she's ready. Even so, she manages to shoot me a smile and a wink. I like Emma, and she seems to like me. A fact that's mostly surprised me. I didn't have a lot of friends in my last school.

Hell, I've never had a lot of friends.

Who needed them when I had Margo?

I was always lucky just to have a person to talk to in any given class as a kid. It was always Margo who was constantly surrounded. But Emma seems to genuinely like me. Our first week, I helped her with her bulletin, and I always grab her mail from the box in the office when I grab mine because I have to pass her class anyway. She even invited me to dinner twice.

Twice I've declined, but one day I might actually say yes.

Baby steps.

Today, like always, she sits with four other teachers.

One woman, Linda or Lynette I think, is midsentence and doesn't stop for a breath even as I sit down. "The press conference was useless. I don't even see what the point is of having one if you're going to keep reiterating the same garbage. And that's what pisses me off. They have to know something, right?"

"Of course, they do," Mary interjects. I remember her name mostly because she looks like a Mary. A biblical, puritanical plain Jane. It's certainly a dichotomy to the dirty jokes she has a penchant for. "We have children to protect. How do they expect us to do our jobs properly without all the information? We need to know if something is going on. It's bad enough she was missing for so long before anyone even reported it."

"I don't know. I'm sure she just took off with a boyfriend or girlfriend. She's done it before, is what her parents said. Kids do it all the time." Koa is also easy to remember. She reminds me of a friend of mine from high school. One of my only friends. A native Pacific Islander who hated our town as much as me. She missed the beach. I didn't have anything to miss. I just knew I wanted out. After Margo died, she was the only one who talked to me.

"This is different. Everyone knows that. That's why the police aren't saying anything. I'm telling you, they know something. They just wasted our time with this press conference to get the public off their back."

"What are you talking about?" I ask, and four heads bob in my direction. They look surprised. Probably because I usually don't talk much. Haven't since Mary made a Stephen King's *Carrie* joke that ended with everyone blushing and giving me looks.

Dead prom queens will always link back to me. Especially in this town.

Linda or Lynette swivels in her seat toward me. Her frizzy red hair is twisted at the nape of her neck and there's a piece of lettuce between her top two teeth. I surely won't be the one to tell her it's there when all her friends have been staring at it for minutes now. I glance at her name tag, but it's flipped backward.

"You mean you haven't heard?" she says. "Tina Drexler. Missing for the past couple of months. Her parents and the police are only just now beginning to take it seriously. They didn't even report her missing for the first month at least. They thought she ran away and would come back, but when she didn't, they filed a report. When the police finally started look-ing into it, they realized she hadn't used her debit cards or cell phone the whole time. Obviously something happened to her, and everyone is kind of peeved that the police aren't telling us anything. I mean, we should know if our kids or students are in danger, you know?"

I remember the conversation I'd overheard earlier from the girls outside my class. This must have been what they were talking about too. "Did she go here or something?"

"Went to Rosemary Academy. A private school nearby. She graduated this past May."

It's a strange feeling once you've experienced tragedy of your own. I held my sister's lifeless body. I watched her die. At this juncture, it's hard for me to summon the appropriate responses when someone tells me something tragic. It's like I'm in a war, bloody and riddled with bullet holes, and someone yelps beside me as a stray bullet catches their hand.

Yes, it hurts.

Life is the only thing more painful than death.

I unwrap and take a bite of my peanut butter and jelly as the rest of the women sink into whispers. The girl from earlier is running through my mind still. Only her sobs are getting mixed up with Margo's. Margo behind a closed door. Me pressing my ear against the wall, feeling my chest compress.

What kind of heartbreak makes a girl cry like that?

Why is my sister crying like that?

*Stop it.*

If I was alone, I'd say the words out loud.

*Stop it, Ren.*

I'm only half listening to the women at the table until I hear Bryson's name. "What did you say?"

Emma stops speaking, clearly taken aback. "Oh, uh, just that maybe we should ask Bryson about Tina Drexler. That's the school he transferred from last year. He was there while she was."

The sandwich weighs heavily in my stomach.

Being here in Benton, I live in Margo's shadow. Wear it like a trench coat. I always have. First in life and now in death. Sometimes the shock of being there, in the darkness of where she once stood, makes my mind drift, makes me think things I shouldn't.

The girl from earlier. The tears staining her face. The tie Bryson no longer wore. And now the missing girl from Bryson's old school. All these things on their own aren't meaningful. They're no smoking gun. They're more like a partial thumbprint, a lack of alibi, or a motive, when you need all three to tell a complete story.

Yet I can't help it. There's something inside me itching to learn more. Maybe it's being once more in Margo's shadow, swallowed whole by her memory even now, or maybe it's the fact I'm sitting at a lunch table eating a PB&J when something awful *could* be happening. I mean, most likely it's all nothing.

But I can at least find out.

I should, right?

"You going to save her, Ren?" Margo says from her place beside Linda/Lynette. "You think that will make up for what you did to me?"

"What do we know about him, anyway?" I ask, voice lowering, ignoring my sister. "How was he able to move here in the middle of the semester. How did that work?"

"Whoa, Ren. Take it easy." Lynette—she finally adjusts her name badge and then plays with the end of her straw. The action gets my attention. It's one of my pet peeves. Why touch with your fingers something about to go into your mouth?

And why haven't any of her friends mentioned that piece of lettuce?

"Just wondering."

"Why are you asking all of this, anyway?" she asks.

"I'm curious."

"Seems like a strange thing to be so curious about."

"You have lettuce in your teeth, Lynette."

Lynette covers her mouth and starts digging in her purse, and I think of Bryson.

The crying girl.

The missing tie.

The *missing girl*.

Just then a group of kids at a table to our right start getting loud. A drink gets thrown. The women hustle into motion, toward the table. Trying to stop a fight before it happens. When they come back to their seats, the subject has changed.

But for me, I know I won't be thinking of anything else.

Not for a long time.

---

I only have five minutes left of lunch and head straight for the library. Roughly half the size of the gymnasium, it's mostly empty, bar a cluster of tables and chairs and rows of dusty books. There are various posters and banners on the walls touting the benefits of reading. A book club that meets on Tuesday and a fantasy club on Thursday. The librarian is a tall man with mahogany skin and tortoiseshell glasses. I remember him from the faculty meeting, and when I walk in, he smiles, a kindness on his face that seems surprisingly genuine.

"Ren Taylor," he says in greeting, looking up from a rolling cart of books.

"I'm sorry, I don't remember your name."

"Samuel Williams." He slides a book under his arm and holds out a hand for me to shake. "I've heard a lot about you."

"That I can confidently apologize for."

He chuckles, takes the book from under his arm, and places it on a shelf. "Do you need help with something?"

"Just a computer. I'm still waiting for IT to troubleshoot my laptop," I tack on at the end when I notice his curious expression.

"Oh." He nods knowingly. "Always waiting for IT. I hear that. Computers are in the back."

"Thank you."

A student walks in and heads straight for Samuel, distracting him from what would surely be his next question. I don't know what I'd say if he asked. Certainly not the truth. I like to research in libraries for obvious reasons. Hard to know who made any particular search in shared computer spaces. It's supposed to be a little more anonymous, but maybe not with Samuel's eyes on me.

Not that it matters. I have nothing to hide. No reason to cover my tracks. It's all just a habit at this point, researching in public places. And the way my gaze skims the room for cameras, that's a habit too. As suspected, there aren't any. I guess the school's security budget stopped with the metal detectors.

On my way to the back, I trace a finger over the spines of a row of books, and each step I take is a step into the past. The artwork on the walls melts and shifts into something new. The walls are the same heather gray, faded and worn, but the posters are different. The covers of books blur and change. The librarian, a grouchy woman in her sixties, eyes me over her glasses as I disappear into the stacks. I enter the sci-fi section, where there's a whole shelf dedicated to a book that was just made into a movie. Some teen dystopian I never understood the craze for. Those kinds of books made my brain hurt. But *he* said it was his favorite genre. I felt his presence behind me before he could say anything, and it seemed to confirm all of my thoughts. All of my wants. He knew I'd be here.

He came for me.

My body tightens and tenses beneath his gaze. The red in my cheeks, my neck, my chest. His eyes seemed to follow the spreading warmth just as Margo rounded the corner, looking as surprised to see me as I was to see her.

I blink, and I'm back.

Or maybe I'm not actually back, and I'll always be doomed to reside in both places at once. My past. My present. Forever intertwined.

Samuel's voice is a gentle hum in the background. Not the cranky elderly woman who haunted this library in my youth. A student slides a chair away from a desktop noisily. Looks at me curiously before shuffling toward the entrance. I choose a seat in the very back, clinging to here. To now.

I check over my shoulder, and with one eye on the door, I boot up the computer.

Finding an article on Tina Drexler is easy. Though her story hasn't quite gone national yet. No one has picked it up. Too many missing girls to compete with.

I can picture the reporters clucking their tongues, swiping left on missing girl posters like they're searching for a Tinder date. *Nope, not enough extracurriculars. Not pretty enough. Not rich enough. Not skinny enough. Not white enough.*

When Tina's picture loads, I realize she doesn't quite check all the boxes either. I imagine some eyes glazed over when they looked at her. *Can't sell this story*, an editor might have said. *Find someone blonder. Perhaps a cheerleader with a stepdad in finance.*

Tina's a quiet-looking girl. Forgettable really. There are only a couple photos of her floating around. In each one she has harshly dyed black hair. Pale skin. Bracelets up and down her arms. Heavy eyeliner. You see this girl, and you think rebellion. You think this is a girl who wanted to start trouble. Or at the very least, deserved what she got.

I keep scrolling through the various hits on her name without really knowing what I'm looking for. It's all the same information regurgitated over and over again. Been missing for two months. Has a mother and brother at home who never have much to say either.

Backing out again, I try another tactic and type:

*Rosemary Academy missing teen*

I expect to find more about Tina. She wasn't a current student, but she had just graduated. Instead, I stumble into something else entirely. My breath gets stuck in my throat.

*Rosemary Academy Teenager Found Dead*

I look over my shoulder before clicking.

*The students of Rosemary Academy are mourning the sudden death of their classmate. On October 15, seventeen-year-old Alejandra Gomez was reported missing. Two days later, her body was found in shallow water in a wooded area near the school. The police initially ruled her death incon-clusive before discovering a heart condition that they believe*

*led to her drowning. Police Chief Derik Browning said in
a recent press conference, "We suspect Alejandra went into
the woods that day without the intention of swimming, and
something happened with her medical condition that caused
her to fall into the water and subsequently lose consciousness
and drown. At this time, we do not suspect any type of foul
play."*

*Friends of the young volleyball player remember her
bright smile and school spirit as they try to cope with the
unimaginable tragedy.*

I exit and try another source.

A Reddit thread with Alejandra's name in the title.

*Anyone else not convinced this nearly grown teenager
drowned in shallow water by herself?*

The original poster also included a link to a news article and a
photo of Alejandra. A white toothy smile, chocolate eyes, and long
caramel hair—the girl was beautiful. That's the first thing I notice.
She reminds me of Margo, the way my eyes are instantly drawn to
her. This is the kind of girl who makes headlines.

There are over a hundred comments below. Some people say it
was an accident. Some even say suicide. But there's one comment
that catches my eye.

*Cyber-Mick: If she so-called "had a heart attack and
fell in," where were her shoes? Even if she'd taken
them off, they'd be there somewhere. It isn't a robust
river. They wouldn't have floated away.*

Another commenter:

*NurseKat: Maybe an animal?*

*Cyber-Mick: An animal? Not likely. This was no accident. Someone did this to her.*

*NurseKat: She may not have had shoes. That's what the Police Chief said in his full statement.*

*Cyber-Mick: Who goes on a walk without shoes?*

*JoeNinjaxx: u/Cyber-Mick She clearly stopped to put her feet in the water when she fell in. Not to mention, she was known to take her shoes off after big games and practices because of foot pain. If she knew she was going to be soaking her feet, she might have just walked the path without them.*

That was the last comment.

My heart stalls, and I go back out, searching through articles. There is only one other that mentions Alejandra's shoes being missing, and it repeats exactly what one of the commenters said. Alejandra had a big game the day before and was known to walk around barefoot after those types of tournaments.

There is a simplicity to this case.

An almost unbelievable simplicity.

A barefoot teen walking into the woods and dipping her toes into the creek. That same girl having a heart attack, making her pass out and, ultimately, causing her to drown in water she could have easily climbed out of.

It's possible.

But there's something niggling at me. A girl dies in this school and then another recent graduate goes missing. Even more incredible, these events both took place not even a year apart. And there's Bryson, who left Rosemary Academy midsemester, right when Alejandra died. He would have been long gone by the summer when Tina went missing. But he would have known both girls.

I rock back in my seat, staring blankly forward.

"You're overthinking it," Margo says from beside me. She's leaning over my shoulder, staring at the screen and then at me. I can feel her hard gaze like rays of sun on my cheek. "You haven't been yourself since you saw that girl crying."

"There's no harm in me looking."

"Isn't there?"

"What if someone looked closer at *him*? Wouldn't things have ended differently?"

Margo pulls away, chuckling darkly. The sound echoes through my skull. "No, Ren. I don't think it would have changed anything at all."

# 5

The sun is hidden behind storm clouds when I back out of faculty parking that afternoon. Fall can sometimes bring volatile weather. Particularly September. The bitter chill of winter crashes violently into summer's humidity. At any given moment the fattest of raindrops might fall, a tornado siren could sound, forcing everyone out of their homes—both mobile and stick built—and into the community storm shelters that are diagonal from the baseball fields and across the street from the Dollar General.

I'm looking through my windshield at those threatening clouds when I see her.

The girl who'd run from Bryson's room.

Her head's down, arms swinging at her side. The white of an earbud is visible in her left ear as her long blond hair catches the wind and whips around her opposite shoulder. There are no signs of the sadness I'd seen earlier. No sign of any emotion at all. Teenagers are like that. One minute roaring and wailing about the unfairness of life and the next apathetic to it. Could that be all this morning was? A teen being a little over dramatic? A few innocent coincidences?

She glances sideways at me. Makes eye contact once again. I hold the brakes, unwilling to move and unable to look away. Her eyes. They're Margo's.

The thought hits me suddenly and painfully. But it doesn't make sense because this girl looks nothing like Margo physically. Margo walked with her shoulders back. Smiling and laughing. Throwing greetings and comments to every student she passed. She was friends with everyone. The girls who called radio stations trying to score boy band tickets all the way to the guy dressed in black with chains hanging from his jeans. Margo never knew a stranger.

This girl walks hunched over. Eyes alight with awareness. But there's a quietness about her that's almost painful to look at.

Margo was a bouquet of sunflowers, and this girl is ivy growing up the side of a Victorian house. Yet there's something there. A string connecting them only I can see.

Like a skittish animal, she averts her face and speeds toward the student lot.

When I'd seen Bryson in the halls after lunch, he'd tried acting like his old self. Cracking jokes. Winking at students. He'd even managed to put his tie back on. But something was off about him. The forced way he responded to his students. The careful distance he kept between them. He'd even talked to me on my way out, right as I was locking up. "Sorry about earlier," he'd said good-naturedly, running a hand through his wavy hair. "I was just distracted."

I murmured something back, something equally as bland, and as I walked away, I could sense it. He was aware.

Aware of what I knew.

The girl is gone now. Disappeared behind the athletic building. But I'm still locked in place, debating what I should do next.

"You shouldn't do anything." Margo is tenser than usual, and I have no idea how long she'd been sitting there. Watching me. "He's just a teacher. Just a random guy who enjoys getting his ego stroked by impressionable students." She tells me like she sees the wheels spinning in my mind and needs to slow them down before they really get going.

"She was sobbing, Margo."

"Girls are emotional."

I make a sound in the back of my throat, and Margo laughs. "You've hated that saying since before feminism was cool, haven't you?"

"Something happened in that classroom. I know it." My fingers tighten on the wheel. White knuckles. Pressure. I feel as if I could rip it clean off my car if I wanted.

"Because you're so familiar with student-teacher dynamics?"

There it is. The piece connecting this girl and Margo. It's glowing red hot now, even as it's summed up into three tidy words.

"That what killed you, Margo? *Student-teacher dynamics*?" I ask, but she isn't here. Margo's always been good about leaving when things get difficult.

Someone honks behind me.

I finally start moving.

It wasn't hard to find Bryson's address. All teachers are provided a faculty directory. What was difficult was giving myself an excuse to find it. I hadn't meant to look for it earlier today. Not really. I was only curious.

I especially didn't mean to come here now.

His home isn't what I expected. It's a small ranch-style house in a residential neighborhood almost fifteen minutes from the school. His car is parked in the driveway under a dilapidated basketball hoop. There's no net, but I can picture him on the weekends, shooting hoops, making conversation with neighborhood kids. Hoping someone is watching him. Appreciating him.

His house is at the end of a cul-de-sac, and I park on the opposite side of the road, facing the other direction. Gives me a decent vantage point through my rearview.

"What do you think you're going to see?" Margo is back and thankfully much more relaxed now. It always did stress me out when she was upset.

I decide not to answer Margo. I don't know what I'll see.

I hope I don't see anything.

I hope I do.

There's a flash of movement behind his windows as he walks past and takes a seat on the couch. There are no blinds or curtains. I can only assume that's the way he likes it. He's the zoo animal and the rest of us have gladly bought tickets to his exhibit.

"Confirmation bias." Margo snorts. "You're reading too much into the lack of curtains. He's a bachelor. Show me one man who buys blinds and curtains. Not nefarious, just lazy. I bet he doesn't have a bed frame either. He's totally sleeping on a mattress on the ground." When it's clear I won't be talking, she leans back and closes her eyes.

The sun sets.

The streetlights come on.

Several cars pull into surrounding driveways. Kids hop out with backpacks half their size. Tired-looking parents holding base-ball bats and duffel bags herd their children into cars, into their houses while shouting reminders to not forget hats and shoes and sandwiches.

I sink low in my seat.

Avoid eye contact with a twelve-year-old boy on a bike.

Coming here was a mistake. This neighborhood is just too busy. And even if it wasn't, I don't know what I'm doing here anyway. Look at me. I read a news article and see one upset kid and suddenly I'm acting like a detective. Like I have any right to be here. I sit up in my seat and reach for the keys just as the lights turn off in Bryson's house.

I hesitate.

Perhaps I should turn the key and drive home. Perhaps I should forget this address altogether. But if I squint, I can see the shadows dancing on the wall from Bryson's TV.

I relax back into my seat. Get comfortable. I'm looking. Just looking. There's no harm in that.

Even if everything is in my head.

The neighboring cars eventually come back. Dirt-stained and drowsy children are ushered into their respective homes. The kid on the bike doesn't look in my direction once as he passes, drop-ping his bike in his yard and running inside. He shuts his front door and takes the light with him, the warmth. I roll my neck and wonder again what I'm still doing here, why I can't seem to leave, why I feel a responsibility to be here at all.

The neighborhood breathes out like an exhausted mother after the baby finally closes their eyes. I reach into my middle console for the pair of black leather gloves that I always keep there.

My fingers close around them.

"Don't do anything stupid, Ren," Margo whispers uneasily.

"You sound like Mom." I grit my teeth. Slip on the gloves. "Margo will be Margo. Ren will be stupid." And I'm out, walking silently toward Bryson's house.

Margo is in front of me now, her hands up to stop me. "What are you doing with those?" I go around her, but she's persistent. "You can't go inside, Ren. That's ludicrous."

Bryson's grass is freshly cut, and his hedges are neat and trimmed. It makes maneuvering to his window quite easy. He's asleep on the couch—one hand under his head and the other in his pants. There's an empty frozen dinner package on a TV tray in front of him, a TV mounted on the wall, and a gaming console on the ground below it.

I bet Margo was right about the bed frame.

Seeing him like this in his own space, vulnerable, exposed, and nothing like his usual self, it's like looking at a *Scooby Doo* villain without the mask. It makes you wonder what you were even scared of in the first place.

It makes me hesitate.

But then I remember we all have two sides, and I guess Bryson has one that's pathetic. I'm on the right side of the house. His back is to me, and I can almost hear him snoring. My fingers skim along the bottom of the window. A quick nudge upwards—

No resistance. It's unlocked.

Show me a single woman with the confidence to leave her windows unlocked.

"Men are monsters," Margo says. "But sometimes women are too."

"Equality and all that," I mutter without looking at my sister.

I'm sweating now, a feeling unraveling inside of me that's something between excited and compulsive. Margo is at my ear, the scent of her breath—cherry bubble gum—sending me straight back in time. "What's your plan, Ren? You still have time. Go back to the car."

I'm focused on my sister now, her eyes wide and pleading. One of my fingers rests at the base of the window. On how easy it would be to slide it up, to go inside his home. Examine his bedroom and kitchen junk drawer. See who he really is. Then I'd know for sure, and if it's all in my head, it wouldn't even matter because no one would ever know.

No one would get hurt.

I'm preoccupied enough that I don't notice Bryson's movements. So quickly I almost don't have time to move, he tilts his head over his shoulder and looks behind him. At me.

I duck, my heart dipping to my toes, all feeling leaving my fingers. He shouldn't be awake. I didn't expect him to wake up.

Margo won't say I told you so, even if she's thinking it. What do I know about this man really? Why am I so consumed by him? What in the hell am I doing here?

I'm frozen against the side of his house, pulse hammering so loud he must hear it from inside. His front door opens. I close my eyes. Wait for his accusing voice. Think of what I could possibly say to him to explain this.

*Hey, Bryson! Remember how you accused me of not liking you earlier? Well... you were right.*

There's a creak as if he has one foot hovering over the porch, contemplating.

I wait. But there are no footsteps.

Then the door closes.

My breath stutters. I won't acknowledge the knowing look on Margo's face. Won't admit how close I was to making a huge mistake.

I flee to my car, ripping off my gloves before I'm fully seated. I shove them to the bottom of the console, knowing I should just throw them away. Throw them from my car window and never wear or think about them again. And for a second, I almost do it.

I shouldn't have come here.

Not just here to Bryson's house but *here.* Home.

This place is supposed to be different. I'm supposed to be different here. But how can I be? How can I change myself when this town brings out the darkest parts of me?

In the window of the house nearest my car, I think I see a pale face. Another watcher in the dark. Another person to carry the brunt of my secrets. But when I look again, there is no one there.

"I see you, Ren," Margo says from the passenger side, her voice quiet, defeated. "Isn't that enough?"

I don't answer.

Instead, I start driving.

# 6

My body hurts when I wake.

I flex my left hand and wince. The deep gash runs along the inside of my palm, covered haphazardly by a bandage that's now soaked through with dried blood. It's so swollen I can't even bend it.

"Shit," I mutter aloud, holding my hand up to the light.

"Yeah," Margo says from the edge of my bed. She snaps her gum. "You really messed up last night."

———

I check every square inch of the hood and inside of my car before leaving for school, searching for any clues as to where it's been. Traces of last night.

There's a small indentation above the headlight. I can't remember how long it has been there.

I wash it with the strongest chemicals I can find. Scrub the driver's-side door and then open it to find dry blood on the wheel and door handle. I roll up my sleeves and get to work.

Then I go to school.

My foot is heavy on the gas. I try not to look at my hand. Freshly bandaged. No more blood leaking through. I could almost forget it was there. Almost.

"Do you even remember what happened?" Margo doesn't sound angry. More concerned than anything, and that bugs me. I hate that she still gets to be the unruffled big sister while I'm stuck playing the vexatious little one.

I cut my eyes at her. "It was an accident."

"You don't accidently do something like that, Ren."

One traffic light in town, and of course it's red. I ease to a stop, careful not to look out my window. There are a group of men standing outside the gas station to my right. My cheeks warm as they look at me. Stare right into my window.

A cold chill breaks out over me.

Were they there last night?

I try and picture all the faces, but it's all muffled and fuzzy. Broken up by the other memories. The man holding out a drink, a charming smile on his face. His clammy hand in mine as I followed him to his room.

A scream.

The searing pain in my hand.

"Come on," I mutter. The light is blaringly red as traffic slowly piles up behind my car.

A fog descends, locking me in a hazy gray. Filtering into my brain like slow poison, snuffing out all other sounds, all other sights. Fourteen years ago. The butterflies in my stomach. *Me* in *his* classroom. Standing at his desk. The room smelled like him, cinnamon and spice. He gave me that look, and I leaned a little too close.

The door was open, but really, I wasn't thinking of anything at all.

Nothing mattered except him.

Until Margo's voice rose sharply behind me. "Ren? You need a ride?" She stood there, fingers tight around the straps of her backpack. I twisted around, putting space between me and my teacher. Her curious gaze shifted back and forth between us, and I hated feeling like there was something to be embarrassed about. Something I should be ashamed of.

Not us.

Not this.

A horn blasts from behind me. An angry mom in a blue minivan pointing at the green light.

I hit the gas.

When I park in the faculty lot, there's a clawing, restless need growing inside me getting harder and harder to deny. I step out of my car and breathe. A hand braced against my car and the other on my stomach, trying to make it look like I'm searching for something in the middle console. Someone slams a car door behind me, and I jump, nearly slamming my head into the ceiling. I breathe in through my nose and out through my mouth, aware of the cheerleaders nearby, practicing on a patch of grass at the front of the building. There are also a couple stragglers near the baseball field on the back side of the building. Hunched-over girls in dark clothing staring down at cell phones that blast music I can hear from here.

I breathe in deeply again.

"Morning, Ren." Someone calls out behind me.

I wave over my shoulder.

Center myself.

Last night went too far. But it was an accident. It doesn't matter what Margo says. I'll be more careful. I won't make the mistake again.

I'm fine.

Everything is fine.

One more breath is all I can afford before I force myself to straighten and walk toward the building.

Margo falls into step with me. "Think about why this is eating you up. Think about what you've done. You shouldn't have been there at all. Maybe the problem is you."

I clench my jaw. She's right.

Last night. Fourteen years ago. Bryson.

It's all jumbled together. One death. A runaway teen. A girl leaving his classroom crying. These are common scenarios. These are tragedies in life that happen every day. There's no real connection to Bryson. At least nothing that should lead me to believe he's been anything other than truthful.

Nothing that should make me feel like I am losing control.

Nothing that should make me do what I did last night.

"Ren." Margo's voice is quiet, calmer. She must sense me wavering. "Maybe you shouldn't be here. It's this town. It isn't good for you. You're not ready."

Maybe she's right. The thought is paralyzing.

After all, the whole reason I came back was to work on my relationship with my parents, and I haven't even made contact with them yet. The only thing I've done so far is hyperfocus on a man until it felt like I was sliding against my will, nails dragging on the ground beneath me, back in time. And I'm tired. So tired.

How long until last night happens again?

How much farther will I sink before I hit the bottom?

"You can get help," Margo whispers. "It isn't too late. This isn't the right place for you. You're not ready yet, Renny."

I stop abruptly, heels sliding over concrete. The cheerleaders are louder now. Directly in my ear. I see a few heads tilt in my direction, and I turn and keep walking toward the front entrance.

Margo follows.

She's right again, and it hurts. It hurts to know that I'm so messed up from my past that I can't handle working here. That I can't just be normal. That I have to find the worst in every situation.

The screaming and clapping fades to a buzz, and that's when I see her.

The figure sitting on the bench. Margo's bench. The girl from Bryson's class.

"Her being here doesn't mean anything," Margo says, quickly, urgently. "There are lots of people out here, Ren."

Technically, kids are supposed to wait for the first bell to ring in the gym or cafeteria. But, like the girls near the baseball field, not everyone adheres to the rules.

"Ren."

The way she's sitting now makes me think she needs a minute of solitude. Her shoulders are curved down, and her face is stormy.

The restless feeling is back, tugging on my hair like an unruly child.

"I only want to talk to her." I don't know if I'm convincing myself or Margo. "Just to make sure. Then I'll know I can leave."

I walk straight for her.

She has her earbuds in and clearly hasn't spotted me yet. It gives me a moment to look at her. The girl is small. A few inches over five feet give or take. She has long blond hair that hangs in corkscrews over her thin shoulders, which are being drowned in an oversized jean jacket. It's a style I've seen the other kids wear. Though their jackets are clearly new and made to look vintage, hers looks like she pulled it right out of her mom's closet. And I know she must have, because Margo wore one of my mother's just like it over a decade ago, all the way to the blue patch on the shoulder.

The spot where my heart is supposed to be pulses.

Her head darts up, and her overlined lips thin and pinch tight. Her eyes, a seafoam green, narrow. There's something about her that's unique. Something that makes you look twice, though you're not sure why.

I greet her once I'm several feet away. "Hello."

"Ms. Taylor." Her eyes flit from my face over my outfit. A gray pencil skirt and white blouse. Nothing special, and she must notice. She looks away, back at an open notebook on her lap. "I'm sorry. I can go back. The gym was just getting way too loud."

"No, stay."

She looks up, eyes widening like she hadn't expected me to say that. They get even bigger when I sit next to her. Neither of us say anything for a long moment. I take another second to watch her. I'm trying to see everything. To understand who she is.

To understand how I could have made all this up in my head.

A spider crawls over her thigh, and she doesn't flinch. Just lays her palm down and lets it crawl in her hand before placing it on the ground carefully.

Her cheeks heat when she sees me watching. "I never did understand why everyone smashed spiders. What about them is so horrible that they need to be killed without question?"

Something burns within me. It's like sitting next to my sister. Margo wouldn't even swat flies. She'd dance around our house like an idiot, trying to shoo them out windows. "I saw you yesterday, didn't I?" I ask.

"What happened to your hand?"

Her question takes me off guard, and I fold my hands in my lap. Flashes from last night pierce my brain. The blood leaking down my wrist, sticking to my steering wheel while driving home. The palm print on my front door I didn't realize was there until this morning. I'd had to clean it on my way out the door, hoping no one had seen it in the bright light of day. "I got a little too excited and did something foolish," I say quickly, deciding that was as close to the truth as I could get. "That was you yesterday, wasn't it?"

If my questioning throws her off, she doesn't show it. "Uh, I don't think so."

"Coming out of Mr. Lewis's room. Before B lunch."

Something else trickles onto her face now. A tightness like someone is stretching plastic across her skin.

"You were upset," I remind her gently.

"Oh, yeah. No. It wasn't like that."

"You weren't upset?"

"I mean, I was. But it's not a big deal. Just—problems with my ex-boyfriend. I was talking to Mr. Lewis about it." She looks down at her own hands, and her left leg starts bouncing.

Bryson told me she'd been crying about a family situation at home. "Is everything OK with your ex now?"

"Define *OK*." She unlocks her phone, flashing me the screen. It's a picture of a teenage boy in front of a stadium with another girl on his back. They're both laughing. She scoffs at it before sliding it in her pocket. "We only broke up at the start of summer."

"Does he go here?" I ask carefully, trying to feel her out. I'd been so close last night to making another mistake. I remember the back of Bryson's head. How easily his window inched up.

What if I'd gotten it all wrong?

What if he'd been telling the truth?

"No, thankfully." She's still avoiding eye contact. "It really isn't a big deal. We weren't together long."

A teacher I recognize but can't name walks past, looking between us curiously. I nod, forcing a smile, but don't say anything until she's inside the double doors. I look back at the teenager next to me. "You were pretty upset to not have dated long."

The girl groans dramatically. Another Margo-like thing to do. How many times had I stood behind her while she paced the room, talking expressively on the house phone? Her hands in the air, in her hair. Her face pinched up as she alternated between gasping and laughing with her friends. Every time she made eye contact with me in the mirror she'd stick her tongue out or roll her eyes playfully.

"You sound like my brother," she says quietly, but now there's a smile playing on her lips.

"Does he go here?"

Her eyes narrow. "Why are you asking me all this? Do you think I'm lying or something?"

As long as I've taught students, I still get surprised by their directness. Especially from students like her. The ones who come off the most quiet are often hiding the most strength.

"No, that's not it. I was just worried about you."

"You don't even know me." She looks at her feet now, scuffing her shoe onto the concrete.

"You're right. I don't know you. I'm Ms. Taylor. You are?"

She looks up at me with two furrowed brows, hesitating only a second before answering. "Olivia Green."

"You're in Mr. Lewis's third period?"

First bell rings, and she springs up, shouldering her backpack. There's a faint sheen of sweat on her face that likely matches my own. I flap my blouse, feeling it stick to my body. It's not even 8:00 a.m., but the September sun is piercing, and the humidity is so thick you could stick a fork in it.

"Olivia," I say, standing and placing a hand on her arm just to get her attention—but only for a second before I pull away.

She doesn't look at me.

Everywhere except me.

"Yesterday, after you left, Mr. Lewis wasn't wearing his tie. Did he take it off in class?"

"Uh, I don't know. I didn't even notice. I should get to first period. I think we're dressing out in gym today." She pulls away, risking one more glance in my direction before hurrying inside the gym doors.

"Ren." Margo's voice is a whisper behind me, and I know everything she wants to say. Everything she's not saying.

She knows me just as well, so I don't have to answer out loud. She already knows.

I can't leave yet. Not when I know, deep down on a gut level, Olivia Green just lied to my face.

# 7

I watch Bryson the first half of the day. Watch his goofy smile. The way he welcomes students into his classroom. And I can't fight the feeling he's watching me right back.

*Had* he seen me last night?

"You OK today, Ren?" he asks while we stand in the hallway, side by side. The weird energy fluctuating between us.

"Why do you ask?"

"You seem distracted," he says, and his eyes shift down to my hand. "Whoa, what happened there?"

"Just me being thoughtless."

"Ouch." He raises his eyebrows dramatically. But there is something off in his tone. He doesn't believe me.

Guess the feeling is mutual.

———

Before lunch, the same two girls as yesterday corner me about the pig carcass we're set to dissect on Monday. "We were thinking," Delilah says. "Instead of an actual essay, we could make a video about pigs."

"We saw this video that these biology students did for a project. It went viral. We think we could do something like it but focus more on the life of the pig instead of the death."

They continue talking, but I'm watching the door. Searching for Olivia or Bryson. Something that will tell me my suspicions aren't crazy.

Margo sits on the edge of my desk, picking at her chipped purple fingernails. "Is this really who you are now? Invasive. Suspicious. Borderline creepy." Her molten brown gaze meets mine. "And what will that mean for Bryson when you snap, Ren?"

"Ms. Taylor?"

I blink at the empty space my sister had just occupied and look at the girls. "Pardon?"

"Uh, did you hear what we said?"

"The video project is fine. Just make sure it covers chapters five and six. Use the vocabulary. I need to see you're making an effort."

When the girls leave, I lay my head on my desk. The feeling is toxic. Olivia. Bryson. His tie. His *lie*. Olivia told me she talked to him about her boyfriend. Why would he say it was a family matter? Which one of them is lying?

Are they confused? Or am I?

"Oh, sorry, I can come back."

I lift my head. Our custodian. My old classmate. Billy. He stands in the doorway with a giant rolling trash can. He's tall. Taller than I remember. He has stubbled cheeks and hair that is in clear need of a trim. Not quite the gangly boy I knew in high school but close enough to it that it makes me want to look away.

Reminds me that none of us ever really change.

I've only seen him in passing since the day of the faculty meeting, and he hasn't looked at me twice over the month since. Once I'd even thought of approaching him, making conversation, and it's like he knew the direction of my thoughts and went in the opposite direction. It made me wonder if I imagined the whole thing, the way he stared at me that day. Maybe he never recognized me at all.

But the way he looks at me now, it brings it all back.

"You can come in, Billy. I was just about to leave anyway."

His cheeks redden. "You remember who I am?"

"You were in Margo's grade. This school wasn't that big."

"No, it's just, I remembered you," he says. "I didn't think you knew who I was."

"Of course, I do. I've been meaning to talk to you. I just haven't really seen you around. How've you been?"

"Good. Yeah, really good. Hey, I should get started. If I don't get this whole hall done before lunch ends, then I'll get behind, and Smart will have my ass."

"Come on in."

He smiles, and his lips twitch like he isn't used to it. Then he gets to work on emptying the trash cans in my room. Eminem blasts from his earbuds, and when he walks, he bobs his head with the music. Billy catches me looking and another red blush covers his cheeks, blooming all the way down his neck.

"Sorry, I don't mean to be weird," I tell him.

"What?" He pops an earbud out.

"I don't mean to be weird. I just haven't seen any of Margo's friends in a long time."

I didn't think it was possible, but somehow his cheeks get even redder. "Me and Margo weren't friends."

"Of course, you were. Didn't you do that presentation together in a history class? I remember watching you study in our kitchen."

"The teacher made us work together. She wanted to partner with Nancy."

"She liked you."

"She was nice to me." He shrugs and gathers the bag, hauling it to the door to drop in the giant can. "I don't mean to be a dick."

"No, I didn't think—"

"I am. I can hear it. It's my own insecurities. Your sister was really nice to me, and I'll always appreciate it."

I watch him closely for a second. See the very insecurities he mentioned playing on his face. "You thought she pitied you?"

He looks up sharply, and for a second there are too many emotions on his face to name. But all of them I recognize because the same ones come over me whenever I think of my sister too.

"I know she did. She only agreed to partner with me that day because she felt bad for me."

"She's dead, Billy. She's the one deserving of pity now."

"I'm sorry, Ren. About Margo. Clearly, I'm still holding onto a bunch of stuff that doesn't matter. But you're right. She was good, and I'm sorry she's dead. I have siblings, and if something like that went down with them, I would lose it."

"Thank you."

Billy makes like he's turning to leave before stopping. "I

remember the rumors. I know what they said after everything went down. I never bought into any of that. It was all *him*."

*Him.*

It's like everyone is afraid to say his name.

Or maybe they're just afraid to say it to me.

Billy bobs his head a little too roughly. "Anyway, I should get back to work, but maybe we could hang out sometime. Catch up. I don't know." The words take me by surprise. Nobody from school spoke to me after Margo died. No one asked me on a date. There were no tearful goodbyes at graduation. His invitation feels like a sucker punch.

"There's this bar right up the road," he says. "The Blue Lantern. Across from the corner store. I go there sometimes. Few others you may remember from school. We hang out there on Fridays."

I know the place. I can remember driving by as a teen, watching middle-aged, washed-up people come in and out, wobbly and holding beer cans. The country music always bled out onto the street, and if you were unlucky enough to drive past at night, you'd almost always see the flashing lights of the police in the lot.

I used to think I would never set foot somewhere like that. That was before Margo. "They won't care if I come?"

Maybe Billy can hear the discomfort in my tone or the steady clip of my heart that's been on a sharp uptick since he mentioned *him*. Or it could just be written on my face.

"Of course not," Billy says. "Ain't nobody there who cares about something that happened so long ago."

With one last wave, Billy backs out of the room.

And inside my head, everything feels like it's boiling over.

"Where do you think it comes from?" Margo asks from her spot leaning against a lab table.

"Where does what come from?"

"The anger inside of you. It can't just be because I'm dead."

The answer is there. Burning in technicolor. The brush of his hand along my shoulder. His laugh, floating across his desk. An exchange of candy, of jokes, of anecdotes. Of attention.

He'd call on me when no one in the room could give him the correct answer. *Shortstack?*

The other girls would roll their eyes. *Suck-up,* they'd mouth. *She wants to suck something,* they'd say.

But his gaze, his eyes on me, they'd give me all the confidence I needed. I only ever had eyes for him.

Until that night.

"You never really saw me the way I saw you, did you, Renny?" There's hurt on her face. But not anger. Never anger with me. Perfect Margo.

"No." I shake my head honestly. "But I'm finally seeing something." And I don't say it, but she knows. She knows that I have to do something.

I have to do what I didn't do all those years ago.

# 8

Principal Smart stares back at me from across his desk.

The room is more open than I remember. His windows aren't covered like my principal kept them. The one time I remember coming in here as a teenager was after my sister died. The room had been dark except for the lines creasing the edge of the blinds. It had smelled faintly of cigarettes and potpourri as Principal Marx gave me a speech that was probably supposed to be comforting. I'd left with a blinding headache and a bleeding heart.

Principal Smart's environment is different. Clean. Muted colors. A cougar bobblehead on his desk. A small couch in the corner of the room with a blanket thrown over the back, our school's mascot and logo smiling toothily from the fabric. Principal Smart himself is a lot like his office. Nondescript. Perhaps a little too spirited.

"Ms. Taylor, I have to say, it was a surprise when you requested to meet with me. What can I do for you? How are you adjusting?"

"Good. I like it here."

"I've heard great things." He clasps his hands in front of him. "Students talk and all that. I didn't realize you were a Benton Cougar when you interviewed either. It wasn't on your resume, and I didn't think to ask." He sighs a big gusty breath. Minty. Like he'd popped one when he saw me coming. There's a sandwich wrapper in the can beside his desk with what looks like mayo smudged on the side.

"I'm so sorry about your sister," he says. "You saw the tribute in the main hall? Some have wondered about taking it down, but I think it's important to remember the past. Particularly, members of our Benton family who have passed on. Really moves me, seeing her face every day like that. Think it does the same for everyone here. Especially those who knew and taught her. Reminds us to appreciate the little things."

I try to force the thickness from my throat. This is the worst part when someone you love dies. How you have to share them with others. Even people who didn't know them. They look at me like they understand my grief, like they're active participants in it.

*I hate that.*

*I can't even imagine.*

*I don't want to.*

Every time they try and placate me with meaningless words or talk of Margo like she was theirs more than she was mine, they take a little piece of her from me. One day I figure I won't have any of her left.

I begin. "You're probably wondering why I'm here—"

"If it's about your sister, if things are difficult seeing—"

"I'm here concerning Bryson Lewis."

"Oh." He sits back in his desk, his smile falling away. "Oh. What about him?"

"There was a situation on Friday." I explain what I saw. Olivia leaving his room in tears. His missing tie. I don't bring up Rosemary Academy, mostly because I don't know enough about the dead or missing girl to claim that they're somehow connected to Bryson, regardless of my own personal feelings on the subject. And I get the feeling if I say too much, push too much, he'd write me off as obsessive.

Principal Smart is silent. Watchful. There's a deep silence before he sighs. This breath is different. Sour. Annoyed. "Ms. Taylor, I appreciate you coming to me today with your concerns. Particularly, in lieu of speaking these concerns to other teachers. Thank you as well for keeping such a close eye on our students here." He clears his throat and sits forward in his desk.

Margo is behind him, hands on his shoulders. "But," she says with a smirk.

"But Mr. Lewis is a well-qualified—honestly, overqualified teacher. The students love him. We haven't had a single issue with him since his transfer. Well, except students fighting in droves to get into his class."

"I've seen him teach. I know they like him. But if you had seen—"

"Ms. Taylor," he interrupts, his voice irritatingly calm. "You're understandably having a rough transition being here again. If it's the photo of your sister that's making you so agitated, then I can remove it. Perhaps find a more private area for it."

"What?" I recoil sharply. "This has nothing to do with Margo."

"It's a normal response for you to see things the way you do.

Make these…connections. After everything that happened to your sister, it's understandable."

"You think I'm making this up because I'm traumatized by what happened to Margo?" *Tell me more*, I want to demand. *Tell me more about my pain and where it comes from. Tell me how I feel.*

"No," he says too quickly. "Not making it up. You're just understandably prone to being mistrustful. Bryson is a young, male teacher. He must remind you of the man who…uh…"

"The man responsible for her death? You can say his name, and you can say hers for that matter."

"I don't mean to upset you."

"This has nothing to do with what happened to Margo." I sit forward in my seat and try to lower my voice, deepen it. Anything to make him take me seriously. But I feel immediately silly. "It's about what I saw. And it may not have to do with anything, but he left his old school in such a rush."

"That business at Mr. Lewis's old school had nothing to do with him. Rumors. Surely, you're familiar with the rumor mill." There's a pointed measure to his tone. A reference to the rumors that have haunted me my whole life. Not a good point for him to make, especially since a lot of the rumors about me were true.

"That business?" I ask incredulously. "You mean the girl who died or the one who is still missing?" I didn't want to say it, didn't mean to say it, but after throwing my dead sister in my face, my reasons for biting my tongue don't seem so important.

To him, I was too emotional before I opened my mouth.

"I'm not sure what you're insinuating. Students cry, Ms. Taylor. In fact, one leaves my office crying once a day, at least." He chuckles to himself as if expecting me to join. He looks irritated when I stay silent, like I missed my cue and this conversation derailing is all my fault.

"Look," he says. "I meant what I said. If you need help, counseling, or anything at all. If you can't handle being here, we can look into other options."

That's enough to bring me to my feet. I stand stiffly. "If I can't handle being here?"

"You're emotional, Ms. Taylor. Like I said, it's expected."

Margo, still behind Principal Smart, watches me. "What did you think, Renny? That he was going to *believe* you? That he would *help* you?"

Hadn't I?

I came in here with every intention of going through the correct channels. Righting my past wrongs. Protecting girls who needed it. Girls like Margo before they became like Margo.

Victims.

Dead.

My fists clench at my sides, but I force myself to breathe, to relax. "I'm sorry," I say without looking at my sister. "I shouldn't have wasted your time."

My walk is brisk, face bloodred with anger. The secretary says something to me on my way out, but I pretend to not hear her as I swing open the office door a little too harshly. There is only five minutes left of lunch when I make it, and by then, my blood is a steady roar in my ears. It drowns out all other noises in the cafeteria. The women glance at me curiously as I slide into our table empty-handed, but none of them ask where I've been or why I'm not eating. They talk about Koa's mother-in-law and Lynette's shoes.

I think of Olivia.

"Hey, you coming?"

"Pardon?"

Emma's face comes into focus, her braids flipped over her shoulder, a blush blooming over umber skin. She strokes her tummy through her floral dress. "The bell rang, Ren."

"Right." I stand too quickly. My center of gravity shifts, and I brace myself on the table to keep from stumbling.

"You sure you're OK?"

None of the other teachers have stayed back, and most of the students around us have already filed toward the doors.

I lean closer to Emma. "Actually, I wanted to ask you something."

"OK?"

"The rumors about Bryson Lewis. From his old school. Do you know anything about them?"

Her eyes ping-pong around us. "Why are you asking about Bryson again?"

"You've been here a lot longer than me. You're friends with a lot of the staff. You've had to have heard something." I don't mean to sound so desperate, but I can't help it. I can feel that I'm running out of time. The clock is quickly counting down, and I don't know what's going to happen when the buzzer hits zero.

The last few students trickle out, and Emma looks at the door uneasily as a new wave of students filter in.

"Really quickly," I add. "I know you need to get back to class."

"Look." She lowers her voice. "My husband plays golf with Smart. That country club off I-10. They've done it for years. This is something Smart mentioned to him. Not something everyone knows. I'm not even supposed to be saying it to you."

"I won't say anything to anyone."

"Will you tell me why you want to know at all?"

"If I had an answer for you, Emma, I would. But I can't explain it right now."

Her teeth snap together sharply, flashing a bright white that I could never manage no matter how many times I brushed. "All I know is this: Principal Smart told Jack that there were rumors about Bryson and a teenage girl. Some girl on the volleyball team he coached. According to him, they really were just rumors with absolutely no evidence to back anything up. But when she died, people started talking."

Hearing those words outside of my own head makes my stomach drop. I was right.

"Alejandra Gomez." I nearly whisper her name. "The girl from Rosemary Academy who was found in the woods."

"You've heard of her?"

"Yes."

"Apparently, the principal and superintendent pressured him into resigning. Didn't really give him much of a choice. Said he was too much of a distraction. Smart goes way back with Bryson's family and let him transfer without asking too many questions. That's it; that's all I know."

Smart looked me in the eye when I told him my suspicions. Looked at me with pity while telling me I was too emotional, and it was all in my head.

God. The anger. It rivals anything I've ever felt. Bitter storm clouds gathering, violent and black.

"Thank you," I say hoarsely. "Seriously, Emma. This has been a lot of help."

"You'll tell me what this is about when you know?"

"I promise."

The halls are silent as I walk to class. My students are probably anxiously waiting at the door, but I can't bring myself to speed up. Somehow, I end up in front of the trophy case. Margo's smiling face. Blond, perfectly curled hair. A shiny crown. A lovely smile. A future flashing in her eyes she would never see.

Encapsulated here forever.

Suddenly, I'm in this same main hall but fourteen years before. Head tucked low, thinking of my next class. A project due. Biology. Ms. Gats is a stickler, and I could tell from the first day she wasn't my biggest fan. I didn't color in the packets as well as other girls. Didn't try as hard. Didn't see the point.

Which is what every single boy in my class did. It's just unacceptable when a girl does it too.

Someone bumps into me. I look up just before slipping into my own class. That's when I see him.

Mr. Henry.

Tall, with brown hair that glints blond in the sun. The girls always talk about the way his dress shirts stretch over his shoulders. The way he smiles crookedly at them. His eyes meet mine, and my heart skips a beat. *Morning, shortstack.*

*I'm not that short.*

*You're not that tall either.*

When I walk past him into class, he pats my shoulder, his hand lingering a second too long.

The years fade to dust. The hallway lightens. The lockers age badly.

And I'm back.

I place my good hand over the glass of the trophy case. Over Margo's face, nearly lost behind stacks of trophies and ribbons and medals. Various awards and honors for students over the passing years. Mr. Henry isn't in his classroom anymore. Margo isn't giggling on the stage during theater or waving from a borrowed Mustang in the homecoming parade. But I can see her face over my shoulder in the reflection of the glass, feel her warm breath tickle my cheek. Feel the pain emanating from her, from all she's lost.

"You couldn't stop it when it happened to you. What makes you think you can stop it now?" Her voice is a hushed whisper.

I turn quickly to face her, but she's gone.

Just like the night she went into the water.

"I don't know," I say to no one. "But I have to try."

———

That night I go home to a dark house.

I turn on the TV to drown out the noise in my head.

The news anchor's voice pierces me in the heart. "…was found dead outside of Stefan's Hotel and Bar downtown. His body left abandoned from what the police say is a hit-and-run—"

The living room is blanketed in darkness and silence as I hold the remote in my trembling hand.

I wait for the regret.

The guilt.

It doesn't come.

# 9

I don't know what motivates me to finally make the drive to my parents. But I do it the next day after school. I haven't been back since that first try. I'd thought about it. Nearly talked myself into it more than once.

But I never could actually do it.

Just like last time, I don't make it up the driveway. From my vantage point, I can just see the roof of the house. See the spot Mom and Daddy used to wait for me and Margo to get off the bus. For a second, my foot pulses over the accelerator like I can drive into the memory and bury myself in it. Margo shoving me playfully as we run off the bus. Mom watching with a smile and two juice boxes in her hands as she waves.

I blink, and the scene is superimposed with another. An after-Margo memory. It started out slow, my mother's descent into her own mind. A gradual fall until one day Mom was outside our house in a bathrobe, on her hands and knees spraying a bottle of bleach into the grass. The school bus dropped me off, and I remember the heat in my cheeks when I saw her. When I saw the look on our bus driver's face and the faces of my classmates pressed into the glass windows. Some were laughing. Some were confused.

*Poor lady*, their faces said, *one daughter dead and the other killed her. It would make anyone lose their minds.*

*These tiny little bugs, Ren,* Mom had said when she spotted me. *They're everywhere in the house. It's an infestation. I have to see where they're coming from. I have to kill the whole colony.* There was blood on the gravel driveway from her knees and sunburn on her cheeks. She must have been out here for hours.

I'm so caught in the memory that I don't see him. My father stepping off the porch, walking toward my car.

I force myself to get out.

He stops a few feet away. "Ren, you didn't mention you were visiting."

"Good to see you too, Dad."

"I didn't mean anything by that."

Dad looks older than I remember. His face sunken in by shadows and a patchy beard. When I'm close enough, I notice he smells the same—tobacco and peppermint. I can't decide if that comforts me or makes me nauseous. I hesitate in front of him, unsure of what to do with myself or my hands.

I didn't plan on actually seeing him. Didn't plan on this conversation. What do you say to the man who raised you? A man you haven't seen in four years and only a handful of times before that? Do you hug him? Do you acknowledge you've been pretending, and you know he has too?

Are you allowed to ask him to pretend just a little longer?

Roughly, he pulls me against him. It feels forced. Like he knows he should do it, but he doesn't really want to. When's the last time we truly embraced?

"It's good seeing you." He breathes onto my head, fluttering the hair.

It almost feels real.

Then he drops his hands. Pulls back and steps away. There's a redness to his cheeks. "How—uh, long are you here for?"

"I'm only dropping in for a few minutes. I wanted to check on you and Mom."

"Long commute for a quick check-in, huh?"

"It's only half an hour."

"Thought you were in Atlanta?" he asks gruffly, his brows furrowing.

"I live just outside of Benton now."

He pulls back sharply. "What about Allen?"

"We split up two years ago."

"I see," he murmurs, clearly troubled. "I must have forgot about that."

"I haven't told you. Besides, sometimes I forget too." It isn't a lie. Looking back at the years I spent with Allen feels like I'm watching someone else's life in a film. I married him right out of college, and as he grew up and outward, toward the sun, life, and the future, I shrunk inward, into my own darkness.

We lasted two years.

He hisses out a breath. "I'm sorry, Ren."

I want to ask if he's more sorry for missing my divorce or my actual wedding? A courthouse affair in the pouring rain.

And what about the other years in between? What is he really sorry for?

"It was amicable." Which is mostly the truth. I don't think Allen hated me completely in the end.

*Who are you, Ren? Why are you doing this to us?*

I close my eyes at the assault of memories. Allen, whatever he felt when things ended, is so much better off without me. Last I heard he's married again with a kid on the way.

"I'm sorry either way, Ren. Now let's have a look at you." Dad's eyes dim as he glances me over. Like he's disappointed. His eyes are an exact copy of my own, and I wonder if he's noticing the lines around them that are starting to match his. The dark circles that have been present since Margo died. Evidence of us aging and changing in ways Margo never will.

There's a steep silence.

I cough and rock back on my heels. "How's Mom doing? I haven't seen either of you since Allen and I came for Easter." The one and only time they met the man nearly five years ago. That was also the last night Allen and I had sex before the divorce, and in my childhood bedroom. He kept his eyes closed the entire time, and when my fingernails sunk into his chest too hard, he'd winced and jerked away, stalking straight to the bathroom for an alcohol wipe and bandage. When he came out, I pretended to be asleep.

Dad sighs, his breath jostling his beard and mustache. "She's gettin' by."

There's another silence where neither of us knows what to say. Margo was always the one filling the void at our dinner table. Dad and I were always content with listening and watching. I think it was the silence, after she died, that chased me away. But I don't think the worst part was me leaving. I think the worst part is how my parents just let me go.

I take a small step toward my car.

"Who's out there?" My mother's voice reaches us from the porch.

Dad's eyes go so wide, and I freeze.

"It's Ren, sweetheart."

She doesn't say anything for a long time before the screen door flaps, and she steps outside in a nightgown that might have been white at one point. Her hair, graying from the roots to halfway down and straw blond near the bottom, spills in ribbons over her shoulders. She looks older than I remember. Older than her fifty-five years. It's not just the gray hair, but the deep-set lines to her face, like roadways on the map of her despair. She looks older. Like she's lived an extra year for each one her daughter has been dead. Her eyes, the same deep brown as Margo's, seem to scan my whole body all at once. "Is it really you?"

This is the hard part. The pregnant moment before I realize which version of my mother I'm going to get. Who is she tonight? Easter she'd been cordial. Made it the whole dinner before having a meltdown. It was my fault anyway. I'm the one who made the mistake of bringing up Margo. She'd gone silent at the dinner table and then started sobbing uncontrollably. No one said anything. We all just kept eating until her cries turned to sniffles, and she picked up her fork again.

Allen and I had left early the next morning before she'd even woken up.

"Yes, ma'am. It's me."

Another breath of silence. My fingers tighten on my car keys.

"Well, come up here, won't you."

My breath stalls as I cross the yard, take the three porch steps in one long stride. The feeling builds. The one right before an avalanche, right before your life implodes. The wait for an inevitable outburst. I don't know if I'm waiting for my mother's or my own.

Her eyes stay wary and hard, her lips a firm line. I stop a foot away from her. She lifts an arm and then drops it to her side. "Have you eaten lunch?"

"Yes."

"You're so skinny. You should eat more."

I tug nervously at my sweatshirt. "Yes, ma'am."

"You and your sister, always trying to be so skinny. So different from my generation." She lets out a shaky laugh, and Dad and I pretend we don't notice her use of present tense. "Have you been painting?"

"Ma'am?"

She motions to my canvas shoes. There's a spot of dried red on the tips. I rub the toe of my shoe on the porch rug until it crumbles away, leaving only a yellowish stain. "Yeah, the kids were at school. Must have missed a spot there."

"You always were great at lying to Mom." Margo's suddenly at my side, clearly enraptured by our mother as well. She doesn't take her eyes off her. "Do you think she believes you?"

There's something about having my sister here with me. Something that makes my breath come easier.

"I don't mean to intrude on you or Dad. I plan on coming around more. I thought—I don't know. I thought that might be nice." I sound like a child eager for her parents' approval. It makes me hate the words as they come out, but not enough to take them back.

"Yeah, Margo, honey, of course. Why don't you come on in? I just made a pitcher of sweet tea."

My body jerks, heart stills. "I'm Ren, Mom. Remember?"

She blinks, all feeling on her face snuffed out right before my eyes along with the levity around her lips. Her shoulders sink, her face dims. "Ren."

"It's me. I know it's been a while since we talked. I thought we could change that. I thought we could try..." I can't even finish the sentence. Don't even know how I want to finish it.

This is my mother.

She feels like a stranger.

What am I doing here?

Why do I want her to hold me even now?

She looks away quickly. "I think I'll go to bed now."

"Mama—"

But she's gone, the screen door flapping behind her. I watch it until it goes completely still. I knew this might happen. Expected it. But it stings.

Worse than I thought it would.

There's a shuffle of movement behind me before my dad's hand lands heavily on my shoulder. "I'm sorry, Ren. Your mother—well you know. You bring up memories."

"I plan on coming around more. Maybe that will help."

"Maybe."

"I work at the high school now." I hate myself in this moment. Twenty-nine years old and still desperately grappling for whatever scraps of love they'll toss at my feet. I give them anecdotes like candy and hope they will eventually like the flavor.

"Oh, I didn't know that."

"I pass by here practically every day."

He seems lost, eyes in a faraway point beyond me. "Been awhile since we've been back there."

Since Margo's graduation, actually. She was dead by then, but her class honored her at the ceremony and of course invited my parents. My mom started wailing during the national anthem and didn't stop. Dad had to take her to the car before a single person even walked.

"What made you come back?" Dad asks suddenly. His fingers twitch at his sides, and I wonder if he wishes he had a cigarette. Wishes I wasn't there so he could smoke it.

"I thought it would be good for me, for us."

He frowns, then coughs into his hand, and I swear something in his chest rattles. "Ain't nothing good about that school."

"It's not the same. The people there are different."

He makes a derisive sound. "I've found that most people really aren't that different after all."

It's a direct hit, and we both know it. "What's that supposed to mean?"

"Nothing, Ren."

"I'm an adult now. I'm not a child anymore."

"I know. Guess it's the children I'm worried about."

"I would never hurt anyone."

"No, of course not." He winces. "That's not what I meant. I'm sorry. I really wasn't trying to insinuate anything."

"Will Mom be OK? Maybe I should go in and talk to her."

"Why don't you give her a little space?"

I nod slowly, backing toward the steps. "Space. Yeah, sure."

"You said you'd be back? We can try again then." He sits

heavily in his rocker, and I think when I drive away it will be as if I never came here at all.

"Sure. Bye, Dad."

"Bye."

Margo sits in the passenger seat on the drive home. "It isn't your fault."

The night Margo died plays on a loop in my mind. The way I screamed at her. My nails sinking into the skin of her arm. The way she looked at me like she didn't recognize me at all.

"Whose fault is it then?" I ask.

The rest of the drive is in silence.

# 10

My dark green bungalow with wooden shutters, a rental I'd found only a week before the start of school and rented sight unseen, sits quietly beneath the shadow of a cluster of sassafras trees. The leaves are bright green, an oddly soothing color even now. Even knowing what I did two nights ago.

What I caused.

Gathering some papers that need grading and my sweater from the passenger's seat, I don't see the woman until she's right next to me. "Ren Taylor?"

I start, nearly dropping everything in my arms. "I'm sorry. Do I know you?"

"I'm Detective Wu, Baldwin County Sheriff's Office," she says, flashing a badge. She looks at the hood of my car and back to me. "Do you have a few minutes to talk?"

*Shit.*

My stomach rolls.

The woman is several feet away with a sheepish smile on her face. Her black hair brushes her shoulders, and her rumpled blouse looks as if she's been wearing it awhile or maybe sitting in her vehicle for too long.

Watching my house.

Waiting for me.

"Who did you say you were again?" I hoist my items back in my arms. I know I am a picture of calmness. The surface of a deep black ocean. I'm good at that. Concealing how I really feel. She doesn't know what's really going through my mind at this moment, how I'm thinking of my house. Picturing it, trying to confirm I left all my curtains closed without glancing over to check. Thinking of the bloody smear I'd noticed at the bottom of the stairs last night but didn't clean. Even if a curtain was open, she wouldn't be able to see it, I don't think.

She can't hear the way my heart rate is climbing. Doesn't feel the sweat pooling under my arms.

"Sorry, I didn't mean to sneak up on you. Are you Ren Taylor?"

"Yes."

She motions to my porch. "Mind if we talk for a few minutes?"

"What's this concerning?" But I know. I've known ever since I saw the segment on the local news last night.

I knew they'd come for me eventually. Just didn't think it would be the next day. How did they even find me?

She lowers her voice. "It might be better if we go inside."

"Let's go to the porch. It's so nice out tonight."

She nods thoughtfully, glancing around once more. There aren't any neighbors out, and in the month since I've lived here, that seems to be the norm. Everyone keeps their head down, keeps to themselves. I glance across the street where I know an elderly woman lives. Her curtain twitches, and I swear I see the shadow of someone standing there.

"Ms. Taylor?"

"Right." I look away and clear my throat. "Sorry. This way." There are two rocking chairs on the porch, left here by the last owners. Both chairs, white at one time, are now draped in cobwebs and flaked with black. I swipe at the seat before sitting, holding my papers in my lap tightly and gesturing to the other. "Please have a seat."

The detective eyes the other rocking chair before sitting slowly.

"I was expecting you earlier. You're a teacher, aren't you?" As she says it, she pulls a small notebook and pen out of her jacket pocket.

"I had errands to run. It always takes me so much longer than I think it will." I eye the pen and notebook curiously. "I'm sorry. Can you tell me what this is all about?"

"Where were you last night, Ms. Taylor?"

She almost catches me off guard with the question. The way her whole demeanor shifts. But I'm too prepared. I barely slept last night just thinking of how I'd respond. How measured I'd be. How controlled. The exact inflection of my voice.

"The bar in the lobby of Stefan's in downtown Baldwin."

"Were you with anyone?" Her gaze switches from me to her notebook.

"I met a man named Casey. We had a few drinks. I headed home around nine." All of this is the truth. I force myself not to look at my hand. Not to remember the rest of that night. Everything I'm not saying.

"Were you alone with him?"

"This is about Casey?" I ask in surprise. "Did something happen?"

"Ren, if you could just tell me everything you remember from last night."

"All right. Yeah," I say indignantly, grinding my teeth. "I'll tell you what happened. That asshole is married. I drank with him the whole night. Touchy feely. The whole thing, right? It had been a long week, and, well, you know how it is. So we get up to his hotel room, and everything is going fine if you know what I mean—"

"You were being intimate?"

"Yes." I nod sharply and let out a breathless laugh. "Unfortunately, his phone rings. His wife. Can you believe that? Anyway, he tells me to be quiet, and when he hangs up, he just tries to pick up where we left off. I'm obviously not into it, and I leave." It's all true, I remind myself, soothe myself. Like stroking a purring cat. I didn't do anything wrong.

Not on purpose.

"And that's all that happened?"

"I was tipsy, and it was late. That's all I remember."

Her eyes scan my face, my body. She stops at my bandaged hand, clenched around the papers. "What happened to your hand there?"

"Slammed it in my car door. Why are you here? Why are you asking me this?"

She rests her pen on the paper and trains her gaze on me. "Casey Ballard is dead, Ms. Taylor, and you were the last person to be seen with him."

I breathe in. Out.

"What?" My grip on the papers loosens. "What do you mean?"

"What time did you leave?"

"At nine." I remember because I had his phone. I work my jaw back and forth, staring blankly across the yard. "Whew, this is…a lot. I mean, I didn't know the guy very well. But I certainly wouldn't be speaking so ill of him if I knew—I'm sorry." I look at her. "This is awful. How did you even find me anyway?"

"The bartender identified you from the security footage. Said he remembered your name from your ID because he has a brother called Ren. We pulled the credit card records."

"I'm sorry you went through all that trouble, and I'm not more help." I try to stay casual, but there's a tremor in my voice. "Oh, Lord. This is all so wild. Can you—I mean, can you tell me what happened to him?"

"Hit-and-run."

"Damn."

"When you left the hotel, what was he doing?"

I lick my lips, aware of a slow passing car. The sounds of children playing from somewhere down the street. "Just lying there. In bed."

"Was he clothed?"

"Mostly. His pants. Shirt was on the ground I think."

She raises a brow, jotting something down. "He didn't act like he was going to be leaving anytime soon?"

"Not that I remember."

I didn't do anything wrong, I remind myself. All I need to do is tell her the truth. Most of it.

I didn't do anything wrong.

"Didn't you?" Margo says from the railing of the porch. She's standing perfectly straight with her arms folded. "I told you to be more careful."

I breathe in through my nose. Try and calm my racing pulse. Detective Wu doesn't miss anything. "Are you OK?"

"Just surprised—and confused."

"What are you confused about?"

"I hung out with a rando last night, and suddenly you're here telling me he's dead," I say, wanting to stand up and pace but unsure if my knees could even hold me right now. I bend the corner of a piece of paper down and fold it back. Smooth it out. "I'm sorry. This is just a lot."

"Shut up." Margo's blazing eyes are on me. "Shut up, Ren. You know how this works. You need to stop talking."

I snap my mouth closed.

"You're not in any trouble." Detective Wu tries to sound reassuring, but it doesn't quite ring sincere. "Really, I went through the trouble of hunting you down because I wanted to know more about what you talked about last night. How did he seem to you throughout the night up until you had to leave?"

"I remember it being a typical conversation at first. We hit it off. Talked about work. He mentioned going to some hockey game this weekend." I shake my head. "I really wish I could be of more help. I had a few drinks. It's all a bit fuzzy."

"How did his demeanor change after his wife called?"

"Like I said, he tried to go back to where we left off, but I was done at that point."

"Did that seem to piss him off?" She stares at me as she asks.

"I was the one pissed, Detective," I say. "He seemed…annoyed. But I wouldn't say he was angry."

"Did he mention a wife?" Detective Wu asks.

I make my eyes widen. A tinge of panic in my tone. "No. No. He wasn't wearing a ring, and frankly I didn't get that impression at all."

"What do you mean by that?" Detective Wu narrows her eyes. Tilts her head.

"I told you to shut *up*, Ren," Margo taunts from somewhere beside me. I don't look in her direction.

"He invited me to his room. I didn't think for a second the man was married."

"Huh," she replies. "Another interesting thing, he was found outside at roughly nine fifteen. Still bleeding. Body still warm. It must have happened very quickly after that phone call. Right after you left, actually."

I pull back sharply. "What are you trying to say?"

"Not trying to say anything. I just have a lot of questions, and I'm really hoping you can help me make sense of it all. You said you didn't think he was going to leave, but he left right after you. You didn't see him? Didn't hear anything?"

"No."

"Where were you parked?"

"The lot in front of the bar. The one beside the side entrance."

"Hmmm…"

"Look, I don't know what that man was thinking or where he was going when he was hit. I really don't know." I make sure to hold her gaze a little longer. "Again, I'm really sorry I can't help you more."

She doesn't look away. "And you came straight home after leaving the bar?"

"Yes, I had an early morning. Hey, I'm sorry you drove out here for this." I stand, hoping she gets the message.

A moment passes, and her expression eases. She stands, digging a small card from her pocket. "You'll call if you remember anything?"

I take it, tucking it into the other papers in my arms. "Of course."

"You have a good night, Ms. Taylor."

She climbs into an unmarked sedan parked on the street. When her taillights have dissolved into the night, I go inside. Rest my back against the door, face-to-face with the dried bloody palm print on the railing of the stairs.

I sink to my knees, papers falling and scattering all around.

Here are the things I know: I know Olivia lied to me this morning outside of school. I know Bryson is hiding something. A girl from his old school died. A recent graduate went missing.

I know it could all be a coincidence.

"What else do you know, Ren?" Margo asks. She's sitting on the stairs watching me. I keep my gaze on the smear of blood.

"OK." She stands, walks slowly down the stairs. "I'll go. I know you think you're onto something, but you don't really know anything at all. I know you're so obsessed with Bryson Lewis that you're not thinking straight. A detective literally just questioned you, and all you can think about is him. You're making mistakes. People are getting hurt. So tell me, Renny, do you know how this is going to end?"

I pull my gaze to hers, sadness tugging at my heart. "I won't make another mistake again. This is about Bryson. I can't stop until I know for sure. I can't stop when I could help her."

"Help her? That girl? Olivia?"

"I can help her, Margo. I can save her."

"From what?" she asks, desperately. "What do you think you're saving her from?"

"Something more awful than me. Something worth losing myself for."

Margo is standing over me now, looking down. "Just what are you going to do to find the truth, Ren?"

# 11

My laptop hums to life as I pull up a private browser. To find out what Bryson is hiding, to find out why Olivia lied, why Bryson moved to Benton at all, I have to start at the beginning. The first girl in the puzzle. Alejandra Gomez. The first search pulls up a bunch of similar articles. A tragic accident. Nothing else to see here.

Switching to her social media, I find an Instagram account. The very first post—or rather the last—was right before her death. There are hundreds of comments.

*Rest in peace*

*Fly-High Baby Girl*

*We will never forget you*

It is a picture with her volleyball team. They're huddled around a gold trophy. Alejandra looks deliriously happy. Her perfectly straight teeth take over her entire face in a smile.

*We won BIG tonight. I love my girls!!!*

I scan the other faces and stop at the coaches in the middle.

Bryson and another man looking just as enthusiastic as the girls.

It was posted on October 13. Two days before she died and her very last post. How did this happy and excited girl go from playing a volleyball game to being found dead in a creek?

And how did Bryson go from coaching his team in a championship to resigning only days later?

I start scrolling back, closer to the last team photo, and stop suddenly. A picture of Alejandra in the front seat of someone's car. I'd passed right by this one earlier without paying close attention, but something stops me in my tracks. There's another girl with sunglasses, sitting in profile. But I recognize her. It's an instant injection of ice into my veins.

Tina Drexler.

Alejandra was friends with Tina, the missing girl.

Tina's account is more low-key than Alejandra's. Artistic. She only has several dozen followers, and most of the people she follows are tattoo artists or indie bands. Her photos are never of her but of random objects with filters. Two concert tickets to a band called Mayday Parade. A cup of coffee with a lipstick stain on the edge. A pair of red Converse high-tops at the foot of her bed. The headlights on a car. A cat curling into her windowsill. It's only a few scrolls to reach two years back. Clearly, Tina hadn't updated her profile much.

So different compared to Alejandra.

I scroll back up to a picture of a slightly younger Tina with shorter hair, posing next to an older guy who is holding a guitar. It's one of the only pictures of her. Neither are smiling, and there's a black and white filter that gives the photo an edge. Like I'm looking at a picture from a Joan Jett autobiography. A photo that belongs in the eighties.

I click the image and his name pops up. Fallon Drexler. A brother? I click his profile. His bio reads: *Just a good ole' country boy.*

He posts nothing but pictures of half-drunk glasses of alcohol and bottles. Captions inviting friends to join in for *a couple.* There's a fluorescent sign in the background of several photos. I zoom in.

The Blue Lantern.

It doesn't click at first why the name is so familiar. Then I get it. It's the bar Billy invited me to.

A million puzzle pieces swirl around my head, and I'm not sure if they mean anything. They may not fit together at all. At least not yet. I decide to end my search on Rosemary Academy's website. The prestigious private school has all their extracurriculars listed. Their championship girls' volleyball team has frequent practices.

The next one is on Monday.

I write the time and address and save it in my phone knowing that there's really only one way I can get answers.

I have to talk to the people who were there.

—————

I don't find his photo until the end. I know I shouldn't. I really shouldn't be looking him up, but I have to know. I have to understand the man who died two nights ago. Casey Ballard. He made the local news but not much else. A grown man in the back of a seedy bar isn't front page worthy. The article mentions a bereaved wife and child.

A kid.

That part I didn't know.

But maybe it wouldn't have changed anything even if I did.

———————

Margo is lying across my bed when I finally put away my laptop and pull the covers to my chin. There is no warmth emanating from her. She isn't real.

"You still think it's not your fault?" she asks.

"It's all my fault. Everything. Except that, Margo. He—Casey—didn't leave me any choice."

"You shouldn't have been there."

I roll over and look at her. "Now that I'll agree to."

"With those girls. Alejandra, Tina, Olivia. You're trying to find meaning in something that could be nothing. That's why you're losing it." Margo is lying on her side facing me and looking intensely sad.

"The only thing I regret is not having done it earlier. I'm fourteen years too late," I murmur, and it's true. There were so many chances. So many signs I ignored.

Margo lifts a hand as if to stroke hair from my face, but she pulls back, tucks it under her cheek. I think she's going to argue.

Tell me why I need to stop this. How much is at risk. How losing control could mean losing everything. But she doesn't. Her next words surprise me.

"Maybe I should have been the one to protect myself. I was the older sister."

Was. Another reminder that Margo will be seventeen forever. As my hands wrinkle and crease, as the lines and indentations become increasingly prominent, Margo will be smooth and supple and flawless.

And so very dead.

"Ren?" Margo whispers. "Do you think he would want you now? Or me?"

"I'm old and you're dead. I think it's anyone's game."

Margo laughs, and it's something good. "We were way too competitive back then."

It's true. Video games. Board games. Races up the driveway. With Margo and me, it was always a competition. "I always lost," I say.

Her eyes flash with a sadness so severe I have to look away. "I think you won in the end."

———

I spend the weekend grading papers and cleaning blood.

Sometimes I think about what will happen when Detective Wu comes back. Mostly I think about Bryson and about my next steps.

Soon Monday is here and flies by like a child's flip-book, one image careening into the next. Lecture, lab, test, lecture, lab, test.

It keeps my hands and mind busy. Which is good. I can't overthink what I'm doing this afternoon. My upcoming trip to Rosemary Academy.

By the time lunch rolls around, the last student exits my room, and it's the first time all day I truly breathe. Light seeps in with a warm breeze from a cracked window, and I close my eyes, leaning a hip against a lab table.

Someone knocks, and I open them, prepared to tell whoever to get lost.

Olivia stands there looking back and forth into the empty classroom, clearly unsure. "Can I come in?"

I step back quickly and hear myself say, a little too desperately, "Of course."

She glances over a shoulder at Bryson's door before stepping inside and closing my door behind her.

"We should probably leave it open."

"This will only take a second. I don't want anyone to hear." The way she says it—*anyone*—lets me know that there is a specific someone she's thinking of.

"I'm not a victim," she says right away, playing with the ends of her blond hair. Today she wears the same oversized jean jacket over a pair of bell-bottoms. Rings cover her fingers, and it looks like she's drawn something with a Sharpie on her wrist, but I can't make out what it is.

"OK."

"Nothing weird is happening to me or whatever." Olivia avoids my eyes, but I keep my own face cool and controlled even though my pulse must be strong enough she can see it leaping in my neck from across the room.

"OK."

"Mr. Lewis is really nice. He's not—I mean, sometimes he...
He doesn't do anything bad."

"OK."

She pauses, lifts her gaze up to mine, and I see pure turmoil
there.

I see Margo.

And everything else slips away, falling into the past, taking
me with it.

# 12

There were two knocks on my bedroom door before she pushed it open. "Hey, Ren? You in there? You didn't ride—" The words were dead on her tongue when she saw me.

Did I look that awful?

I wrapped my arms around my knees, drawing them to my chest and sinking further into my bed. Margo stood perfectly still. "Sorry," I muttered, wiping my face with my sleeve and attempting to avert my head. "Yeah, I wanted some air, so I just walked home."

She didn't speak. Didn't move.

"Ren?"

"Just let it go."

My sister moved across the room and sat on the edge of my bed, her fingers playing with a ring. One of many peppering her fingers.

"What happened?" she asked.

"Nothing." And that's the truth, wasn't it? Nothing happened. Nothing was wrong. Nothing was wrong and nothing could be. Because I'm nothing. I meant nothing to him.

A sob hitched in my throat, and I clenched my eyes closed.

Images from earlier flashed in my head. The way he stared at his phone with that weird little smile on his face. The smile usually reserved for me.

The commotion in the hall that made him drop his phone on the desk.

The way I walked across the room, unfinished test in hand like I was turning it in. Really I just wanted to peek at his phone. See who he was talking to. The messages were irrefutable.

*I can't want to see you.*

*I had the best time last night.*

*I need you.*

Messages with another person in his phone. Someone named Pearl. I'd left my unfinished test on his desk, grabbed my stuff, and left. There was his voice calling out to me, "Shortstack?" but I kept going, unable to face him.

I was being stupid.

Just a stupid little girl.

"Ren, please. You're scaring me. You left school early. You didn't ride with me. What's going on? What happened? Was someone mean to you—" She stopped, and I slowly looked up.

She was staring at my hand too intensely. I looked at it, and a blush covered my cheek and neck, hot and uncomfortable. *Ren Henry* is written in swirly cursive with a heart at the end.

I shoved my hands under me, but it's too late. The damage was done. And she could only stare at the place my hand was. "Henry," she whispered. "Like Mr. Henry?"

"It's a joke."

The way she watched me. Analyzed me in that way she's always done. "Is this about him? Is that why you're—"

"I was just playing around."

"I think there's something you're not saying."

"Just leave it, Margo!" I spat the words at her, anger spilling out of me that I couldn't keep contained. Margo didn't understand. Her life was too perfect. She'd never been in love like us. She didn't know what it's like. But the hurt on her face made me pause. Take a breath. I turned away from her. "Just leave me alone."

Her face crumpled, and just like that, she turned her back and left.

———

Olivia's in front of me. So real. So reminiscent of my dead sister. She's watching me in that same way. Like she wants to know what I'm thinking.

"I don't know why I'm here." She threads her hands behind her neck. "I just see the way you watch me in the halls. I know you think something is wrong. I just wanted you to know that there isn't anything wrong."

"There isn't anything wrong."

I caught her in the hall. It's dimly lit. Faintly, I could hear our parents downstairs. The TV blared some sports game. I lowered my voice. "I don't mean to be bitchy. I've just had a bad day, but there's nothing wrong. Not really." The panic overcame me as soon as Margo left. The last thing I needed was Margo getting too worried and taking this to our parents. She needed to think everything was OK.

She needed to think there was absolutely nothing going on between me and Mr. Henry.

Margo's back was to me as she stared at the wall. A photo. Me and her at the entrance of Disney World. We were ten and fourteen. Her arm was thrown over my shoulder, and she looked effortlessly beautiful, even then. Not like other teenagers in the midst of puberty. She'd never had an awkward stage. At ten, I was all gangly limbs and crooked teeth, but Margo—she was something else. Always had been.

And I finally thought I could be someone else too. Someone a man like Mr. Henry saw.

The pain was a needle prick to my heart.

*Pearl? Who is she? Why would he say those things to someone else?*

"What does it mean?" She turned to look at me. There was no anger. Only concern. Hurt.

"What?"

"His name is on your hand, Ren. He's your teacher."

"I know that. I told you it was a joke."

"You…like him?"

There's a flustered moment where I'm not sure how to respond. Like him? It seemed so…childish. What I felt for him and what he felt for me was beyond like. It was connection. It was pure kismet. The way his hand felt when he walked past and squeezed my shoulder. The way he winked when no one was looking.

"I've seen how you look at him," she said quietly. "You've acted different since you've been in his class."

"All the girls like him, Margo." I tried to sound flippant, casual. "He's hot."

"I know you. I can see it on your face."

"See what?" I asked sarcastically.

"See how close you are to being hurt." She sighed, and I hated how patronizing it was. How much older than me she was. How she thought she just knew everything.

"He's a grown man," she said. "You're just a kid, Renny. You know…you know that would never work. You and him."

"Shut up! I told you." I tried to lower my voice but couldn't even hear myself past the pounding in my ears. Mostly because everything she said was my worst fear, and it was all true. "There's nothing there. His name on my hand is just a silly joke."

"Other people have noticed too."

"What are you even talking about?"

"You know what they say, Ren? The times you leave his classroom last or get there early? When you eat lunch in there? Do you know what I have to listen to them say about you?"

"He's my friend. My teacher. None of that means anything." But could she hear the lilt in my tone? Or perhaps the tiny voice screaming into the canyon between us that I was nothing but a liar. Mostly. Mr. Henry and I hadn't done anything. Not yet. But the energy between us was growing and building to something. Something bigger than me.

Or at least I thought it was.

"I love you," she said. "I don't want you getting hurt."

"He wouldn't hurt me."

"He'll never love you, Ren. Not like that."

I reel back, and for a single breath she looks regretful.

"I'm sorry," she said. "I'm trying not to—God, I just don't want you getting hurt."

———

"I still don't want you getting hurt." Margo is the same but different. Light pours in through the window, slanting over Margo, over Olivia. My classroom falls in place around me, anchoring me.

For the first time in years, tears prickle my eyes. I force them back.

"Ms. Taylor? Are you OK?"

I look away from my sister. Focus on this student. This girl that reminds me of the most vulnerable parts of two other girls. But Olivia isn't Margo. Olivia isn't me. I swipe my eyes casually and clear my throat. "Sorry. Yeah, I'm OK."

"Keep telling yourself that," Margo says and swings herself to sit on a stool, watching us like all she's missing is popcorn.

Olivia follows my gaze to the empty lab table, then back. "I shouldn't have come. I knew I shouldn't—"

"Olivia," I say, and she stops. "Sometimes things happen to us that are confusing. Things we think are OK because we don't understand."

Mr. Henry grabbing my hand. Pushing my hair behind my ear. Brushing the back of my neck when he walked past.

She's oblivious to the bedlam in my mind and fidgets near the door still. Like she's ready for a quick getaway. "He's never hurt me or like done anything. We're not—I'm not some kind of victim, and I don't want you to treat me like one."

"Olivia—"

"I promise. It's innocent, OK? He's just friendly."

"Does he make you uncomfortable?"

She wipes her nose with the sleeve of her jacket, and I want to hand her a tissue, but I'm so afraid she'll stop talking. That she'll lose this momentum.

"No," she says.

"What made you cry that day?"

"Nothing is what you think."

I stand and walk around my desk, facing her head on. She looks everywhere but my eyes. Lying. She's clearly lying. "Olivia, I'm just trying to look out for you. I'm concerned about you. After everything with that missing graduate—"

Olivia jolts. "Tina? From Rosemary Academy? Why are you bringing her up?"

I'm only surprised for a second that Olivia knows Tina. But of course she does. She's been missing for a while. It's a small town.

Or could it be something more?

Could she have learned something through her connection to Bryson?

"This is how rumors are started, Ren. This is how they get out of control," Margo says, still here. And for the first time since her death, I don't want her to be. I regret the thought as soon as I think it.

Ignoring her, I look at Olivia. "I just think Tina is another girl who might have needed help at one point."

"What?" Olivia still appears confused. "From Mr. Lewis? You must be joking."

"No, that isn't what I'm saying. I'm just letting you know that I'm here to help you. You can trust me."

She takes a step back and then another, a scowl covering her face. "I don't even know you, and I shouldn't have come here at all. It was a mistake."

And she's gone. Just like that.

I'm left staring at the space she just occupied, wondering what I should do now.

"Whatever you do…" Margo is sitting on the stool, swinging her legs without a care in the world. "Don't help her the way you helped me."

# 13

I watch him through the doorway. Casual glances as I walk past.
Bryson claps a young man on the shoulder. Fist-bumps a
girl. Laughs when someone shows him something on their phone.
He teaches loudly, with a booming voice that fluctuates to keep
his kids engaged. When he teaches, he walks the room, dragging
his finger across the desk of a student nodding off.

There are no lingering looks that I've seen. No secret touches.
But I wouldn't see it, would I? He wouldn't let me. That's
what makes some men such deadly predators. They're adept at
camouflage.

When the last bell of the day rings, I don't gather my stuff as I
usually do. I wait with my door open. When half the hallway has
gone dark and all the students are gone, Bryson waltzes out of his
room, whistling under his breath. I wait until he's a few feet away
before I poke my head out to see where he went. The copy room.

I grab a random sheet of paper someone left on the lab table and head that way. The copy room sits across from the restrooms. Inside there's a small table and fridge. A tiny microwave pushed into a corner next to a geriatric coffee machine. At this time of day, there shouldn't be anyone else in there. That's why I'm surprised when I hear two voices.

I pause at the corner.

Bryson and another man.

"I put my neck out for you."

"I know that," Bryson whispers.

"Then I don't understand what all this is about. Who is she?"

"I told you it was a misunderstanding—"

"Like the key?"

Bryson makes a frustrated sound in the back of his throat. "I lost it. What other reason would I have in keeping it, Jack?"

Jack? Emma's husband is Jack. The basketball coach and lower classman history teacher. There's something else said. Something Jack hisses under his breath that I don't catch, and then a warm body rounds the corner, nearly slamming into me.

Jack Davis. I remember him from the faculty meeting. A tall, nondescript man with a prematurely graying beard and balding head. What had Emma said? He plays golf with Principal Smart at a country club. Jack's eyes widen just a fraction before his face tightens, and he pushes past me. Bryson is right behind him and, unlike Jack, stops so suddenly he almost loses his balance.

"Ren? What are you doing in here?"

"Making a few copies."

"Right. Yeah. Of course." He eyes the crumpled and marked-up paper in my hand, and I pull it further into my chest.

"Are you and Jack friends?" I ask.

Bryson rolls his eyes playfully, but there's still an undercurrent of anxiety he's clearly trying to mask. "Most of the time. He's a bit irked with me now. Sore loser. This is why I don't make bets with him."

"Bets?"

"Fantasy football." Bryson steps around me, all earlier intensity gone from his eyes. "I should get going."

"Everything OK? I couldn't help but overhear. You lose something? A key or something? I can keep an eye out for it." Maybe I shouldn't have said it, but I'm not eager to let this moment go. Not when I'm still so confused by the interaction between Bryson and Jack.

"You were listening awhile, weren't you?"

"It just sounded serious, and I didn't want to interrupt."

A shadow crosses his face as he palms his jaw. "Listen, Ren, I know what you think of me."

This gets my attention. My fingers tighten on the paper. "What do you mean?"

"I know you mentioned my interaction with Olivia Green to Brad—Principal Smart."

"He told you that?" Fresh waves of anger course through me as thick as blood.

"You wanted him to talk to me about it, right?" Bryson takes a step closer, and I'm suddenly aware of how alone we are. Billy must have already made his rounds, because the hall lights are off, and whatever light is present comes from uncovered windows. It makes the shadows on Bryson's face more defined. "I think it's good you care that much. I think it's good to be careful. But I can't for the life of me figure out what I did to make you think I was...involved with a student in any type of way."

"It's small things." So many small damning things.

"It's what happened at Rosemary Academy," he says. The garish shadows shift and move. Almost like he's wearing a mask. "If you had just talked to me about it, if you had given me a chance to explain, then you'd know those were all rumors. I transferred here for personal reasons. And yes, I'm friendly with my students. Yes, I want them comfortable. I want them to feel like they can talk to me. That's all that was. I told you Olivia was speaking to me about a family matter. Her boyfriend, to be more specific. She got upset. That's honestly all there is to it." He stops and takes a small step back, threading a hand through his already ruffled hair. He looks tired. Exasperated. A person beaten down by rumors. It's something I can relate to. I know, more than anyone, how it feels to grow beneath a shadow.

I take a step away from him too, crunching the already wrinkled paper to my chest.

"Look." He straightens and sighs. "Next time I would appreciate you coming to me first. Give me the opportunity to explain before running with the first theory you come up with. That's a privilege I wasn't given at Rosemary."

It's my turn to be exasperated. My turn to want to bang my head against the wall. Everything about him, his reaction, his words—it all seems so genuine. He seems tired of running from the rumors of Rosemary Academy, and he doesn't appreciate me bringing them up again.

"I didn't mean to be intrusive," I say and mean it. "I was just looking out for Olivia."

Olivia.

The only thing more important than hurting a potentially innocent person's feelings.

"I get it." His eyes soften with the edges of his face. There it is. Bryson's humanity coming in full force. Like I'm the one to feel sorry for. I'm the pitiful girl seeing ghosts where they don't exist because of my own past "After what happened to you and your sister, I get it. I just hope we can start fresh. Become friends, even. I really want that, Ren."

I pause. "What happened to me and my sister, Bryson?"

His hand goes back to his now disheveled hair. Nervous Bryson. "Not all men are him. I'm not like that. That's all I'm saying. I should let you make your copies. I have somewhere to be anyway—"

It erupts within. The anger. It comes on so fast and ferociously there is no way to fight it. I'm sick of everything coming back to Margo. I hate that my trauma becomes their easy out, a way to excuse themselves.

"That day after Olivia left, I saw you leave, and you weren't wearing your tie. It had been on when class started. She was clearly upset. Those are signs that have nothing to do with me or my sister."

He pauses, a weird expression crossing his face. "I got something on it. Was scrubbing it with one of those stain pens while Olivia was talking to me." He shakes his head sadly. "You can't live in the past like this, Ren. It isn't good for you. Isn't good for anyone."

He walks away, leaving me alone in the dimly lit hall.

"What are you thinking?" Margo asks.

"I think," I say, "I think that was a threat."

# 14

Rosemary Academy isn't what I expected. On television private schools are most always looming brick structures with green gardens and pristine fields. The private school I taught at in Atlanta could be pulled straight from any teen drama, only with a lot more security. It makes Rosemary Academy seem even stranger. It's not that Rosemary Academy is dilapidated; it's just slightly unkempt. The hedges are a bit overgrown, and weeds sprout through cracks in the sidewalk. There's no gate around it. No guard watching the entrance. It's a place where you'd picture any normal teen going to school. Hell, there's a YMCA next door. It's just so…normal. Not a dark, ominous school with one dead and one missing girl. Not a place where a predator lurks.

I try to picture Bryson here. Parking in the lot. Ruffling a student's hair as he pushes in the gray double doors. He'd fit in easily. He *did* fit in. They must have loved him. But, regardless of Bryson's excuses, something went sour. Something forced him out.

And there's really only one way to find out the truth.

I park next to a group of boys, shirtless apart from football pads, who stand around a truck bed. They watch me as I climb out.

"Could you point me to volleyball practice?" I ask.

One of them points without saying anything and nudges the boy beside him.

"Thanks."

There's a wave of snickering as I walk away. Guess it doesn't matter how much your parents pay for your education. Kids are still kids.

The gym doors are propped open with a giant fan. Over the whir of its blades, I can hear the squeaking of sneakers on hardwood.

No one looks twice when I slip inside. There's plenty of space on the bleachers, but I choose to sit behind a group of men and women who I assume to be coaches. There are a few other parents in the room: a woman on her laptop at the very top, two sitting near the coaches, whispering to one another, and a man in three-piece suit who glances sideways at me and cuts his eyes almost instantly, like I'm not even worthy of the glance.

The girls are sweating. Playing as hard as they would at a game, that's for sure. They'd won the championship only last year, so it makes sense that they'd take each practice seriously. This is their life. I was never into any sports like that. Margo enjoyed drama club. She was passionate about it enough to try to get me into it. It took one theater class for me to realize I'm more of a backstage girl myself.

That's when I notice the red ribbons. Each player has them pinned to their uniform. Some even have red shoelaces. It takes a second of watching and scanning for me to see that I was wrong. Not *all* the girls wear ribbons.

One isn't.

She's tall. A head taller than all the other girls at least. She has braids that are held back by a headband and a look of determination on her face. But no ribbon.

Maybe it fell off? Maybe she lost it?

The whistle blows. "That's it. Carly will lead stretches, and you're good to go. Don't forget about tomorrow morning. The gym will be closed in the evening, so we'll be practicing before school."

Everyone groans but brings it in for stretching. I note the way the ribbonless girl stays a few paces behind and sits alone. She's actively participating, but I can tell there's a clear divide between her and her teammates. After several minutes, the girls stand, huddle together, and the parents shuffle down from the bleachers. The girl without a ribbon stands off to the side, stuffing something in her bag. It's clear she's completely alone, even amongst her teammates. Suddenly, like she feels my gaze on her, she looks up.

There's stubbornness in her eyes, with an edge of pain. Way too much for a girl her age. I stand and begin to walk toward her.

"Michaela," the coach calls out, walking toward her. The girl doesn't react but turns to her coach with a seemingly careful expression. A wariness.

They speak to one another in low voices while I stand frozen in place. Michaela says something to the coach and turns back to her task of digging through her bag. I restart my descent down the bleachers when the coach looks in my direction, finally noticing me.

"Hey."

Their coach is a short woman with petite features. She seems too small and delicate to play any sports, but I can tell by the way the tendons in her arms flex as she waves me over that there's strength packed into those slim arms. "Are you with one of the girls?"

Crossing the gym floor, I'm vaguely aware that girl, Michaela, is only a few feet away, sliding a pair of sweatpants on over her shorts.

"No. I'm not. I actually wanted to talk to the head coach."

"That's me. Who are you?"

"My name's Ren. I teach at Benton."

Something crosses her face too quickly for me to name. "I guess you're going to tell me what you're doing all the way over here?"

I clear my throat. "I wanted to talk to you about someone I think you knew. Bryson Lewis."

She stiffens, steps back. "No, no, no. That's old news. I don't need this. *We* don't need this."

"I know the subject is upsetting."

"Upsetting?" Her teeth grind. "Everyone wants the story. Everyone wants to know what *really* happened. What really happened was a damn tragedy, OK? Bryson is a good man. He doesn't deserve people like you asking about him. He certainly didn't deserve to be forced out of his position."

"He was forced out?"

"I'm done. You need to leave or else I'll call the cops. You have no right or reason for being here."

I want to press, want to ask more questions, but the severe

look on her face stops me. I back away from her. "I'm sorry. I never meant to upset you."

A few more girls look our way curiously, and the suit-wearing man with the phone to his ear is clearly paying more attention to us than the phone call. My cheeks burn as I walk out.

The boys are no longer lingering by my car, but there is a condom stuck under my windshield wiper and note with someone's Snap on it. I rip it down and shove it in my bag to dispose of later. That's when I hear her voice.

"Hey, wait." Michaela is jogging toward me. "Wait just a second."

Even after her practice and sprinting to the parking lot, she still isn't out of breath. The girl doesn't appear winded at all when she comes to a stop in front of me. "I heard you," she says before I can get a word out. "Heard you asking about Coach Lewis."

"Yes." I look behind her, checking to make sure no coaches or parents are nearby. "You're Michaela?"

"How do you know that?"

"I heard your coach say your name. I'm Ren. A teacher from Benton."

"I heard." She coughs into her fist. "You were asking her about Coach Lewis."

"Yes."

"Why are you asking about him?"

"I want to know more about him."

"Is this about Alejandra?"

"Why do you ask that?" I narrow my eyes at how quickly she made the connection. Could just be the rumors, I remind myself.

But it could also be something more. A stronger thread connecting Alejandra to Bryson.

Michaela glances down, a stormy expression on her face. I recognize it. Remember when I had that same look. Maybe I still do. Jaded. Pained. The face of someone who has lost something but has not yet accepted they'll never get it back. "She's why everyone is asking about Coach Lewis."

"Did you know her well?"

"She was my best friend."

Something in my chest chips away like ice. "I'm sorry, Michaela."

"Have you ever lost someone?" There's a film over her eyes. A tremor in her voice. God, she's just a kid.

"I lost my sister when I was about your age." I don't love talking about Margo, but I appreciate talking about her only when I'm speaking to someone who I know understands.

She looks away, and the tears spill over her cheeks. "Does it get easier?"

"Yes," I reply honestly. "At least, the shock wears off. The jolt in your heart when you think of her. When you forget for a second. And at the same time, you'll get stronger. The pain won't go away, but you'll learn how to carry it."

"Everyone says they miss her. They talk about her and post about her. I can't stomach any of it. And these ribbons—" She grits her teeth, shaking her head.

"The ribbons everyone was wearing today? Those are for Alejandra?"

"Heart disease awareness." There's a bitter edge to her voice.

"You didn't want to wear one?"

Her eyes connect with mine, and in them I can see agony, bright as day. "What's the point? A heart attack wasn't what killed Alejandra."

"What do you think killed her?"

"Not what," Michaela corrects grimly. "Who."

# 15

Her words are icy water pouring over me, chilling me from the inside out.

"What do you mean by that?" I ask, hesitantly. "The police said she had a heart condition, and she fell in the water and drowned."

"I'm not saying that didn't happen."

"So, what are you saying?"

Her jaw tightens and eyes flash with anger. "Why do you care? *No one cares.* Everyone just expects me to shut up and go along with it."

"Is that why everything between you and the other girls seemed strained today? They don't believe you?"

"Strained?" She laughs. "They hate me. I've got a college scholarship I'm working toward, otherwise I would have quit a long time ago."

"Why do they hate you?" I ask, recognizing the despair as it passes over her face as she desperately tries to cover it with defiance.

"Because I care more about my best friend then that man. Coach Lewis."

"They liked him?"

"Worshipped him."

"What do you believe happened to her, Michaela?"

"No one has an explanation for why she was even out there, you know. She would never go into those woods alone. Alejandra was skittish. She didn't even like to drive alone at night. She wouldn't have gone there after sunset." Michaela lifts a pleading hand. Her whole body is tense, like an animal preparing to be attacked. She's on the defense before I've made a single move. "And I know you're probably thinking I'm wrong. That I just can't accept the truth. That's what everyone says. But this is different. I know—knew her better than anyone. There was a reason she was out there. Someone was out there with her."

"Maybe she needed a little privacy," I offer.

"No. Not her."

"What do you think happened?"

Her nostrils flare, and it looks like she's gathering herself. Debating. Somewhere behind me on the main road a car honks, an engine revs. All mundane noises, though none can drown out the beating of my heart.

"You never answered me," Michaela says. "Why do you even care when no one else does?"

"I know you don't know me," I say urgently. "But anything you tell me can help."

"Help who?"

"There's someone else. Another girl I'm worried about."

"What does she have to do with Jondra?"

"I'm not sure, but there's one person connecting them."

Michaela lets out a shaky breath, and it's like all her energy nose dives at once. "Coach Lewis."

"I'm a science teacher. Biology. So I'm used to the scientific method. Observations. Asking questions. All to form a hypothesis."

"Why are you telling me this?"

"Because I started with a hypothesis, Michaela. I formed one the second I met him without even meaning to. Then I started noticing things. The way he talks to his students. A particular student. Now I'm gathering data to support what I think I know. To see if I'm right. And…" I pause, letting the weight of my words crash over me. "I really don't want to be right."

Michaela sighs. "They were close."

"Who?" But even as I ask, the crack in her voice gives the answer away.

"Alejandra and Coach Lewis. They had common interests. He teased her at practice. She respected him. Listened to him. I mean, we all did. He had that way about him. And he was hot." She doesn't smile as she adds this. She says it like someone filled her mouth with vinegar, but something is preventing her from spitting it out. "All the girls on the team were obsessed with him, but with Alejandra he was different."

"Did they talk outside of school?"

"Snapchat. I didn't know who she was always snapping, and it wasn't like Jondra to have secrets. One day I saw the screen. It was Coach Lewis. He snapped a bunch of his students. But it seemed like she was constantly talking to him."

My stomach twists painfully. As a teacher, the boundaries dividing the students from the adults meant to teach and protect them are clear. I see those boundaries like lines on the ground. Like someone drew them with one of those rolling machines to paint field lines in bright red. I would never communicate with a student outside of class by any means apart from my school email address. Yet, I know of teachers who do, who send friend requests and DMs.

Do they have lines? Wavier ones them mine? Grayer ones than mine? What happens when there are no lines at all?

"The thing is there was nothing in my face, you know?" Michaela seems bothered by this. She clearly blames herself for not noticing. "Sure, they talked a little. But in public there weren't any signs. That's why, after everything happened, no one really listened to me."

"You thought there was something going on between them?"

"Yes, and I told them. I told the cops. Alejandra's parents. The other girls. Anyone who would listen. But what was I telling them really? I hadn't seen anything wrong. At least nothing I knew for certain."

"What do you mean by that?" I ask, stepping closer to her, aware of how much time we're taking. Any second someone could walk out here. Another parent. The coach. A person who wouldn't understand.

What would they think?

"There was one time at an away game. Our championship game." Her voice quivers, and her hand covers her stomach like something is physically bothering her. "We were staying at this hotel out of town, and I remember Alejandra locking herself in the bathroom. I knew I shouldn't, but I pressed my ear to the door trying to listen in. She had the shower going, so I couldn't hear anything, but

I knew she was talking to someone. And when she came out, it was clear she'd been crying." Michaela glances at the ground. "I asked her who she was talking to, and she wouldn't tell me. I know I said we didn't have secrets. And we really didn't. Not until then."

"Who do you think she was talking to?"

Michaela's burning gaze meets mine. "I don't know. I don't know a lot. I don't know what happened to her that day in the park either. The only thing I truly know for certain was something was happening inside of her. Something was happening *to* her, and I don't know what role Coach Lewis played. I only know one thing: if Coach Lewis had never been here, then Alejandra would still be alive."

It's a lot. I glance around the still quiet lot, fighting the feelings building inside me. Feelings I'm not yet ready to identify.

"What about the day she died, the day after the championship game, did you talk to her?"

"I spoke to her the night before. When we got off the bus."

"How did she act?"

"I don't know." Michaela throws her hands up. "I don't know, OK? Normal? I was distracted. Some stuff was going on with my stepmom, and I wasn't really paying attention. That's how it was with me and Jondra. Sometimes we both needed space, but I knew she'd talk to me eventually." Her voice breaks. "She always did."

"And you never saw anything concrete? She never told you anything?"

She shakes her head, and her face transforms with pain. "Maybe that's my fault. If she had just trusted me, then things could be different. I could have helped her, and no one else would have gotten hurt."

My breath catches. "Who else has gotten hurt?"

Michaela shifts uncomfortably. "I can't say for certain. It's just a hunch."

"What is?"

She doesn't speak right away. I can see the wall come up in her expression. "I don't know."

"Anything could help," I plead. "There's another student. A girl. I told you. Something you know might help her."

She gnaws on her top lip, still looking unsure. "It's just a thought. I don't have any proof."

"Please, Michaela."

"Tina Drexler," she whispers, eyes meeting mine.

I blow out a long breath. There's still no one else out here, but I hear voices. Can't tell which direction they're coming from or how much time we have. I step closer to her. "Were you friends?"

"No. Not really. She graduated this past spring. She was a grade ahead of me and Alejandra. Kept to herself from what I heard. But she knew Alejandra."

I think of the photo I'd seen of Alejandra and Tina online. "They were friends?"

"It was a weird matchup, but yes. They were close. I wasn't as close to Tina but because of Jondra, I ran into her from time to time. It's not that I didn't like her; we just didn't have anything in common. Wait." Her brows furrow. "I think Tina picked her up after we got off the bus. She drove this little car. A Honda I think. I only remember because she had this stupid bumper sticker on the back. You couldn't miss it."

The voices get closer now, and I see a group of teachers coming over the hill. I glance toward them, knowing we don't have much time. "Why do you think her disappearance has anything to do with Alejandra or Bryson?"

"Because…" Michaela seems to consider her words carefully. "Before she went missing, she was really vocal about something."

"About what?"

"She didn't think Jondra's death was an accident either."

———

There are no detectives waiting for me today. That's a good sign, and I attempt to hold on to that goodness. To let it replace the acid filling my body. A forest fire burning through me.

After we exchanged numbers and parted ways, I'd tried to be objective about what Michaela told me. She's a heartbroken, grieving kid. Of course, she's bound to have some wild theories.

But the things she'd said.

Tina picked Alejandra up the day before Alejandra died. The day before she walked into the woods alone. Something the people close to her can't explain. Something *Tina* couldn't explain, and now Tina is missing.

My bungalow looks unusually sad and empty in the deepening darkness. I sit inside my car staring at the black windows. The curtains are pulled, but even if they weren't, there would be nothing to see.

"Don't feel sorry for yourself," Margo says, sounding bored from the back seat. "It isn't a good look on you."

My eyes flash to hers in the rearview. "There's something I'm missing."

When Margo speaks again, she sounds different. "Because

there's a whole puzzle piece you know nothing about. An unknown variable."

Then I get it.

I go inside and head straight for my laptop, powering up my private browser. One quick search, and I'm looking at Olivia Green's social media. She doesn't have many followers. Just a few hundred. But her page is carefully curated like she cares enough to make it beautiful even if no one is there to see it. I click on a post from three days ago first. The day I'd caught her crying.

A picture of her lower half in a green hammock. An open book on her lap. The caption is: *In the end, the monsters are never who you expect.*

A chill ripples through me. The topsy-turvy feeling I'd had in my gut since speaking to Michaela intensifies. And like Michaela, I don't know what's happening either. I don't know the role Tina played. If Alejandra's death really was an accident. But two things are for certain: Olivia Green is the unknown variable, and I don't trust Bryson Lewis.

Not one bit.

# 16

It's funny how time passing doesn't ease the ache inside. The urge to find the truth. One day, two, three. A whole week. I'm tense the whole time, and even my daily runs do little to stop the throbbing in my head. I just keep waiting to loosen, to stretch, to come out of it, but I don't. My body stays coiled tightly. Waiting.

Michaela.

Olivia.

Bryson.

The detective.

Which domino will fall into the other next?

It turns out to be none of them. Thursday morning the news alert catches my eye while I'm hurriedly eating yogurt at my breakfast bar, still sweaty from a morning workout. One week after the meeting with Michaela, one week of watching Bryson carefully, looking for Olivia in the halls, one week of quiet. I'm not expecting today to be different. That's why the headline steals my breath.

*Body of Missing Teen Girl Found*

I click, numbly. The words fill my head up with more acid until it must be bubbling out my of ears and seeping over my body.

Margo glances over my shoulder at the phone. "Shit," she says, and for once seems at a loss for words.

*Yesterday evening the police were notified of human remains in the woods near Locklear Road. The remains have been confirmed to be that of missing teen Tina Drexler. Tina was last seen on July 16 and has not been heard from by friends or family since. The police have not yet released an official statement on the condition of...*

I throw my yogurt away, get ready, and drive to school.

———

The hallways are buzzing.

The news report is playing on every tiny screen. Every face alights with energy, like hordes of bees crawling beneath their skin. Every person seems to be too afraid to speak above a whisper, yet they all have something to say. And I hear her name on every parted mouth.

Tina Drexler.

Tina Drexler.

Tina Drexler.

Dead.

Dead.

Dead.

There are hardly any details online. Her remains were quietly found last night. After identifying them and speaking to the Drexler family, law enforcement held a press conference early this morning.

"It's about drugs. My cousin told me…"

"Human trafficking. I read an article…"

"Probably her boyfriend. It's always the boyfriend…"

"She was so young."

"Just not fair…"

"Ren?"

I blink through the vortex of warm bodies and voices. Emma is standing at her door, one hand supporting her growing tummy. There's a look of confusion on her face. "Are you OK?"

"Of course."

"You're just standing there."

I look around me, blinking.

"Can I talk to you for a second?" she asks, waving me inside before I even answer.

"Uh, yes. Sure."

Her room is empty, and she closes the door behind us.

"First period prep," she says under her breath. "I used to not like it. Felt like I needed the break more often at the end of the day, but I don't mind it so much anymore." She sits on the edge of her desk, a serious expression on her face. "I wanted to talk to you. About Bryson."

Just hearing his name sends me spiraling, thinking of what Michaela told me and Olivia's cryptic post and Tina Drexler's cold pale body.

*In the end, the monster is never who you expect.*

And sometimes the monster is exactly who you expect.

"Ren?"

"Pardon?"

"Did you hear me?"

I shake my head, rubbing my temples. "I'm sorry. It's been a long morning already. What were you saying?"

"I know." She sighs. "Ugh. You're right. I'm being insensitive. After everything with your sister. I'm sure this kind of thing…with that missing girl…hits close to home."

She's right. Not that I want to admit it, but I remember what it was like after Margo's death. The feeling like my chest was always at risk of caving in.

Margo is in the back of Emma's class, flipping through a notebook like she's bored with it all. I don't pay her any mind. She wouldn't understand. After all, she wasn't there. She didn't know what it was like when she died.

"But this is different," Margo says, looking up at me. "This feels different already, doesn't it, Ren?"

"It's OK," I say to Emma, ignoring Margo completely. "I'm fine. What is it you wanted to talk about?"

She seems unconvinced but opens her mouth anyway. "It was just about Bryson. I wanted to know if you learned anything new about him. How you were feeling about everything, I guess. I don't know. I don't mean to pry. I'm just worried about you."

"There's no reason to worry about me."

"It's just—you seem tired, Ren. Distracted constantly."

I take a mental step back and try to see myself the way she does. The way others do. I haven't been sleeping as much as I should have. The dark circles under my eyes are quite noticeable even to me. But the thing is, I don't feel worn down. I feel invigorated by each piece of the truth as I uncover it. I'm following a rope, and it's leading me somewhere. Sleep seems like such a small sacrifice for what's at stake.

I don't *feel* exhausted.

I'm filled with a new sense of purpose.

A part of me wants to believe I can confide in her. It would be nice to have someone to unload on. To tell these things to. Someone who'd listen and tell me I wasn't crazy and they understood my choices. But I don't know if that person is Emma.

"I heard him arguing yesterday. With your husband."

Emma doesn't seem surprised. "Jack told me he saw you yesterday. Said you were listening to his and Bryson's conversation."

"I was going to the copy room, heard them talking, and didn't want to interrupt."

"It's not a big deal anyway. Jack was just asking him about the key he lost. To the chiller."

"The chiller?"

"Sorry, yeah. A room below the stage in the gym. The coaches use it to store equipment. The kids call it the chiller because it's like a meat locker in there."

"I know it. It was a thing when I went to school here." Though back then it was full of old volleyball nets, random theater props, and dust. "Why did Bryson need to get into it?" Bryson doesn't coach anything here. What reason would he have to enter that room? To need access to it enough that he would ask for a key.

"He needed something out of there for an object lesson for his class. Something about a basketball, energy, and the physics of bouncing a ball. I don't remember now. But that's where all the sports equipment is stored."

It makes sense.

Plus, I remember him carrying a basketball and a bag full of ping-pong balls in his room a couple weeks ago. The story checks out.

But why does my stomach feel like I'm free-falling?

What am I missing?

"Hey, what are you thinking about? You look really serious."

The bell rings, long and loud. My first period is probably standing outside my class wondering where I am.

"I don't know," I admit, backing toward the door. "I really need to get to my class though."

She nods quickly and stands, hobbling over in that way pregnant women do. Like any second the bottom is going to fall out and the contents of their stomach will hit the floor like rushing river water.

"You'll tell me though?" she says. "Once you know?"

"Tell you what?"

"What you're really thinking."

"I'll see you at lunch, Emma."

The kids are in fact in a line outside my door when I make it to the top of the stairs. Though none of them seem especially perturbed by this turn of events. They're either huddled together talking quietly or leaning against the lockers on their phones.

"Sorry, everyone," I mutter, unlocking the door and letting them file past me.

"Was wondering where you were." Bryson leans against his

doorway with his arms crossed, making the shoulders of his sport coat pull taut.

"Sorry, Emma caught me. We lost track of time." I say it distractedly, watching the emotions play out across his face. Wondering what the person who killed Tina Drexler would look like the day after her body was found. Nervous? Angry? Scared?

Bryson looks like none of those. He's utterly normal. The same guy from the past week. His guard is up, I sense that. But that's something he's saved just for me based on our past few interactions.

He nods, lips shifting into an almost smile. "Well, I'm glad you made it."

"Thank you. And thanks for keeping an eye on them."

"No problem."

He doesn't close his door, but he disappears into his class, going straight to his desk. I watch for a second before turning and going to my own.

"Ms. Taylor?"

"One second." I ignore the boy in the front row with his hand raised. "Give me two minutes guys."

The class settles into murmurs as they talk amongst themselves. I boot up my laptop, going into our Benton High faculty database, INOW. I search Olivia Green's name and find her schedule. First period gym. Maybe I could pop my head in. Pull her out just for a second to check on her, see what she's thinking after the Tina news.

I scroll further down, my brows furrowing at the word on the screen.

*Absent.*

I check yesterday's date and the day before.

Absent both days.

That same feeling from earlier comes back. Like I'm missing something that's right in front of my eyes. I'm so consumed with these thoughts that I don't notice at first. The way every phone in class seems to buzz or vibrate at once.

The way the room sinks into eerie silence.

It's the silence that gets my attention. I look up. Every kid in the class is staring at their cell phones completely unashamed. "You know the rules. No phones in class." There's a gasp from the back of the room. Shuffling as more students pull out their phones. Murmurs of shock and confusion.

"Hey." I stand to get their attention. "Phones up. You know you're not..." But I stop. They're not listening. Not even pretending to.

More gasping.

"Holy shit."

"Who is that?"

"It's that girl!"

That's when I see the blinking icon in my email. I lean down and click over, not recognizing the sender. It's some kind of spam email, but I click it anyway. The pictures load instantly.

I grab on to my desk to keep from stumbling back, then force myself across the room, holding my hand out for the phone of the nearest student. She hands it over reluctantly. On the screen is a photo. The same one on my computer screen.

A topless Alejandra Gomez is smiling, holding her phone selfie-style over a sleeping Bryson Lewis.

# 17

There's something artistic about the photo. Something familiar. It reminds me of Tina's Instagram grid. Alejandra's hair is gracefully splayed over her shoulders, not quite covering her breasts. The lighting is sultry and shadowed. Her head is tilted just so. Lips pursed. Her head on Bryson's shoulder. His chin, covered in day-old stubble, is tilted toward her.

Clearly this was an important photo to Alejandra.

And clearly no one was ever supposed to see it.

"Who sent you this?" I ask, working past the numbness in my lips.

The girl shakes her head in confusion. "It was a mass text from a random number. Can I have my phone back?"

"Put your phones away." My voice is louder now. Sharper. "Put them away. Now." I lock the screen of the phone in my hand and pass it back. The students all watch warily. Just then, there's the sound of footsteps. Everyone in class cranes their necks to look at a pale-faced Bryson stepping into the hall.

His classroom is dead silent behind him. Sweat dribbles from his forehead, over his neck. And every emotion that I expected to see a few minutes ago on his face is there now. Fear. Nervousness. Stress. His lips are in a hard, tight line. His eyes are wide and afraid as they meet my mine.

"Ren—"

"Mr. Lewis?" Principal Smart is at the top of the stairs. Next to him is the school resource officer. Neither look in my direction. "You'll come with me."

Bryson gives me one last look, heaves out a breath, and nods. Principal Smart follows without making eye contact with me.

There's a flash of movement, and Mrs. Caldwell hurriedly bustles past the three men and into Bryson's room, shushing the already deathly silent class. She catches my eye before looking away quickly and closing the door firmly behind her.

"Looks like you were right, huh, Renny?" Margo stands at the top of the stairs looking down before glancing back at me. "How does it feel?"

I open my mouth to answer her, but nothing comes out.

———

The announcement slides into my inbox by second period.

An official statement from the board and Chief of Police. It made it clear all students were to delete the text sent to their phone immediately as the photo contained explicit pictures of a minor; anyone possessing or distributing the image could face criminal charges. Faculty are to do the same thing with the email. The police are currently looking into the person behind distributing the mass text and email. Until then we are all to pretend it didn't happen.

Seems reasonable.

There is no mention of Bryson.

Bryson doesn't come back to class either.

Not that I expect him to. Not that I thought there'd be any type of explanation for that photo that would grant him access to his classroom. Him sleeping beside a naked student. There's really only one explanation for it.

I go through the motions for the next few hours. Standing in front of my students, pretending I don't notice their cell phones unsuccessfully hidden or their restless whispers. There is a lab to go over. Equipment to clean. Vocabulary words to assign.

But it's all an act. I teach, but I'm watching the doorway the entire time. They listen, but they're staring at their phones.

When the resource officer comes back for Bryson's stuff— everyone notices that. They break out in whispers when they see his laptop case, bag, and cell phone. When the bell rings, I stand in the hall, watching the faces of each passing student for Olivia, willing her to be here.

The hour creeps by, and right before the lunch bell, like I'd done every half hour since Bryson was escorted from his room, I check the faculty database.

My eyes nearly pop when I see the green check mark by Olivia's name. She checked into class. Bryson's third period.

I stand abruptly, earning the curious stares of a few students. They only look a moment before turning back to their worksheets. "Give me a minute, everyone," I say to no one in particular and step out of the room.

I close my door behind me and cross the hall. The door is open, and Mrs. Caldwell is sitting at Bryson's desk on her phone while a film plays on the projector. Olivia is at the back of the class, her head folded on her arms. Her face is tilted away from me so I can't tell if she's awake or asleep.

"Ms. Taylor?" Mrs. Caldwell says my name like a question. "Can I help you with something?"

By now, every kid in the class is looking in my direction. Including Olivia.

"Actually, can I borrow Olivia just for a minute?"

Mrs. Caldwell nods slowly, still looking confused.

Every eye in the class is on Olivia as she stands from the lab table and walks toward me. The room is dark, making it difficult to read her expression. But just seeing her here, healthy, in one piece—it does wonders for my psyche.

"Am I in trouble?" Olivia asks when she's right in front of me.

I nod for her to follow me into the hall. I lead her down a little ways to a snack machine and water fountain tucked into an alcove.

It's the first time, beneath the harsh fluorescents, I get a good look at her. Her eyes are rimmed with red, and there's a gray pallor to her skin. She looks flustered.

"Why did you think you'd be in trouble?" I ask.

Her jaw tightens, and she seems to look anywhere except at me. "I don't know."

"Olivia—"

"Why did you pull me out of class?" Now she does look at me, anger flowing into those wide blue eyes.

"I've been looking for you. I wanted to check on you. Make sure you were OK."

"Why wouldn't I be?" She shakes her head, looking exasperated. "Wait, you still think something awful about me and Mr. Lewis don't you?"

"Olivia."

"I told you, I'm not a victim." She opens her mouth as if to say something else but stops. "You know what? I can't. Please, just leave me alone." She walks away, back to her class.

I have no choice but to go back to my own.

———

Emma and the other women are gathered around the table when I slide in with my own lunch tray. A rubbery slice of pizza and an apple. I don't even know why I got it. I have no appetite. Not since Olivia stormed away, and I was left wondering why she's still lying to me and who she's trying to protect.

I pick at the pizza, halfheartedly tuning into the low murmurs of the women around me.

"It went all the way to the board," Koa whispers while nibbling on a roll, clearly not trying to be overheard by any students. "I have a friend at the BOE, and she texted me this morning. The police are involved."

"Why police?" Emma asks.

"Because she was his student. It's illegal. Then there's the way she… you know, the way she died. They may have to reopen her case."

Emma leans back, shaking her head to herself. "What? They think Bryson killed her?"

"He was having sex with her, Emma. Clearly we didn't know him as well as we thought."

"None of us could have known. How could we? And who knows what he's capable of at this point," Lynette mutters before taking a bite of pizza. Grease dribbles down her hand.

"Really?" My tone comes across dryer than intend as I stare at each woman at the table. It's funny that when something bad happens, when truths are yanked out, roughly pulled into the light while dragging their fingernails across the ground, they somehow never knew. Whenever an evil man goes off the rails and murders his whole family, there's always a slew of people on those stupid documentaries saying that he was such a nice guy and they had no idea. I've always found it so hard to believe. "You really had no clue? No idea at all?"

To me, the answer is so much simpler. There are moments of unease, feelings we push to the back of our minds and write off with explanations that never fully make sense. We get thoughts and impressions. And we shove them down. Stuff them back in. Because we are raised in a world that makes us doubt ourselves before doubting others. A world that teaches us it is better to be uncomfortable than bring discomfort with our truths.

"Ren," Emma warns under her breath.

I stay focused on Lynette.

"What's your problem?" Lynette asks, through slitted eyes.

"I just think it's funny that when things like this happen, everyone suddenly never heard or saw anything."

"I don't know what you're insinuating."

"I—" I cut myself off with a shake of my head, and the hopelessness of the situation nearly crushes me. The thing is, I'm angry. At them. At every teacher who was supposed to protect me when I was in high school. Mostly, I'm angry at myself because I knew. I *knew*, didn't I? I recognized the signs in Olivia.

Now she won't even talk to me.

"It doesn't matter."

Lynette's brows stay raised, and she looks like she wants to say something else. Luckily, Koa takes back control of the conversation. "Why don't we talk about something else? We can't keep rehashing this. It won't change anything, and we don't really know anything. Not yet."

I stand abruptly, sliding my barely touched tray off the table with one hand. "I need to go, anyway."

"You just got here." Mary's brows crease with concern.

"I know, but it's been a long day. I need a minute."

Emma stands with me, and we both pretend not to see Lynette's scowl.

I dump my trash, ignoring the looks from the students at the table nearest us. Last thing I need is to give them more to talk about.

"What was that back there?" Emma asks with a low voice.

"What do you mean?"

"You were right," she says, mimicking exactly what Margo had said earlier. "You were clearly right about Bryson. You never said why you kept asking about him, but it obviously had to do with this. Ren, I know you have to be feeling a lot right now, and I'm here for you if you need to talk, but you can't take those feelings out on us. We really didn't know what kind of man Bryson really was. No one did."

"But that's not entirely true, is it, Emma?" I ask, quietly. "You told me the rumors Jack told you. You knew what happened at his old school."

"I just thought they were rumors," she replies, and there's so much distress in her eyes, I almost feel bad. Almost.

She reaches out, grabbing my arm. "I didn't know, Ren. Please."

I step back, and her arm falls away and flaps to her side.

"That's the thing, isn't it? We never do. These men squeeze through the cracks in our armor, slithering in like snakes. And when they do something sick, there's always someone there excusing it. Boys will be boys and all that."

"I never doubted you, Ren, and you know that. I didn't know the truth, not for certain. But I would have supported you."

My jaw locks at those words. I want them to be true. But I also remember the condescending look from Smart. The way he refused to meet my eyes. The way Emma told the story about Bryson so casually. So quick to assume the rumors were just that—rumors.

"I just—I need some time to think, I guess."

"OK." She steps back, a protective hand going over her stomach. "I can give you that. I'm here for you though. Whenever you're ready."

I turn and push out of the heavy double doors, letting them slam behind me.

———

After that interaction with Emma at lunch, I finally gave up and put on a video for my afternoon classes. My mind was too muddled. It wasn't fair to my students.

Besides, they were distracted too.

It's in my final period of the day when my phone rings with

an unknown number. "I'm stepping out into the hall for just a minute," I say, though no one gives me a second look.

They all pull their own cell phones out before I've even made it fully out of class, and I'm too preoccupied to say anything about it. "Hello?" I answer, closing the door firmly behind me. The halls are completely empty. Doors are all shut. I revel in the solitude, leaning back against my classroom door.

"Is this Ren?"

I recognize the hesitant voice instantly. "Michaela?"

"It's me. I've been wanting to reach out all day. This is the first chance I've had. Did you get the picture too?" She's whispering, and I can imagine, with it still being school hours, she's probably hiding in a bathroom or closet somewhere just to make this call.

"Yes. Are you OK?" A fresh wave of anger washes over me. I hadn't even considered anyone outside of our school getting that photo. I hadn't considered what seeing that would do to the people who loved Alejandra.

It sounds as if she's been crying when she finally speaks again. "I knew it," she says, thickly. "But seeing it like that. Seeing her with him—it feels so wrong somehow. Now everyone has it, and she's naked, Ren."

"I know. I'm so sorry you had to see it. I'm sorry this is happening. They'll find the person who sent it." Even as I say the words, I know they aren't good enough. Nothing can fix what happened here today.

"Who would do that? Who would send it to everyone like that?"

A door opens at the end of the hall, and a student glances my way before walking to the bathroom with a long wooden pass in their hand. I lower my voice. "I don't know."

"I knew this was happening, but having it confirmed... I didn't realize how much her secrets could hurt even now."

"Michaela, do you have any idea who would send this photo? Who would have any reason for this to happen?"

"No. Especially not now. If someone had this, why wouldn't they have come forward right after Jondra's—" She cuts herself off. "Why now? Why wait so long?"

"And you've never seen that photo before?"

"Of course not." She inhales sharply. "But there is one thing."

A dark-clad figure comes out of the bathroom. Hair curtains her face, and her head is angled away. My body tenses. "Olivia?"

The girl glances back. Not Olivia. She looks at me confused before heading toward the stairwell.

"What did you say?"

"Sorry," I say to Michaela without looking away from the direction that girl just went. "I thought I saw someone. What were you saying?"

"There's something I noticed about the picture. The bed Coach Lewis was lying in. That comforter was the same one as the hotel we stayed at for our away game. I only remember it because it's in one of my pinned TikToks. The night Jondra locked herself in the bathroom to talk on the phone—" A bell rings from somewhere in the background. "Shoot. My mom is picking me up. Taking me away for a long weekend. Says it's to spend more time together, but I see right through it. It's like she thinks I'm suicidal or something."

"She's worried about you."

"She's outside. I have to go. But there's one more thing I wanted to talk to you about. I don't really have time, and it would be better in person anyway. Could you meet me on Monday? After school? There's a park near Rosemary Academy. It's the only one with a dog park if you look it up."

"I'll be there. Michaela? Take care of yourself."

There's a burst of sound before the line goes quiet once again. I have to check the screen to be certain she didn't hang up. Finally, through a thick clog of emotion, she speaks. "I wish I could have seen his face today. They got him, didn't they?"

"Yes." I think of Olivia and wonder how this will affect her. Then I think of Alejandra. Tina. Their names are just sparks, burning into something bigger, something more important. All the girls at the mercy of men in power. Too afraid to speak. Too scared. Too beat down by a system intent on keeping them that way. Too dead.

Their voices snuffed out forever.

My heart squeezes in my chest. "They did."

It doesn't seem like enough. Nothing will ever be enough.

But maybe, I think, maybe I can make it good enough.

# 18

I inhale night air as thick as tar. My fingers lace and unlace on the steering wheel, and my knee bounces up and down.

I shouldn't be here.

And what's my plan anyway?

Why come at all?

Bryson's house is dark. No lights anywhere except the living room, where his TV flickers.

I stay in my car. Picturing Bryson. Is he inside, watching an old movie to take his mind off today? Is he looking up lawyers on his phone? Desperately trying to get rid of evidence?

And so what if he is? The police are investigating. They're doing their job. I've done mine already. It's in their hands. There's no reason for me to be here.

But I think of that night with Casey. The smooth leather of my gloves as they slipped over my hands. How I felt so powerful. Like someone else entirely.

Maybe it's the way a man feels.

"You honestly think this is a good idea after what happened with the man at the bar?" Margo sits beside me, chipping at her nail polish. She's nervous. "What are you even doing here, Ren?"

"I just want to make sure."

"Make sure of what? That there are no teen girls screaming for help in his basement? So, he messed around with a student? Many teachers do. Most never even get caught. You should be happy that he did." Her face is serious for once, hands fallen to her sides. "Look, clearly Alejandra consented. I mean, she did take the picture, Ren." When I stay quiet, Margo's voice lowers and deepens. "Why are you here?"

I swallow back a harsh sound trying desperately to fight its way out of my chest, and I think. I *think*. First about that night nearly two weeks ago when Casey died. How the evening spiraled. The bump of his body on my car. The silence on the drive home. I was too shocked to panic, too sick to cry.

Then another night. The worst of my life. The sound Margo made when she fell. The smell of lake water. Mud squishing between my toes.

Then the all-consuming quiet that came after.

Two bitter silences.

"I can't go through that again," The anguish is so visceral, I feel it in every nerve ending.

Because what if someone stopped Mr. Henry before that night? What if the wife and child Casey left behind will be much better off without him? And what does consent even mean when the man asking for it is your teacher?

What if the silence of these men, their absence from the world, is a lot more peaceful than the quiet they cause?

"Ren." Margo doesn't say anything else. Just my name. She knows exactly what I'm thinking, after all.

"They're just thoughts. They don't mean anything."

"Then why are you here?"

"Because." I'm blisteringly angry though I'm not sure at who. "Because, Margo, there's something connecting those girls. Alejandra. Tina. Olivia. That something is Bryson, and now two of those girls are dead."

"That's not a question though, is it?" Margo asks. "Whether he did anything or not isn't the question. The real question, Renny, is what do you intend to do about it?"

My fingers close over the latch of the middle console. I can already feel the cool leather over my fingers. The jump in my pulse as I walk toward his door. I can feel it all, and I want it. More than I ever wanted anything.

"Listen to me," Margo says urgently, staying right with me. "This isn't you. It isn't you."

I don't look at her.

Make it to his front door.

Place a hand on the handle.

"Ren, if you do this, you won't be able to go back. If you do this, then everything changes."

I glance at her. Weigh her words in my mind while I grit my teeth against the urge. Every cell in my body is pulling me forward.

How am I supposed to stop?

"This isn't you," Margo whispers. "You can't do this, Ren. Not tonight."

Like there's a fire burning on the other side, I release the door handle.

The bar sits on the corner of a main highway in Benton, across from a corner store and burger joint. It's the saddest bar I've ever seen. The Blue Lantern has sat in this same spot since I was in high school, but I've never been inside.

Until now.

The room is dimly lit, smelling faintly like cigarettes and liquor. Waves of smoke make the room hazy. Two men lean over a pool table, beer cans lining the edge. Two more sit at the bar with several spaces empty between them.

As the door closes behind me, every head turns my way. I make a beeline for the person at the very end of the bar.

Billy glances up when I slide in next to him. There's a moment of confusion on his face before he smiles. "You came."

"I know you said you usually come on Fridays. I thought I'd take the risk."

He laughs, and I notice the sour scent of beer and the empty bottles in front of him.

"Sometimes I drop in a little more than once a week." He shakes his bottle at the bartender—an older woman with gray-streaked hair down to her waist and sun-damaged skin.

"What can I get you?" she asks when she slides him another brown bottle.

"Club soda and lime please," I answer, watching her fill a glass quickly and push it in my direction.

I finally take in Billy. He looks distracted. His hair is disheveled; clothes are wrinkly. Though I'm positive I can't look much better. Not after what I almost did. The insanely stupid decision I almost made without thinking of a single consequence.

"Are you OK?" he asks.

"I'm fine. You?" I take a sip of my own soda. "You look kind of preoccupied. I can go if—"

"No," he says quickly, eyes widening. "You're good. Please. Stay. It's just been a long one."

*You have no idea.*

No doubt this news about Bryson probably shook him. Hell, he probably had the photo sent to him too.

"Did you know him well? Bryson?" I ask.

His eyes flash to me, and for one second, I think he won't answer. Like I've pissed him off or something. "Not really. Well as you did, I reckon."

"I wouldn't say I knew him well. But he was across the hall from me. We spoke from time to time."

"Huh." He takes another long draw of beer and then lets out a low chuckle. "Guess we should have seen that shit coming."

"What do you mean?"

"It's always guys like him. Same as last time."

I take a sip of my soda. It's flat, but my throat is dry, and I nearly finish the glass anyway. It's a relief to hear Billy reference the last time something like this happened, because no one else ever does. Anytime I reference the past or what happened to my sister, people get uncomfortable. Even though I don't know Billy well, it feels good to talk to someone who was there back then. Who understands the shock of it.

"You're talking about Henry?"

He laughs again. "Girls just loved him, didn't they? You too. No offense. What is it about those douchebags?"

I bristle, trying to force the memories back. Keep them at bay. "Did you think Bryson was like that? A douchebag?"

He glances around us for a second. The men at the other end of the bar are nursing drinks silently. The bartender is only a few feet away and has been drying the same glass since I sat down. He looks at her and then back to me. "Need a smoke. Want to come outside a minute?"

I follow him out. He doesn't go out the front door like I'd expect but passes a door that must be a bathroom and leads me to a side entrance. Neither of us say anything as he lights up a cigarette and leans against the dirty brick wall. He closes his eyes as he exhales. "I know this is a bad habit, but I can't make myself give it up."

"I know the feeling," I say.

"You want one?"

"No thanks. I was actually wondering if you could tell me more about Bryson. You were there last semester, weren't you? How did that go? Him transferring midsemester. How did he seem?"

"It might have been strange, but I honestly didn't think much of it. 'Sides, he seemed like a nice enough guy. To answer your earlier question—no, I didn't think he was a bad guy. Didn't think he was like Mr. Henry at all. Till today of course."

"But you paid enough attention to know that girls liked him?"

His eyes open, and he takes another long drag of his cigarette. "Is it strange that I did? It's almost natural, isn't it? Noticing people like him."

"People like him?"

"Smart. Good-looking. Nice. The trifecta." His face darkens. "And most of 'em are snakes. Ain't they? It just pisses me off that

Bryson was one too, and I didn't notice it. Most likely, he'll get away with it all."

My fists clench and unclench at my sides. "The police are involved."

"You think that means anything for a guy like him, Ren? Mark my words, our system is messed up. Guys like him get off with a slap on the wrist while there are men rotting in prison for smoking weed." As he speaks his voice gets louder. "And if that girl was my sister or God forbid my child…" He trails off with a shake of his head.

"What would you do?" I ask. I already know, but I need to hear it. Need to know I'm not the only one.

He cuts his eyes to me. "I'd kill that son of a bitch."

# 19

He finishes the cigarette and stomps it out before leading me back inside to our stools. The room has settled into some semblance of normalcy, but everyone does go a little quieter when we walk back in. Clearly, news of what transpired at Benton High School this morning has spread.

"Billy." I hesitate as the front door to the bar opens, and something in the air shifts as a man steps in.

I don't recognize him until he's fully inside and in the light, and then the blood drains from my face.

Tina Drexler's brother looks almost exactly like the picture on Tina's Instagram. Tall. Probably the tallest man in the room, with a thick red-tinted beard and a beanie pulled low over his head. He stops as one of the men at the pool table approaches him. They exchange words, and the man claps him on the back.

"That's Tina Drexler's brother."

Billy's head swivels to me. "You know Fallon?"

"I've seen a photo of him online."

"He looks tore up."

Billy is right. Even in the dimly lit room, the man's eyes are clearly red-rimmed, and the bags under them are dark purple. His sister's body was found today after being missing for months. I imagine he hasn't slept in a while.

He may never sleep again.

"What's he doing here?"

"He comes here a lot."

Fallon approaches and slides the stool out beside him.

Billy takes a long drink of beer before clearing his throat. "I'm so sorry, man."

Fallon turns his head and blinks as if he's just now registering that Billy is there. "Hey, Billy."

"Listen, if there's anything I can do."

"I'm good. Just stopped in for a beer." He faces the front, waving for the bartender, who scurries right over.

I can't stop looking at him. I have this thing about fresh grief. A few days after Margo died, I'd gone to a coffee shop. I still remember the way the barista smiled at me and told me to have a great day. I remember how much I wanted to scream at her, at the world, that nothing would ever be OK again, much less great. But the world just kept turning.

Ever since, I've sought out grief in others. Analyzed the way it kneaded them like dough. Wondered if they felt the same insular agony I'd felt. A feeling I've never been able to forget. A deadly cocktail of shock and revulsion. An inner animalistic panic.

Fallon looks up suddenly, catching my gaze. "Do I know you?"

I don't even blink. "You want to crush something, don't you?" I hold a palm up. "With your hands. Just grind it to dust or powder."

The bartender slides his beer forward, but Fallon doesn't look at it. He doesn't look away from me.

"I know the feeling." I take a sip of my club soda, which is only melted ice at this point. "I'm sorry about your sister, and I'm sorry that all words are useless."

His chin trembles. "I don't know you."

"I'm Ren. A friend of Billy's."

"Margo's sister." Billy's words are quiet, and they take me by surprise. I haven't been introduced as Margo's sister in fourteen years. I'm like a cat who can't make up her mind. I want to purr happily. I want to scratch and claw his eyes out.

I am Margo's sister.

I am so much more than Margo's sister.

Something flashes in Fallon's eyes. "So you understand."

"Better than others. How did you know Margo?"

"Everyone knew Margo. Knew of her at least. Me and my buddies spent hours at the quarry trying to get her attention."

The quarry sat near the county line. Teenagers would go there for bonfires and to hook up in truck beds. Last I heard, it's now a residential neighborhood.

He takes a long drink of his beer, but his body still shakes. "She was just a kid, you know. Like your sister."

"Too young," Billy says. "A damn shame."

"How do you get past it?" Fallon stares past Billy at me. "The anger."

I take in this man. He's a fresh cut, still pulsing blood. Hemorrhaging with no medical care in sight and asking me for a shortcut to stop the bleeding. "You don't."

"Someone did this to her."

That gets me. I hold my glass tighter. "How do you know that?"

"I don't know. Maybe it's just something I say to make myself feel better that she didn't choose to leave on her own. Isn't that sick?" He cuts himself off and downs the rest of his beer. "Another."

The bartender obliges.

"Who was she?" I ask.

"What?"

"Your sister. Who was she? What was she like? You knew mine. It's only fair."

"She was a bitch." He laughs, and it looks like it was the first time he's done it in weeks. "She was mouthy. Wouldn't let you get anything past her." He sobers, and the smile falls away. "She was loyal. Tried hard in school but was never really good at it. She didn't have many friends, but the ones she did have were for life."

"Alejandra was her friend."

Fallon stiffens, and his gaze shifts around the bar. "Why would you say that?"

"You know her?"

"She was Tina's best friend before—" He takes a drink. "Now they're both dead."

Billy cuts in. "Ren thinks it has to do with him. The teacher who was arrested today."

"Billy." My voice is unusually sharp.

Fallon only has eyes for me, and something flashes deep within them. "What's he talking about?"

"There's nothing to tell."

It's not that easy. Fallon's whole expression darkens. "You know something about what happened to my sister?"

"No. I really don't." *Dammit Billy.* I shoot him a look.

Billy looks sheepishly down into his empty beer bottle.

"If you know something, you better say it—"

"I don't know anything. It's just—isn't it odd that two best friends are found dead in unusual circumstances only a year from one another?"

"What are you trying to say?"

"I don't know yet," I answer honestly.

"That why you're here? Looking for me? Looking for gossip? Her body isn't even in the ground yet."

"I had no idea you would be here."

"Everyone out there thinks they're a detective these days. Listen to a couple true crime podcasts, and suddenly you're Sherlock Holmes. You want to know what I think? I think my sister said something to the wrong person. She finally pushed the envelope a little too far. There is no conspiracy. No special reasoning to explain. She's dead, and sometimes it doesn't have to make sense." He finishes his beer and slams it on the counter. Lays a crumpled ten-dollar bill next to it. "Now if you'll excuse me, I have to go check on my mother."

"Fallon." I stop him with a palm to his shoulder, and I hate myself for pushing it. But I would hate myself more if I didn't. "She was asking questions about Alejandra before she went missing, wasn't she? She was making accusations."

There's a fire burning in his eyes now. "How could you possibly know that?"

I don't want to bring up Michaela. Instead, I say, "I just need to know, was she ever in Benton? Did she have any connection to this place?"

"No, she—" He stops, and his face shutters.

"You remembered something."

"Why would I tell you anything?"

"Because you know me," I say before I can stop myself. "I know what it's like to be chewed up and spit out. To lose something that can't be replaced. To physically ache with a need that will never be satiated. Because you don't want what happened to your sister, what happened to mine, to happen to anyone else's."

"I shouldn't say any of this. I haven't even talked to the police yet." He blows out a heavy breath. "Shit. OK. This probably doesn't mean anything, but the day before she went missing, she visited Alejandra's family. I don't know the details. The only reason I know that is because I called her on the way there, and she told me where she was going."

"Did she go home after?"

"To a park, I think. Uh, the one where Alejandra died. I figured she was upset. Needed space. She came home way too late. Didn't speak to me or Mom. Just went straight to her room and locked the door. That was common for her." His voice breaks, and if I could visually see it, I'm sure it would look like a glass shattering into millions of pieces. "That morning we woke up, and she was gone."

"I'm so sorry, Fallon."

"I don't know why you're asking these questions, but maybe you shouldn't be."

"What does that mean?"

His jaw clenches. "Things happen to girls in this town who ask too many questions. But you already know that."

# 20

I offer Billy a ride home, but he declines, saying he'd rather walk. It's probably for the best. I just want to be alone. I push outside into the cool night air feeling the breeze slip inside my shirt, wrap around my neck like a snake. October crept up on me. No more pollen dusting my car, now it's constantly blanketed by fallen leaves, burnt orange and bloodred. This fall will surely bring a few more heat waves, but right now, the bite of cold as everything around me wilts and dies seems fitting.

I hurry to my car, thankful my earlier urge is gone. I'm left feeling wrung out. Weak with what I almost did. Weak with the knowledge of what I learned.

My conversation with Fallon. The bombs he dropped. Tina had gone to visit Alejandra's family the day before she went missing. She ended up at that park.

The park where Alejandra died.

How could any of this be a coincidence?

And the bigger question, the one Margo asked me earlier: What am I going to do about it?

———

The message arrives while I'm in the shower Friday morning. I dry my thumb on the shower curtain and check it. A quick statement from the board encouraging teachers not to talk to any members of the media about the email sent yesterday. No updates on Bryson. No apologies for hiring a predator.

I can't help but think Billy is right. It's the beginning of them sweeping everything under the rug.

The beginning of history repeating itself.

———

I search for Olivia that morning. She's not in the gym or cafeteria. When the first bell rings, I hop on my computer. Olivia is marked as present in her first period.

Don't know why that brings me relief.

"You just can't help yourself." Margo sits on the edge of my desk. "Can you, Renny? Is it because you think she's going to die? You think the boogeyman is going to get her too?"

I ignore her.

Two girls in the desks closest to me whisper quietly, their voices rising above the hum of the others. "I heard he's having sex with someone else. That chick—what's her name? Olivia something."

"There's no way that's true."

My back straightens, fingers flattening on my keyboard. Their words nearly unmoor me. Rumors. I know how they work. I know most aren't true. But of all the names they could say. Of all the girls they could mention.

It's not a coincidence.

It can't be.

"That's what I heard. Miranda said she saw her leave his class once, like, after hours. Said Olivia acted surprised to see her and super nervous."

"Olivia who? Who even is that?"

"She's, like, blond. She's always wearing that jean jacket."

"Oh shit. Wait. Yeah. Her?" The way she says it. *Her?* Like that's the most disturbing part of their conversation. Not the fact they're discussing a teacher sleeping with a student. "Come on. No way. You think she's the one he'd risk a felony for?"

"I'd let him commit a felony with me." A burst of giggles.

"Girls." My voice is icy. I can't bite my tongue a moment longer. "That's enough."

The girls straighten in their seats, turning away from each other. Everyone else stops talking to look at us. At me.

"We were only joking."

*Why is she crying? We were literally only joking.*

*She's just upset because she knows we're right.*

*It's her fault Margo's dead.*

A chill sinks into me, bone-deep as I look between them but don't really see anything at all. "Can I speak to you outside for a second?" They look at one another and then nod reluctantly, following me out to the oohs and ahhs of their classmates.

The girls round on me as soon as the door closes. "It was just a joke. We shouldn't have even been talking about it."

"We're not, like, in trouble, right?"

I ignore the question. "You mentioned Olivia. I'm presuming you mean Olivia Green."

They glance at each other again, looking uneasy.

"Look," I say. "I just want to know where you heard that. You mentioned she's in a relationship with Mr. Lewis."

Neither one will meet my eye or say anything.

"It's important that you tell me if you know something."

One of them, Brenda, a tall basketball player, looks as if she's about to cry. I don't know if it's from nerves, embarrassment, or something else. "It's just something we heard. We don't know anything for sure."

"You mentioned someone seeing her leave his classroom after school hours?"

"That was a while ago. A couple weeks, I think. That's it. That's all we know."

But her friend shifts uncomfortably. "Well…there was the video."

I freeze. "What video?"

"It was so weird." She runs a nervous hand through her bobbed brown hair. "OK, so, Olivia posted this weird video to TikTok and then deleted it pretty quickly. But I screen recorded it, like, instantly."

"You have it?"

She looks at Brenda and back to me, nodding. "You want to see?" She digs in her pocket, pulling out an iPhone. A few swipes of her fingers, and she's holding the phone out so I can see.

All words die on my tongue when I see Olivia's face.

Olivia sits against a plain wall. Her hair is neat and pushed behind her ears, and her face is void of makeup. Music is playing while words flash on the screen rhythmically.

*Something people don't know about me?*

*I had s3x with someone I shouldn't.*

*Someone older.*

*Someone who was supposed to protect me.*

*He only hurt me instead.*

*It doesn't matter if no one believes me.*

*It's time I tell my story.*

*I had s3x with a teacher.*

*My teacher.*

*More than once.*

*And apparently, I'm not his first.*

I hiss out an uneasy breath. Every neuron in my brain seems to be firing at once. "When did she post this?"

"Last night. It was shared thousands of times."

"She deleted it when someone sent it to the principal."

Brenda nudges her. "That's what we *think* at least. Someone saw her go to his office this morning, and she hasn't been back in class since."

"Is that it? This is everything you've heard."

There's a beat of silence before Brenda clears her throat. "We, uh, heard it happens here. Like on campus."

"It?"

"You know." She blushes bright red. "There's this room under the stage in the gym. The chiller. That's where everyone thinks they go to…"

She doesn't finish the sentence. Doesn't have to. Because I know.

"OK," I say numbly, nodding toward my door. "Thank you for telling me. Go back inside. Tell the class I'll be back in five minutes."

They look confused, but they don't ask any questions before slipping inside and closing the door behind them.

Before I realize I'm doing it, I'm walking down the stairs, through the empty halls, my shoes clicking on the ground with every step.

Margo keeps pace with me. "You think you can help her?"

"Just like I tried to help you."

"Is that what you called what you did that night?" she asks, an amused lilt to the question.

Principal Smart is in the hallway right outside the gym, whispering to Jack Davis. Both men huddle together with serious expressions on their faces. Both look up when they hear me approach. It's Smart who looks away first, his cheeks reddening by the second. There are no attempts to talk to me. To apologize for brushing me off. He merely looks away. Maybe he's assuring himself it won't happen again. Maybe he even believes it.

He's convinced it's only an accident that I'm right.

That he hasn't done anything wrong.

The fury beats through my veins viciously. A mother hurdling down the halls of her home with a baseball bat when she hears an intruder. There is no fear. There is only primal protective instincts. The anger doesn't let up. It doesn't ease.

Principal Smart told me he fought to keep Margo's photo up. It made him feel better. It reminded him of how important the students are. Principal Smart also laughed me out of his office when I'd told him about his buddy Bryson.

I stare at his avoidant eyes as I pass. If he's wondering why I'm going into the gym, he doesn't ask.

Doesn't matter.

He'll know soon enough.

Inside the gym, I scan the bleachers. The walls. The rolled mats in the corner that several girls are sprawled across. Everyone is lying around on their phones while the gym teachers are huddled in a corner with a few students talking football. I quickly move to the stage, and no one gives me a second look. The stage is a chest-high surface at the end of the gym behind the basketball net. There are no stairs without going through a closed door on either side, so I just hoist myself up.

I look behind me once more, confirm no one, least of all the coaches, are paying attention, before dipping behind the red curtain. It's dark back here. Musty. Clearly they use the space for prop storage when it's not in use.

I exit stage left and go down a small set of stairs. At the end of the short hallway is the door to the chiller. The noise in the gym muffles to nothing, and I can't fight the roiling feeling in my stomach as I reach for the door.

That's when I hear it.

Crying.

It's muted, like someone is crying into their shirtsleeve. Trying their best to stay silent. I pull the door open just as someone pushes. A rumpled Olivia Green stands in the doorway of the chiller, wiping tears from her eyes.

# 21

Olivia starts when she sees me. "Ms. Taylor, what are you doing?"

"Why are you back here and not in the gym with the rest of your class?" I ask. She looks smaller than usual. Huddled in on herself. A weight bearing down on her that I can't begin to understand.

She presses her lips together like she's fighting tears once again. "After he called roll, I came back here to get away from them."

"From who?"

"Everyone. Everything. I didn't know where else to go. I need some space, and I couldn't go home without my mom freaking out." Her voice is raspy and broken. Eyes are glazed with pain. "I messed up."

Those three words. I know those words. "You can talk to me."

Olivia brings an arm up to cover her mouth, and her body shakes with sobs. I don't think as I cut through the distance dividing us and wrap my arms around her bony shoulders. I don't offer words of comfort because I know that's not what anyone needs in crisis. The only thing I can give her is my presence.

My unwavering support.

A whistle blows from somewhere in the gym, and Olivia reluctantly pulls back. "I've been gone too long."

"Olivia, you don't have to go back in there."

"No, I do."

"I'll write you a note—"

"You don't get it." She shoves away. "If I don't come back, then they'll think they won. They'll think they're right. They'll think I'm just a liar."

I bite the inside of my cheek a little too hard. A beat passes where I allow her to catch her breath. One good breath before I steal her next one. "I saw the video."

She flinches but doesn't meet my eyes. "Then you know."

"I know you talked to Smart. I know you told him you made it up."

"That's what everyone else thinks."

"Why are you lying?" I bend my knees just a bit to get eye level with her. "Why would you tell him you lied?"

Now she looks at me. Really looks at me. "You believe me?"

"I *saw* the video."

She wipes a tear away. Then another. "I was so angry. When I saw that picture of Mr. Lewis and…that girl. I was so angry. He told me—he made it seem like he cared about me. But I was just another girl to him."

"You wanted to punish him?"

"That's not it exactly. I didn't even think anyone would watch the video. No one follows me on TikTok. No one that matters at least. It just felt important to say it out loud. So I did it, and as soon as I woke up to ten thousand views, I regretted it."

"Is that why you lied?"

"I never imagined this getting back to the principal. I never imagined everyone in our school watching it. I couldn't risk my parents finding out. I didn't have a choice."

"You can't keep this to yourself."

"It's my secret to keep."

"Not anymore." My voice is sure and strong. There is no room for arguing. There is no getting rid of me. "Let me help you. I don't want to pressure you. I don't want you to be hurt. But I know you can do this, Olivia. It will be hard. It will be awkward, but there's a reason you posted that video last night. A part of you wants people to know. You're tired of carrying this burden alone. Let me take it from you." Her eyes skim to the stage and back to me. I step closer. "I'll be here every step of the way."

A single tear falls. It's lonely, a snail's trail down her cheek, until the rest form and come down with it, and she's red cheeked and wet faced. "I'm sorry."

"No." The ferocity is back. The anger. The mother, with only a baseball bat to protect her children in a gunfight but knowing she's going to do it. Somehow, and at any cost, her children will be OK because there isn't another option. "You have nothing to apologize for."

"It wasn't supposed to be like this. It never was supposed to go this far. We started talking last semester. We'd Snapchat or whatever. I didn't have his class then, and he was funny. There were no lines crossed." She bites down on her lip. "But this past summer, he invited me over to his house, and we…we did stuff. I wanted to. It isn't like he forced me. I liked it at the time."

"At the time? What does that mean?"

Olivia's sobs hitch in her chest. "I didn't want to do it anymore. But he pressured me, you know? Makes me feel like I—" She seems to grasp for the right word. Any word.

"Like you don't have a choice?"

"He said there's no point in stopping. That we'd already gone too far. That we were made for each other. Then suddenly school started, and he treated me like I was…like I didn't exist. It makes me feel crazy."

I grab her hand and pull her to me. Her hair smells like peaches. It makes her seem younger. Makes this whole situation feel even more debilitating. I pull back to look at her. "This is not your fault."

"What's going to happen if I try to tell the truth now? Who will believe me?"

"Hey." I look her in the eye. "We can't control others. We can't control what they think or how they react. We can only control our own narrative. Everything you have to say is important. It's important for you, and it's important for the next girl." Every word is a bullet. A lifeline. Killing me and bringing me back. Because I was her once—young, scared, broken. And I wish someone had said them to me.

She visibly recoils. "I'm scared."

"When me and my sister were kids, we used to do this thing. It was a special promise we'd make only to one another." Olivia watches me warily. I hold up my hand with my fingers in the shape of a *V*. "We called it a vow. It was silly, but when we made one, we knew it was an unbreakable promise. We only used it for the most serious of circumstances. Hold your hand up like this. There. Now touch the tip of your fingers to mine." Our index and middle fingers touch, and I pull back. "The unbreakable promise. I'm not going anywhere, Olivia. I can't promise you it will be painless, but I can promise you it's the right thing to do. I can promise I'll be with you every moment you need me."

"Thank you."

"Are you ready?"

She takes a deep breath and nods bravely. I do too. Just one breath. One moment to remember the last time I made that vow.

The last promise I kept.

When the pain burns too brightly, I shove it away and lead Olivia over the stage to the gym.

Every pair of eyes in the room is on us.

If I was as brave as Olivia Green, Margo might still be here. Faintly, I hear Margo's laughter coming from somewhere behind me.

# 22

The first thing I do is pop my head into Emma's class. First period prep. She looks surprised to see me and downright shocked when she sees Olivia.

"Can you watch my class?" I ask her quickly.

She doesn't ask any questions. "Yes. Now?"

I nod, knowing I'll have so much to explain to her later. "Thank you."

Principal Smart isn't in the hallway when we come out of Emma's room, but we find him in his office. His face goes stark white when he sees us.

"We need to talk." I lead Olivia to a chair. She sits, but I remain standing. I like this position. Towering over Smart. Seeing the unease in his eyes as he looks up at me. "Perhaps we should start by calling Olivia's parents."

Smart's mouth tightens, but he nods without an argument.

We wait on her mother together.

Olivia's mom works at a bank nearby and arrives hurriedly, eyeing the three of us suspiciously. The woman looks a lot like Olivia. Blond with sharp features and crystal-clear blue eyes. But that's where the similarities end. Where Olivia has an easy smile, a goodness that she wears like a familiar scarf, her mother has frown lines. She doesn't sit by her daughter or take her hand. There's a space between them, and it appears to be more than just physical.

"What is this regarding?" Mrs. Green asks, still not looking at her daughter.

"There's been an incident."

"Mom." Olivia turns in her seat toward her. "It's about the teacher who was arrested yesterday. Mr. Lewis."

"What about him?" Mrs. Green's gaze roams from Olivia to me to Smart. Back to Olivia. There is confusion in her expression, but something else. An anger. Suspicion even.

"The girl in the photo. She wasn't his only…she wasn't the only girl who…"

"She wasn't his only victim," I finish for her from my spot against the wall. Everything in me yearns to protect Olivia. From her from her mother. From her principal.

From the teacher who's responsible for us being here at all.

"Olivia," Mr. Smart says gruffly. "You said it wasn't true. You said the video was a joke."

"What video?" Mrs. Green looks between the principal and me. She still hasn't looked at her kid.

Olivia starts explaining. She explains her relationship with Bryson. What happened when school started back. The reasoning behind the video. Every moment she speaks, her voice gets stronger.

I analyze the shock on Mrs. Green and Principal Smart. They both look close to vomiting throughout her whole speech. When Olivia finally goes silent, it's Principal Smart who clears his throat to speak first. "This is all very serious."

Olivia looks down.

I pace the room to stop myself from tilting her chin up. From telling her they are the ones who deserve to look down. Not her.

"I'll have to call the police. They'll want your statement."

"The police?" Mrs. Green chokes out like a statue brought to life. The anger is back. "For heaven's sake, Olivia."

"Your daughter is a child." My voice is chipped ice and sharp edges. "She was taken advantage of by a man with an ethical responsibility to protect her. She doesn't need judgment right now. Can't you see how hard this was for her to even tell you?"

Mrs. Green's teeth clash together angrily. "I don't know who in the hell you think you are, but Olivia is my daughter. What are you doing in here anyway?"

"Mom, this is Ms. Taylor. She's helped me."

Mrs. Green glares over her daughter's head. "Well, she's done helping you. We're calling our lawyer to figure out how to go from here."

"Ma'am—"

Principal Smart is cut off. "No, she's not saying another word. Not to any of you. You all have done enough." Mrs. Green stands, grabbing the back of her daughter's arm, jerking her to stand. "Come on."

I stand too, my teeth set on edge. Olivia's panicked eyes swivel to me. "It's OK," she says. "I'm fine, Ms. Taylor. I'll be OK. Trust me."

Mrs. Green rolls her eyes. "Let's go, Olivia." The woman pulls her daughter from the room, phone already to her ear before the door fully shuts behind her. I stay standing in a state of shock.

"It's best if you don't mention this to anyone else," Smart mumbles from behind me, his hands laced behind his neck. "At least not until I talk to our superintendent. I'm sure she'll want to get our lawyers involved too."

There are so many things I wish to say. So many emotions racing through me. But it's like trying to catch feathers in hurricane winds. Impossible. "This is your fault too," I say finally.

He doesn't say anything back.

The walk back to my class is silent. My mind races, and I can't identify a single thought for what it is. I can only identify the emotions tugging at my chest. The sadness. The regret.

Is this what justice feels like?

This cloying feeling, it's subtle. It almost feels like it isn't enough. Like Olivia isn't getting back what was taken from her. Because what's going to happen now? She reports him and gets embroiled in the investigation. Her mother sues? Pulls her out of school? The rumors keep spreading? Her mother blames her? And we all just go on pretending this was the right thing to do?

Margo had justice, and it felt a lot like this. But her justice couldn't bring her back from the dead. Maybe if it had, it would feel more satisfying.

At the end of the day, I get in my car and sit. My fingers tighten over the gear shift. It would be so easy. Drive to his house.

Slip on my gloves.

Walk to his door—

I clench my eyes closed and lean my head forward on the

steering wheel. It doesn't help when all I see is a twister of faces spinning behind my eyelids over and over. Olivia. Alejandra. Tina. Margo.

I pull out of the lot a little aggressively. The cheerleaders are on a patch of grass again in front of the school, and the coach yells something at my retreating car. I don't feel bad. I can't. Not when I'm running from something far worse than shame.

I'm running from myself, but something tells me I won't be fast enough.

———

I drive to my parents' house after school.

Birds sing cheerfully and a playful breeze teases the ends of my hair as bright sunshine warms my body through my open window.

But when I pull up and shift into park, I know instantly that something isn't right. Dad's truck isn't out front.

They're probably at an appointment for my mother. Maybe they stopped somewhere for an early dinner. Though Mom usually hates eating out and says it's a waste of money. Margo and Dad were always sneaking trips to Waffle House and sharing secret looks when Mom inevitably found the receipt and started ranting about the cost of living.

Maybe she's changed her mind.

That has to be it.

I watch the flash of sunshine through the kitchen window, watch it and the whole scene fade to gray, and I'm left staring at an empty house.

I no longer hear the birds.

And I'm empty too. Even with all the memories.

Margo is next to me. "You wanted to see them. Wanted to feel like a kid again. Back when things were right, and I danced in the kitchen to the radio while dad skinned his fish in the front yard. Mom would be working on the computer, humming along to the music even though she tried wholeheartedly to pretend she hated anything you and I listened to."

I can see it. See all the things I'm yearning for.

I laugh out loud.

My eyes are wet.

There is no radio. No salty fish. No Dad working under a light. No Margo laughing. Mom humming.

There is only me standing in front of an empty home.

Beside my dead sister.

Knowing two more girls just like her are now dead too.

# 23

Detective Wu is sitting on my porch steps when I make it home.

I wipe my eyes quickly and park, trying to mask the emotions from today. I force a half smile. "Can I help you with something, Detective?"

She stands as I approach, swiping at invisible dirt on her pants leg. "I was hoping we could talk."

"I'm afraid I don't have any more information for you about Casey. I've told you all I know."

Detective Wu's eyes stay on my face, the skin around them creasing with clear concentration. "It's about something else."

"Sure," I say quickly, walking past her. Back to the rocking chairs. Feeling like all I want to do is slam the front door on her face and curl up in my bed.

There will be plenty of time for that later.

She doesn't sit. Instead, she stands diagonally from me, hands in the pockets of her slacks. "You're an interesting woman, Ren Taylor."

I don't say anything. Just wait.

"I did a little looking into you. Protocol, you know? Considering the circumstances."

"Right."

She rocks back on her heels, somehow keeping all her focus on me. I resist the urge to squirm, but surely any type of movement would be better, more natural, than my current frozen state.

"Can you tell me anything about the charges brought against you last year?"

I bite down on my tongue to keep from wincing. Use a second, just one, to think. Those charges. I remember him. Steve the lawyer. He was angry when I was done with him. Angry enough to press charges, but not foolish enough to go through with it. "They were dropped. And anyway, it was a little ridiculous. You've clearly looked into it. You know how outrageous it was."

"A man said you threatened him. Said you took his phone and sent his wife explicit photos that were private, resulting in the breakdown of his marriage. He said you did it on purpose. You targeted him."

*Oh, Steve.*

I remember the way his eyes had wandered to me as soon as he walked into that bar. The tan line on his finger where his wedding ring should have been. I remember his hands on me the whole night. The things he said. The things he wasn't saying. And I remember when he slipped into the bathroom, and I was left with his phone. A wife and two beautiful blond children were his screensaver.

But I'm the one who targeted him.

I'm the one responsible for the breakdown of his marriage when he took off that ring, when he approached me in that bar.

All I did was take a few pictures and hit send.

"His statement said he thought you did it on purpose; you brought him into that room, you got him vulnerable. You stole his phone to send the photos. He said you told him he deserved it. Men like him deserved it."

"Yes, that is his statement," I answer carefully, and something in Detective Wu's eyes flash.

"You don't want to explain what happened there?"

"I don't see the point." I stand, and it's my turn to dust off the imaginary dirt. The grime of Steve's memory. "Is that all you needed today?"

Detective Wu doesn't move an inch. Doesn't even blink. "There was something interesting that happened the night of Casey's death, Ms. Taylor. Right after he hung up with his wife, lying to her profusely might I add, he sent her his location."

She waits a beat.

I say nothing.

"That's strange, right? That he would do that. He'd just convinced her he was on a work outing and then sent her a location to a local hotel and bar. It doesn't add up. I don't know. I guess it got me thinking."

I want to step around her, make for the door, but something in her expression has me absolutely still.

"Did something go awry, Ren?" she asks, suddenly. The pretense seems to fall away, and she appears genuine. Vulnerable, even. "You were upset he lied to you. Maybe you retaliate by doing something you've done in the past. You snag his phone, send the location, and then take off. But he follows you. Maybe he's angry. Violent. Something happened in that parking lot didn't it, Ren?"

"I think," I say roughly, pushing thoughts of Casey and Steve and all the other men not worth my thoughts out of my head. "I think it's time for you to go, and if you feel the need to contact or question me again, I'll have to insist on having a lawyer present."

Detective Wu lets out a breath and takes a step back. "Right. Good talking to you, Ren."

"Good evening, Detective."

She steps off the porch and lifts her hand in a wave. "I'll be in touch."

———

I lie on my side, knees curled into my chest. There's pressure there. The weight of the last few days. Tina being found. Bryson being found out. Olivia being scrutinized.

Detective Wu getting so very close—

"She's going to figure it out, Renny," Margo whispers against the back of my neck. "She already has."

I squeeze my eyes closed. "It doesn't matter."

"What are you going to do?"

I open my eyes to a darkening room. A headlight passing over my window. The thrum of my central heating. "What I've always done," I answer.

# 24

The rumors are worse on Monday. Or maybe I'm just not in the mindset to hear them. I didn't sleep much last night. I couldn't stop worrying. Thinking.

Getting to school today, hearing the chorus of voices vibrating the halls, only makes me want to sink under water and not resurface.

Tina's name, Alejandra's, and even Olivia's. It's not just the students either. Teachers huddle at the ends of the halls, leaning close together. We all try to pretend we grew out of high school, but it's rarely true for any of us.

As students rush into first period, I stare at Bryson's door. At the young woman welcoming students in, and I picture him there. That tie hanging loosely from his neck. His signature smirk on his face.

I think of him curled up beside a naked Alejandra.

"He was arrested."

"I heard he's on bail."

"Everyone is saying it's a deep fake."

The whispering doesn't stop until I stand at the front of the room and get their attention. But the silence doesn't last long. It never does.

I barely make it through my early classes, and come lunchtime I check on Olivia's schedule. She was marked absent from all her morning classes. Did her mom keep her out of school? Is she hiding out in the gym again?

I can't help it. I have to check.

The gym reeks of sweat and musk. Somewhere on the bleachers a girl screams and giggles, stomping away from a boy. Kids walk side by side in duos and trios around the gym floor in jeans and thick hoodies. No one is dressed out. Same as last time, no one is really doing anything. No physical activity.

I don't bother glancing over my shoulder. Coaches aren't paying attention. I pull myself onto the stage and head down the stairs to the left. The sounds strangle until the world around me is utterly silent. It's like pressing mute on the TV.

The door that leads to the chiller appears cracked, but it's hard to tell for certain. Had Olivia left it that way? Or has someone else been in here?

I go to reach for it, to try to open it to see—

"Can I help you?" The deep voice comes from behind me. The PE coach is staring at me, confused.

My hand drops to my side. "I was looking for a student," I say casually. "They're not here."

"You thought they'd be down there?" He looks me over. His throat bobs with a swallow. "In the chiller?"

"I heard this is where students go to skip." I say it lightly like I'm making a joke, but his eyes only narrow.

"No one is down there. The door's locked. It's always locked."

"Oh, good to know. I should head to lunch anyway. Sorry to disturb your class."

"Hey." He stops me after I slip around him, so close to the stairs. "I saw you yesterday, didn't I? Coming out with that girl. Olivia, right? The one everyone is talking about. Is that who you were looking for?"

"Yes." I glance at him over my shoulder. "Guess she decided to stay home today."

He looks contemplative for a second, his hands sinking into the pockets of his mesh gym shorts. "Probably for the best."

I stiffen. "What does that mean?"

"I just mean with girls like that you never know what they're going to say next."

*Girls like that?*

His cheeks tinge red. "I'm just saying, I've heard she can be dramatic. I don't know. Seems weird that that picture goes out and suddenly she's trying to get the spotlight on her."

"Huh." I let out a breath. "You have kids?"

"Two."

"A daughter?"

He's quiet a long minute. "Both girls."

"Well, here's hoping they never spread any silly rumors about their teachers, right? Wouldn't want them to become a *girl like that.*"

"Wait—I don't think—"

"Have a good day, Coach." And I leave before he can say another word.

My stomach doesn't settle the whole walk to the cafeteria.

Grabbing a chicken sandwich and sitting at the faculty table are something I can do without thinking. The women don't stop talking, but they do give me strange looks when I sit, like I'm the last person they expect to see. It irks me at first but then I remember I haven't made an effort to get to know them since I've been here. Not really. And after snapping at Lynette the other day, I guess I can't blame them for being standoffish.

"What did Jack say?" Koa asks Emma. "I mean, he must have heard something by now, right?"

Emma chews her bottom lip, and I pretend I'm not hungrily hanging on to every word. "OK," she relents. "OK. Look, this can't be repeated because things change. But last I heard Bryson is out on bail. Right now, his charges are only for an alleged sexual relationship with his student from Rosemary Academy."

"The girl that died in the woods?" Mary asks. For once there is no humor on her face.

My teeth sink into my tongue, drawing blood.

"Yes. She was seventeen at the time which is perfectly legal. Georgia's age of consent is sixteen. He's saying it was entirely consensual, and he isn't guilty of doing anything wrong."

"It's a felony," I murmur. "He's guilty of a felony."

"Wait." Lynette swallows a piece of popcorn and wipes her hands on a napkin. "Wait, wait, wait. Didn't do anything wrong? Since when is having sex with a student not wrong?"

Emma grinds her teeth "Apparently with the legality of her age and the situation," Emma says, rubbing her belly as if trying to sooth herself. "His lawyer claims that any formal charges are an infringement of his constitutional rights."

"Constitutional rights to screw his students?"

"Only a white man," Koa mutters.

"What about Olivia?" I ask, and every eye swings to me.

Emma only shakes her head. "He says she's just a student. That he has never been involved with her."

Mary snorts.

"Wait, he's telling people that she's lying?" I ask, my voice coming out sharper than I intend. "What about Tina? What does he have to say about her?"

"Tina? Tina Drexler? There's really nothing linking her to him, Ren. Or Olivia for that matter. The only thing linking him to Alejandra is the photo."

"What about Olivia's side? What about her video? Why would Olivia just make it up?"

The women go silent, watching with widening eyes.

Emma lays her hand on my arm. "Hey, just keep it down. We don't want the kids to overhear."

Their voices churn in and out, and my stomach convulses violently. I place a hand on my middle like that will help. But it's a waste of time. Nothing will settle the chaos inside of me.

My vision blurs.

That's when I see Billy. His head is low, and he's holding a trash bag as he crosses the cafeteria to the side door leading to the courtyard.

I stand up, and Emma grabs my hand. "Wait, don't leave, Ren."

"I'm sorry," I say to all the women at the table. "I just need a second."

I go in the direction Billy went before anyone has time to

protest. A couple of students sit at a picnic table staring at their phones. They don't look at me as I pass.

The dumpsters are behind the annex hall at the very back of the school. I hear Billy before I see him. Or rather, I hear music playing from a phone. He's leaning against a wall half-hidden by the dumpster. Cigarette smoke wafts up around him as he fiddles with his too-full key ring.

"How does that thing not completely weigh you down?"

He swivels toward my voice, eyes wide with fear. "What? Oh, it's you." He brings the cigarette back to his lips and jingles the keys "You talking about this?"

"It looks heavy."

"It's a key to every door in this place. Should be heavy." He sighs, and I notice how tired he looks. There are dark circles beneath his eyes. I try and picture him in high school, but I come up short. Whatever he used to be doesn't seem to match who he is now.

I wonder if he thinks the same thing when he looks at me.

"You do this often?" I gesture around him.

"Am I not allowed to have a cigarette?"

"Not really."

He takes another drag, tilting his chin up and blowing smoke at the sky. "You going to tell on me, Ren Glass?"

"It's Ren Taylor now."

"Huh? Oh, yeah. Right. You were married." He inhales once more, then tosses the cherry on the ground, grinding it into the dirt.

"What about you, Billy? Have you ever been married?" I'm curious about him still.

This time when he looks at me, there's a wariness there that wasn't in his eyes before. "You really care, Ren? We really going to make small talk right now? Why did you follow me out here?"

It's a good question. How do I explain that Billy comforts me? That something about him being around reminds me of my sister. It's a weird feeling, not instantly hating a man. "I don't know. I just needed to get out of there, and I saw you."

"So you followed me?"

"I can leave if—"

"Look," he cuts me off. "If you're wanting to know more about Bryson, I don't know anything other than what I've already said."

I stop and look at him. "This is why you're so upset? It's about Bryson?"

He shakes his head and roughly scrubs his hands down his face. "It's happening again right under my nose. In this school with—and I had no idea. Is it me? Am I that much of a dumbass?"

"It's not your fault," I say, surprised that he'd even think so.

"It's all of our faults, Ren. We're the adults. We're culpable."

I wince. But, God, is he wrong?

"Billy, it isn't—"

"Been screwing students in the damn chiller. Right here. Right here, Ren."

I stumble over the word, to his reference to the very place that keeps coming up. "Why would you say that?"

"He had a key, you know."

"How do you know about that?" His words rock me, and all I can think of is Olivia hiding out behind the stage and the door to the chiller being cracked earlier. Had she been down there?

If so, how many times before?

"Jack Davis asked me if I had a copy of one after Bryson lost his. I didn't. No one has access to that room except Jack and Coach Lambert. And I guess Bryson too." He pushes off from the wall. "I really can't talk about this shit. Not today."

I don't say anything, and he sighs. "I shouldn't be taking this out on you."

"I get it."

"You're probably the only person who understands." He looks over my shoulder and breathes out. All I smell is smoke and something sweet on his breath. "I don't know what to do with this anger. I want to kill him."

"It isn't your fault," I force out between dry lips.

"Tell him the truth," Margo says loudly from her spot right beside Billy. "Tell him what kind of girl you are. You're ready to help him hide the body. Right, Renny?" She sings the last word.

Billy's face remains unchanged. His hand shoots out to grasp a strand of my hair between two fingers and pushes it behind my ear. "I thought I might see you at the Lantern Friday."

"I thought about it. I had a lot of work to catch up on."

His cheeks turn red, and he looks away. "Nah, I get it."

"No, you don't. Trust me. This has nothing to do with you and everything to do with me."

His eyes shoot up. "I get that."

"Rain check?"

"I'll hold you to that. You know I will." He walks backward with the first genuine smile I've seen from him. "I should go before another teacher stalks me and finds us back here."

"Bye, Billy," I say, already walking away. But I'm not heading to class. I'm going back to the gym.

And this time I'm going to find out what's behind that door.

# 25

The gym is empty, and it feels like the first stroke of luck I've had in days. Weeks. I was already running through what I'd say to the coach if I ran into him again.

There's no one here though.

Which is rare. Usually if there isn't a class, then there's some sports team practicing. I head toward the stage, knowing I don't have much time. There are only minutes left of my lunch break.

Just like before, I hoist myself onto the stage and go left. The door is right there, and it is partially open. I push it the rest of the way and peer down a set of ominous stairs. The first thing I notice is the temperature. The drop is immediately noticeable as I venture down. It gets colder with each step. The kind of cold that hugs you too tight. My skin prickles, but maybe I can't attribute every one of my bodily reactions to the frigid air. With each step into the deepening darkness, an underlying sense of dread looms. The door to the chiller sits alone at the bottom.

That door too is cracked open.

Hadn't the coach said it was always locked? Had Olivia been down here and left it open on purpose?

My breath rushes out as my pulse picks up.

I glance behind me, listening for the sounds of another person, but there are none. I inch the door open the rest of the way. It takes one turn of my head to scan the entirety of the room. It's small, maybe ten by twelve. There are dusty shelves packed with sports equipment. Boxes scattered around the room. Basketballs, a volleyball net, pom-poms, bats, and gloves. I can't take a step without bumping into something. And the cold is different in here. It permeates me as quickly as the smell of must. Like something wet is sentenced to rot here with no hope of ever drying again.

I don't know where to start, don't know what I'm looking for, until I see a tiny clearing with a crumpled blanket in the corner of the room. I walk over to it, lift the blanket with my thumb and forefinger, and something falls to the floor.

A scrap of cotton.

A pink bra.

Something about it just lying there on the ground is wrong. Something that tiny and bright shouldn't be here in this cold, dark room with all this abandoned equipment.

It shouldn't be here at all.

"What are you doing?"

I spin on my heels, heart dropping into my stomach. Jack Davis is in the doorway. He has a mesh bag full of volleyballs in his hands and a frown on his face. "You're not supposed to be in here."

"It was unlocked." The bra is still in my hand, dangling from a finger. His eyes drop to it, then back to my face.

"I found this in here."

He shakes his head. "Nah. No way."

"It was under this blanket."

He pops his jaw in and out, a blank expression coming over his face. "My girls have changed down here once before a pep rally when there was work going on in the girl's locker room. It must have gotten left behind."

"Girls don't typically forget their bras. They wear them, Jack. Even in their uniforms."

"I don't know." His eyes widen suddenly, and he lets out a strangled breath.

"So if you don't know how this got down here, and I don't know. Then who do you think does? Who had access to this room Jack?" I gently shake the bra between my fingers.

He doesn't say anything, but I can practically hear the wheels spinning in his mind. I go to move past him, but he doesn't budge.

"Excuse me."

"Where are you going with that?"

"Reporting this."

He leans forward, so close I can feel the vibrations of his voice. Amplifying every difference between us. His height. His weight. It all towers over me, making me feel half my size. Solemnly reminding me I'm all alone in the basement of the school with Bryson's friend.

"I told you," he says. "One of the girls probably left it."

"What about Bryson? He had a key."

"No. There's no way."

"Are you still trying to protect him?"

He visibly pales and takes a tiny step back. "This has nothing to do with protecting Bryson. I could get in trouble for giving him that key."

"That slap on the wrist is your primary concern right now?"

"We don't even know if Bryson had anything to do with this. You're jumping to conclusions, and it won't do anything but get Smart on my ass."

I chuckle softly and push past him, bumping my shoulder against his. "Your priorities kind of suck, Jack."

"Wait, Ren."

But I'm already up the stairs and walking purposefully toward the office.

Principal Smart is at his desk when I stroll in and place the bra on his desk. His eyes flash up to mine, filled with pure confusion.

"I found this in the chiller. You should ask Jack how it got there."

"I don't understand." Smart rubs his eyes and sits back in his chair. "Why are you bringing this to me?"

"Bryson. He gave Bryson a key, and there is a teenage girl's bra down there. Is it clicking for you?"

"Ms. Taylor." His nostrils flare. "Girls change down there occasionally. I don't think it's fair to jump to these conclusions."

"Is that what I did with Olivia too?" I ask, tilting my head, hearing the door open behind me. "Jump to conclusions?"

"Look—"

"I'm just asking you to do your job and look into it. If you don't handle this, I will. And if I have to do it, I guarantee it'll be a whole lot more embarrassing for you." There is no wavering in my tone. Nothing but the confidence I should have had with this man from the very beginning. There are girls lives on the line, and

I know Smart would rather brush this whole situation under the rug. Let Bryson fade to obscurity.

But I've learned the best way to kill roaches is to crush their heads.

He glances over my shoulder, and I follow his gaze to Jack.

"Good. You're here," I say, glancing between them and backing up toward the door. "You two have a lot to talk about."

———

"When did my sister become a bad ass?" Margo asks as I merge onto the interstate. My foot is heavy on the accelerator. I'm already late for my meeting with Michaela, and I don't want her to think I'm standing her up.

"Way too late," I reply as I switch lanes and cruise down the exit. The park we're supposed to meet at is at the back end of winding back roads. The same back roads that lead to Rosemary Academy.

"Smart is spineless. Do you really think he's going to call the police?"

"He has to at this point."

The curvy roads wind through walls of oak and beech trees bursting with shades of rusty oranges and reds. I ease off the gas and roll down the windows. The breeze whips my hair, and the afternoon sun warms my face.

I try to relax, but I keep picturing that bra and the bony shoulders of the young girl who wore it last.

"What are you doing, Ren? Really?"

"What's right," I say finally. "Since no one else will."

"What's right or what you think is right?"

Her question echoes in the chasm between us. I have no answer.

# 26

The park is a wide expanse of green fields with a jogging loop that weaves into the woods. There's a fenced-in playground in the corner and a small wooden pavilion. Michaela is at a table under that pavilion, hunched over, wearing a pair of sweats and a T-shirt.

Michaela lifts her head from her phone and slides it into her pocket when I sit across from her.

"Hey, I hope you haven't been waiting long. I got here as soon as I could."

"Just a few minutes. But it's OK. I like it out here." Michaela looks tired. More so than last time I saw her. Her hair is down today with a red headband holding it back. There's a look on her face. An anxious desperation that wasn't there before, like she could break down in tears at any moment.

"Are you OK? I mean, how are you handling everything? That picture…I know it couldn't have been easy seeing that. And then everything with Tina Drexler…"

She wipes under her eye with her thumb. "I could kill whoever sent it." Her words sink into me with the delicacy of a machete. "There was no warning. No nothing. Our phones just went off, and we looked. Of course, we look. And I—" She shakes her head, biting down on her lower lip. "I couldn't believe it. I know what I told you. I know I had my assumptions. But to see it. To know she was…with him. I just don't understand why she didn't tell me."

Margo's face flashes in my mind.

The secrets we kept from each other.

"It just hurts, you know? That she felt like she couldn't trust me. We told each other everything."

"You had no idea at all?" I ask, still finding it so hard to believe. "She never said a word?"

"I knew she thought he was hot. But everyone did. Coach Lewis was good-looking , but he was also nice. He listened to us when other teachers would just write us off. We noticed that."

"She told you she liked him?"

"Yeah, but like I said, every girl did. Every girl had his name doodled in their notebooks. It didn't mean anything."

It was the same with Mr. Henry. All my friends commented on his jeans when he came to football games in casual clothes. The girls would swear they'd marry him one day. Teenagers talk. They say things they don't mean. Perhaps the most suspicious thing should be their silence. What *didn't* Alejandra say?

"Didn't you say their relationship was different? That he treated her differently? What do you mean by that?"

She wipes her nose with the back of her hand. "I don't know. I mean, yeah. He did. They got along really well. Always had inside jokes. She never, like, fangirled over him like everyone else. They had a genuine relationship. Like they liked each other. Not in a weird way, they just seemed…fond of one another."

I want to reach across the table and grab her hand. I want to tell her everything will be OK, but I know better than to make promises like that. The terrible thing is, as she scrambles and grasps at straws, trying to figure out what went wrong, where she messed up, the person who is really responsible for her pain will go on living.

It's the worst feeling.

"Michaela," I say. "You told me the comforter in the picture was the one from a hotel you stayed in for an away game."

"It was the championship game. The last one. We had a tournament that whole day. I forget the name of the hotel, but I remember the comforter. Look." She opens Snapchat and shows me an old photo from Memories. Her and another girl lying on a bed, laughing. "We took this that night. See."

"Is that why you wanted me to come today? To talk about all this?"

She puts her phone down and swallows. "There's something else, and I didn't know who to talk to. I didn't know who to trust."

"It's about Alejandra?"

She nods. "I couldn't say it on the phone. That's why I thought it would be better if we did it here."

"Why here?"

"This is where they found her."

My blood chills. The lovely little park with the playground and walking circle. A mother catching her son at the bottom of the slide, the woman texting at a bench while her leashed dog yaps at her feet, all of it becomes darker somehow. Like I was peering through an Instagram filter and now I'm seeing it for what it really is. Dimly lit. Gray. A headache forms behind my eyes. "Alejandra was found here?"

"Her body was about a mile into the woods and off the trail."

I rub my neck instinctively and feel my pulse jump against my hand. I think about Alejandra's pain. Her suffering. Had she felt a pinch in her chest? Grabbed herself? Tried to keep herself upright on wobbly knees, just to sink into the water and never resurface?

Then another image plays out. One where she isn't alone in these woods at all. She's led out there by the hand of a man she trusts. There are giggles and smiles as they hike through the woods. Maybe she stops at the creek to get her toes wet or wash her hands. He comes up behind her. It wouldn't take much for a man of Bryson's size to fight Alejandra. To keep her head under that water.

But her heart.

Maybe it *was* an accident. Her heart failed her, and she fell into the water. When Bryson realized he'd have to call for help and that would mean people knowing they were alone out there together, he failed her too.

But why? To keep their secret? To protect his *career*? I guess people have killed for less.

Then there's Tina Drexler. A quiet girl with a tiny connection to Alejandra but no connection to Bryson. Is she just a coincidence?

"A man out with his dog found her in the creek. Sometimes people will go off-trail to hike along it. She'd been missing for two days before they found her. At the time, I couldn't read anything about her—about how she was found. The two days of sitting in the water had to have really messed her up." Her voice completely cracks on the last word.

And I'm back there again. On a cold black lake. The flashing blue and red lights. The flurry of activity as they pull something from the water. Someone. Margo. Until that moment, I thought there was hope. That maybe she would resurface. They'd find her on the bank somewhere, irritated we'd taken so long.

But the moment she was pulled out, all hope left.

And it never returned.

The memory convulses, seizes, and I'm helpless to watch. It's not just Margo's slack blue face, lifeless in the boat. Alejandra is there. Tina. Their bodies are stacked on top of one another like a macabre piece of art.

There's bubbling in the warm lake water. Someone calls out, "We've got another one." And they pull someone else from the water. All I see is a tangled mass of blond hair.

Olivia.

A dog barking from somewhere behind me brings me back. I massage my temples.

Michaela wipes a tear away before it makes it past her nose. "But there was something else about that night. Something I want you to know. I told you Alejandra was on the phone. She locked herself in the bathroom and wouldn't talk to me after. When I woke up around midnight, she was gone. It scared me she wasn't in the room. Her phone was on the bedside table. So I thought maybe she was in the hallway getting air or something. I popped my head out. When I couldn't see her, I started walking. And I remember hearing a door open behind me. I jumped out of view, into the doorway of another hotel room." She sniffs. "I knew that was the direction of our coaches' rooms, and we weren't supposed to be out of our room that late. I didn't want to get caught. Someone walked out and in the opposite direction. She had a hood on, and it looked like Alejandra, but I couldn't say for certain until I saw her shoes."

"Her shoes?"

"Jondra had these red high-tops with checkered laces. She drew a heart on the back of the heel with a black Sharpie. They're the ones she was supposedly wearing the day she went into those woods. Anyway, they were missing. Still are. But that night I knew it was her."

"Did you call out to her?" I ask.

"This is going to sound dumb, but her parents were always fighting. Anytime I came over, which wasn't often because she preferred to stay at my house, they'd always find something to get into. I thought maybe that's what she was doing on the phone. That's why she was so upset. Maybe something was going on at home, and she went to Coach Lewis to get permission to leave? She was walking toward the elevators. I don't know." Michaela's eyes well with tears, and this time she can't stop them from falling out. "She said something earlier when I'd been pressing her about that phone call. She asked me why I couldn't just chill and give her space. I was afraid to be too pushy and piss her off. I figured she'd talk to me when she was ready. But I never got the chance.

"I'm so sorry, Michaela."

"Is it normal to do this? To go back to pivotal moments you had no idea were pivotal and wonder how different things could have been if you weren't so stupid or scared?"

Margo standing at our front door, illuminated by the moon behind her.

*Please. Don't say anything.*

My hands clench the metal bench, and I focus on Michaela.

"Yes, that's normal. But that doesn't mean we should do it or that it helps."

"You sound like you know from experience."

Margo scowling.

Me yelling.

Margo gone.

"Yes." I nod, looking at a point far out past Michaela's shoulder. Margo is standing there, arms folded, eyes on me. "You could say that."

———

I sit in my car. All my energy is depleted. I can't even lift my hands to the wheel. That's how it is when I think of that night. When I think of Margo. But now it's worse. Now the pressure has built to something I feel incapable of carrying.

Michaela went home after promising she'd tell me if she thought of anything else. But I'm left wondering if she should or if I'm even capable of doing this, trying to figure this out, protect the girls that are left.

A sound permeates my mind, slowly pulling me back to reality, and it takes a second to identify it. My phone is vibrating in the cupholder. It's a number I don't recognize, and I wouldn't typically answer, but something has me sliding my thumb across the bottom of the screen.

"Hello?"

"Is this Ms. Taylor?"

I hold the phone tighter, every nerve ending in my body coming alive. "Yes."

"This is Olivia."

"I recognized your voice. How did you get my number?"

"It's on your syllabus on the school's website. I hope you don't mind."

"Of course not."

She takes a deep breath, and I can feel the tension through the phone and her emotion seeping out of her as she breathes out. It makes me sit straighter, shift the car in reverse.

"I wanted to talk to you. If you weren't busy." Her voice is hesitant, and I still can't get a read on her.

"No, I'm not busy."

"Could you meet me somewhere? The football stadium?"

And I'm moving, my car roaring to life along with the blood in my veins, reminding me that Olivia's trust in me, Michaela's trust, it's all I need to qualify me to help them.

And I will.

Even if it kills me.

"I'll be there as soon as I can."

# 27

The sun is nearly set by the time I pull into the Benton parking lot. I drive around the faculty lot and onto a side road that leads to the stadium at the bottom of a hill. There's a car parked half on the grass and road; it's a little red beater with a sticker on the back with lettering too small for me to read. I park in front of it and walk onto the bleachers. It's easy to spot Olivia, even as small as she is. Her arms are wrapped around herself, hood up, and, if I had to guess, her headphones are most likely in.

She doesn't seem to hear or see me approach until I'm climbing up the bleachers to sit next to her, directly in her line of sight. She pops two earbuds out. "Hey, you came."

"I told you I would." I sit next to her, more than aware of our proximity. How young she looks huddled up like this. How sad.

I think of the bra in the chiller.

"What's going on, Olivia? You weren't at school. I was worried about you."

"No, I know." She keeps her gaze forward, and I don't miss the tremble in her voice. "I just, like, couldn't face it yet. Everyone is tripping. I don't even—" She rubs her hands over eyes and down her face. I don't expect the gut punch of guilt, though maybe I should have. After all, I am the one who encouraged her to report Bryson. I practically forced her into it. It felt like the right choice at the time. Like I was the adult and needed to make things right for a child who didn't know how to do it for herself.

The thing is, I can't really say it made anything right, or if it helped at all. Judging by the dark circles under her eyes and her bitten-down fingernails, whatever happened over the past few days has been rough on her.

"Is anyone saying anything to you?" I ask.

A glance down to her lap. "Not to my face."

It's then that I notice her earrings. Tiny silver hoops. My sister had a pair just like them. She never left the house without them. Even in the picture of her in the hallway at school, she had them in.

She had them on the night she died too.

The pang of longing in my heart makes the guilt worse.

"Your earrings," I whisper. "Where did you get them?"

She touches her ear. "Some store in the mall. Why?"

"My sister wore those."

"My mom would prefer me to wear pearls. They're not my thing though." She swallows. "That's why I wanted to talk to you. About my mom. She got me a lawyer. It's been…it's been rough."

"What do you mean?"

"I don't think…" Olivia rubs her hands over her jeans. "I don't think she believes me."

The silver of those earrings glint beneath the rays of the setting sun. "Why do you think that?"

"It's not just her. They're calling me a rat. My friends. Well, they're not really friends. At least not now. They think I made it up. That I just want attention."

"Who?" I demand, already feeling my blood pressure rise. "Who is saying it?"

"It doesn't matter."

"Yes, it does. I can talk to them. Make sure they don't—"

"No," she says, cutting me off. "That's just it. Nothing helps. They loved Mr. Lewis. They see me as the enemy. Most of the guys think he's 'the man' for getting with his student. And most of the girls wish it had been them. They think I'm desperate. They said there's no way he would have been with someone like me."

A tear falls down her cheek onto her lap, and my whole body constricts.

"Olivia."

"The worst part is"—she looks at me, eyes full of tears, shed and unshed—"I didn't even want it. I thought I did at the beginning. Maybe at one point I got caught up, but then it just made me feel gross and dirty. I didn't want to be with him, Ms. Taylor. I promise." She loses it, folding into my side and wrapping her arms around me.

The motion stuns me. I haven't been hugged this tight since Margo. Even my ex-husband learned physical touch wasn't my love language and chose to keep a distance. But I remember the last time I hugged her outside the chiller. It seemed so natural. Comforting her. My arms tighten around her, and I let her cry while I sit perfectly still.

Eventually, she sits back and looks up at me, wiping her swollen eyes. "I'm sorry. I just feel like I don't have anyone. My mom called me a whore. Said this is what happens to girls who spread their legs for everyone. They just want me to keep quiet about it. To save the family the embarrassment."

A fresh wave of anger rolls through me, shaking me all the way to my foundation. Her answer reminds me of how I became this way. How my roots started straight, but somewhere along the way became tangled and gnarled, until the girl I was became a woman I don't want to be.

I don't want that for Olivia. "The truth will come out. It has to." My answer sounds weak even to me.

Apparently, Olivia thinks so too. She rocks back, staring up at the slowly darkening sky. "When has the truth ever mattered? What if they're right?" She looks at me. "What if this is my fault? What if I misconstrued everything? I don't feel like a victim. Not in the way others are. No wonder everyone is mad at me."

"You don't feel like a victim, but it doesn't mean you aren't one. And it sure doesn't mean that a victim is the only thing you are. More than anything, you're a survivor, Olivia. He groomed you. He was in a position of power, and you trusted him. That isn't your fault."

"You really believe that, don't you?" Her eyes glaze over with incredulity. Like she can't believe someone finally sees her. Believes her. "That's why I called you, you know. From the beginning you were there for me. More than my own parents. I knew I could trust you."

Something about her words creates a sense of pressure. I'm not worthy of her trust. Of that hero worship in her eyes.

"Can I ask you something?" I say.

She nods.

"I found something in the chiller today."

Her eyes cast downward way too quickly.

"You know what I found, don't you, Olivia?"

Her lips tremble. "He made me go down there. Made me take my clothes off. It's my fault because I listened. I could have fought him, but I listened. I kind of just went numb."

There it is. The jolt in my blood. The confirmation of what I already knew. "It's not your fault. Never say that."

I'm someone maternal and protective.

And I want Bryson to hurt the way Olivia is hurting.

"My parents already hate me. Even my brother won't look at me."

"Hey." I pull back so she can see me. "You got me, OK? I'm here."

"There's one more thing," she whispers. "One more reason I asked you to come. Something else I haven't told anyone. At first because it didn't seem important, but now I feel like it might be."

"What is it?"

"This past summer I stayed with Mr. Lewis. Told my parents I was with a friend, and he snuck me over. After we uh…" Her cheeks turn red, and she doesn't quite meet my eye. "Afterward, he gets in the shower. His phone kept going off. I wasn't trying to be sneaky or to look at his phone. I know it isn't my business. But it wouldn't stop so I just glanced at it. The message wouldn't show up because the screen was locked, but there were several messages from the same person. Tina."

The feeling is back. Me getting rocked to my foundation. I have to grip the bleachers beneath me to stay upright. "There wasn't a last name?"

"No."

"It's a common name."

"Tina Drexler went missing one week after that night."

I want to tell her there is an explanation. Another Tina. Someone else. Anything else. But I can't lie to her. I knew as soon as she said her name.

"Why do you think it was Tina Drexler?" I ask, needing to know her reasoning. "Why do you think they're connected?"

"You brought it up to me, remember? I never really thought about it until then. And it was like everything clicked into place. They were at the same school. The text. I just feel like anything is possible when we don't know what he's capable of."

"What do you mean?"

"Most of the time he's so charming, but sometimes it's like he's someone else entirely. He can be so cold and distant. He scares me. You think I should tell the police? I keep going back and forth with it. Everyone is calling me a rat already. A liar. They're making me second-guess everything. It—it makes me wonder what would happen if I told anyone this."

"You should talk to your lawyer," I say finally, knowing that what I really want to say, what I really want to *do* is not one of the choices Olivia gave me.

"My lawyer?" she asks.

"Ask them what you should do. I don't know what it means, but I know it's important." If it was Tina Drexler, surely the police know this by now. Maybe they're making the connection as we speak. It shouldn't be hard to nail down random numbers she'd been in contact with prior to her disappearance.

"Thank you, Ms. Taylor." Olivia shifts to her feet.

"It's Ren." I meet her eyes. "You can call me Ren. You're not even one of my students."

"Thank you. I don't know what I would do without you. I don't have anybody."

"You have me."

Her eyebrows crinkle and her lips turn up in a sad smile. "Do you have anyone?"

I don't answer, and that must be answer enough. She grabs my hand, and unlike earlier, I don't want to pull away. I want to hang on for a while.

"You have me now too," she says.

# 28

Olivia leaves and I stay still. The breeze has picked up. Fall in Georgia comes in fleeting spurts of chill and heat. It has you cranking the AC during the day and the heat at night.

Tonight is cold. Tonight the air bites my cheeks, nibbles at the exposed skin of my collarbone as I stare out at the vast football stadium. The field.

It's over a decade ago.

The stadium is a beacon of light for the whole town. Football Fridays are the main event, and everyone comes. Even those who have long graduated. Those without children.

They gather on concrete rows, holding hot baskets of nachos and screaming for boys who haven't had a winning streak in decades. My parents are here. Dad is holding Mom's nachos because she has a habit of leaping up during especially good plays, forgetting about any items in her lap. It's senior night, and Margo is a vision in purple and yellow. Shaking her pom-poms.

Tumbling on the grass. Chanting at the football team to *Go, Fight, Win*.

In between cheers and tumbling passes, she's waving at friends. Every so often, her eyes catch mine, and she winks or makes a silly face.

Then something in the air shifts. As if sensing me thinking of her, Margo's smile widens, and I think it's for me. But she's looking past me. I follow her gaze.

There he is.

When I look back at the field, it is dark and empty like my insides. I stand stiffly, intending to walk back to my car. Go home. Draw a bath. Stay home.

I must stay home. I can't do anything stupid. Not now. Not with Detective Wu breathing down my neck and me needing to be here for Olivia.

Light from the school catches my attention. Someone is inside. I don't remember seeing the light when I arrived. There are voices from the front of the school too, carried on the breeze. I walk around and freeze when I see the police cruiser. Two officers huddle beside it, whispering to one another. Through the glass front door Principal Smart is talking to another officer with a grim expression. The officer is holding a paper bag.

The door is unlocked, and both heads swivel in my direction when I walk inside.

"Ms. Taylor." Principal Smart says my name through clenched teeth. So different from the man who'd greeted me that very first day in the conference room.

"What's going on?" I ask.

"You shouldn't be here."

"I forgot some labs in my class. When I came back, I saw the lights."

The officer says something to Principal Smart and walks past me toward the door, holding something. Smart looks older under the harsh fluorescents, the lines of his face sharp and a certain blankness in his eyes. "You shouldn't be here," he reiterates.

I glance past him, down the hall to the gym where the light is still on. The light I'd seen from the stadium. "They found something else in the chiller, didn't they?"

"I can't talk about an active investigation."

But when the police officer walks past with a clear evidence bag, it's impossible not to see. Impossible not to notice, not to understand.

A pair of red Converse with checked laces. And I can't see the back, but if I had to guess, there would be hearts drawn on the back in black Sharpie.

I take a step back and then another. My first thought is how could I have missed these when I was down there? But the room was so full of junk and I was so distracted after finding the bra. Maybe I wouldn't have noticed the sneakers anyway. I would have assumed an athlete left them behind. They wouldn't have meant anything until Michaela told me her story.

Principal Smart shrinks and ages before my eyes. A stupid tiny man. There's a lot I could say to punish him for what he said to me. But it looks like the punishment is internal. And he looks like he's suffering.

"You should be ashamed, you know?" There is no venom in my voice, only sad defeat. I was right, and I didn't want to be. I didn't want to know just how badly we failed every kid in this building. "It's your job to protect them. Not him."

"I'm sorry." His voice is as rough as I've ever heard it. "I never knew. I didn't know."

I look him up and down, my lips curling in disgust. "That's not good enough."

————

I drive to my parents' in the morning again before school.

They should be here this time, and if they're not, then I'll come back later. The point is, I'll come back. Even as the bitterness festers inside of me and the darkness boils over, I'll keep coming back. I'm making things right.

The local radio station is a gentle hum in the background.

"A local teacher has been brought in for questioning regarding the death of seventeen-year-old high school senior, Alejandra Gomez…"

"Are you embarrassed that you want to see them?" Margo asks from her spot in the passenger seat. "Do you feel like a little girl running back to Mommy and Daddy?"

"Missing shoes belonging to the teen were found and the police are reopening the investigation…"

I snap it off with my thumb. The car sinks into silence.

Margo watches me like I'm seconds away from losing it. She doesn't know that I've lost everything already. There's nothing left.

"So what are you thinking, Renny? They found her shoes. The infamous shoes that have been missing since Alejandra's body was found."

I open my mouth, a reply on the tip of my tongue, but something is wrong.

My parents' truck is missing.

Did they go somewhere else or are they still not back from Friday?

I throw the car in park and hop out, heading straight for the front door. It's locked.

"You're overreacting," Margo says like she's bored. "They've got to be around here somewhere."

I move to the windows, trying to peer through the cracks on the edges of the curtain.

"Why don't you just go in, Ren?"

"It's locked." I move to another window, desperately trying to get a look inside. A feeling is unleashed inside me. Dread that's lain dormant since I realized Margo's body went into the water.

"You don't remember?" There's a lilt to Margo's voice that gives me pause. "The key we hid."

I'm only confused for a second. With her comment comes a distinct memory. Me walking into the kitchen where Margo is shoving something purple in her pocket.

The stove had been bubbling with red sauce, and I'd been intimately aware of my mother moving around in the laundry room. I asked Margo what she was doing, and she shook her head. *Later*, she'd whispered.

That evening when I entered her room, I locked the door behind me. She finally broke down and explained. Our parents made us an extra house key to share, but it isn't something they let us bring just anywhere. It's usually special occasions or when they know they won't be home. Because, according to them, it doesn't make sense for teenagers to have a house key when their parents are perfectly capable of opening the door. Margo decided to make a copy of it.

She'd laughed as she rubbed moisturizer on her face in the vanity mirror. "It's no big deal. I just want the freedom to come and go when I need to."

Standing on the front porch now, the nostalgia rocks me. But I go check anyway. Down the porch steps, on the left-hand inside of the deck, right on the ledge. I touch something crunchy as I feel around for it. A cobweb tangles around my fingers. Just as I'm about to give up, they brush something cold and hard. I grab it and jerk my hand back, opening my palm to a tiny purple key.

Margo is smirking on the porch. "Why wouldn't it be there? No one in their right mind would put their hand there willingly."

Then I open the front door and step into the past.

The house is exactly the same. Dark because Mom likes the curtains pulled. Foyer table neatly stacked with mail. The faint smell of the lemon cleaner Mom always favored. Dad's leather recliner is still a tad too close to the television, and there's a groove-like indentation on Mom's favorite spot on the blue couch.

There's not a speck of dust on a single surface.

I move to the kitchen, flinching at the sudden smell of rot. There are gnats circling the trash can, which clearly should have been brought outside days ago. The two mugs on the table are cold to the touch, with a film over the dark liquid and dead gnats floating inside. I stop short at a plate of sliced tomato and bacon on the counter that looks like it's been there for days.

"Dad?" I call out, glancing toward the hallway.

That's when I notice the broken porcelain on the ground. A plate.

"Dad?" I move quickly down the hall.

My parents' bedroom is empty and smells faintly of mothballs. There are two other doors in this hall, but I don't bother glancing inside either one. When I come back to the kitchen, I glance at the ground. "Shit."

Margo follows my gaze.

Blood.

# 29

It's only natural to head to the hospital. Clearly, something happened in my parents' kitchen. Something that required medical care. The Benton hospital is nearly fifteen minutes from my parents' house. There is no parking deck, just a long lot. I spot my dad's truck parked haphazardly as soon as I pull in.

It only takes a minute to park and get inside. To ask the man behind the counter if my parents are here. He confirms, gives me a room number. Margo is silent behind me as we walk to the elevators. Somewhere a woman is crying. The fluorescent bulb flickers over our heads as the ground jerks beneath our feet.

This is an older hospital, one that has been in town longer than I've been alive, and it smells musty. But it also seems like this is the kind of place that no matter how much you mop the floors, the smell will linger. At this point bodily fluids, decay, and death have seeped into the walls.

We step out of the elevator and head down a hall until I see her room number to my left. I knock once before entering. Dad is seated on a stiff-looking chair, his cell phone in his hands and reading glasses on. As soon as he hears the door, he looks up and freezes. But my attention is on the woman in the hospital bed. So still and pale she could be dead.

Dad holds a finger to his lips and walks over to meet me at the door. "Ren, I wasn't expecting to see you. How did you know we were here?"

"I stopped by your house. Saw the broken plate and blood in the kitchen. Took my best guess."

His brows pull down, and he must be wondering how I got in, but thankfully he doesn't ask. The purple key is tucked away in my pocket. I don't have any intention of putting it back. Dad glances toward Mom and sighs heavily. His facial hair is grown in a little more than usual. They've obviously been here for days. Since Friday at the very least.

"Is she OK?"

He nods. "She's fine. She got up a couple days ago wanting to make breakfast. She hasn't done that in so long. She seemed so much like…herself. I didn't think anything of it. I was in the bathroom upstairs when I heard something crash. Doctor says it was a heart attack. She cut her hand on broken glass when she fell."

"What do you think triggered it?"

"She's been under a lot of stress. It's just everything on the news. Those girls." He shakes his head. "It was too much for her. She's been so down lately. And right when it feels like she's coming out of it, this happens."

"I'm sorry, Dad."

"You know Mom. She's a fighter. Her heart's been broken before."

I stumble over his words. There's something unsaid lingering just between the lines. A shot fired at me because I'm the only person who's ever broken my mother's heart.

"What is she doing here?" The voice is weak and raspy, but Dad and I both go still. Mom is flat on her back, her head tilted in our direction. Her eyes look black in the hospital lighting. "What is she doing here?"

"She wanted to check on you, Becks." Those black eyes look me up and down, and there is an absence in them. No love. No hatred. An absence of any emotion at all.

"She shouldn't be here. She shouldn't be here."

"Mom—"

"I can't do this." Her voice deepens, and one of the machines on her left starts beeping loudly. "I can't even look at you."

I move to her side. Reach for her hand. She doesn't pull away. Just glances to where my skin burns into hers. I cling to her tighter, and her jaw shifts, tears pull in her eyes. "I don't know why," she whispers suddenly. "I don't know why, but I can't."

"Please—" But I cut myself off. What am I even begging for? Please love me? Please forgive me?

We're not talking about heart attacks or broken dishes. We're talking about something more. Something deeper.

I squeeze her hand again, and she makes a hoarse sound, tears pooling in her eyes.

"I didn't know," I say. "I had no idea what would happen that night."

"She followed you out there to protect you," Mom says. "If you weren't doing God knows what with that man, your sister would still be alive, Ren." She chokes out the last few words.

"There's more to it than that."

More tears. A tremor in her bottom lip. "I look at you, and I think—I think it should be her. She should still be here. It shouldn't have been her in the water that night."

I release her hand like it's a hot coal and stumble back.

"Becks—"

"I didn't do anything on purpose. I love her," I murmur brokenly, holding my hand to my chest.

My mother's tears change to heavy sobs, and my dad is right there. Holding the hand that was just holding mine. And I wonder if it feels as cold to him.

A nurse rushes past me into the room, and I back away until I'm fully out. Dad doesn't look back at me. No one does.

I turn around and walk away.

Step into the elevator with a pregnant mother and her young daughter. Another hallway. A set of double doors, and then fresh air, but it isn't enough. It's like I'm breathing in fog. Nothing can clear the scent of rot and urine or drown out the sounds of my mother's cries.

My hands shake while I search for a substitute for my class. I can't see past the tears clouding my vision. Teaching is the only job where even a nervous breakdown doesn't warrant a sudden absence from work.

I find a sub and text another biology teacher to ask if she can throw together an emergency lesson plan for my class. I don't wait for her to reply. It doesn't matter what she says. I can't do any more.

I drive for a long time. Until Benton is far behind me. Until my mother's words are an echo of pain in my mind.

Margo is strangely quiet, but she's there. "You can say it," I tell her through my teeth. "You can agree with her. I know you agree with her. It was my fault. You're dead because of me."

"Do you think that, Ren?"

"No, don't give me that psychological bullshit. You were there. You were the one—" But I can't finish. I can't say the words.

"I was the one…what? What were you going to say?"

But I won't finish. She knows I won't finish. There's what everyone thinks happened that night, and there is what *really* happened, and regardless of the differences, there is one really important truth that doesn't change.

Margo died because of me.

# 30

Shocker," Margo says as I slam my car door, stepping out into the muggy midday sun. My shirt sticks to my back with sweat, but I can't say if it's from the heat or something else. "A bar, Ren? You think this is smart? Look at you. You're clearly not in control right now."

I walk past her. Through her. She doesn't understand. I glance back when I open the door. Margo is right there. "You don't get it. Mom loves you. Everyone loves you."

"Ren."

"It should have been me." It's true. It should have been me that night. Me in the lake. Me in the casket. It was never supposed to be Margo.

Margo's lips snap together. Her face crumbles.

The bar is just outside of Benton. A neighboring city. Near enough to be convenient but far enough away I shouldn't run into anyone I know. Inside, high top tables are scattered throughout.

None are occupied. There are only four people in the room—three men at the bar top and the bartender behind it. I flag the bartender. Ask for something that isn't too sweet. And I drink.

There are eyes on the side of my face. Patrons wondering what I'm doing here in the middle of the day. I must not be the usual customer for this establishment. I don't have it in me to observe them. For once, I'm not here for them or anyone else. I'm here for me.

I'm here to forget me.

"This isn't a competition anymore. And if it was, you would have won. I'm dead, remember?" Margo is somewhere beside me, or maybe behind me. She's speaking, but really she isn't. It takes a moment for me to understand what she's saying and why.

And she's right. It isn't a competition. It's not now, and it wasn't then. Even when I thought it was. Even when I thought I had a chance. Thought I had something just for me. Finally. None of it had been true. Everything, all things, eventually led back to Margo.

"Clearly not dead enough," I say, and the bartender glances over from her spot drying glasses.

"Of course, I am," Margo insists, snark slipping into her tone. "You made sure of that."

"Another," I say to the bartender.

———

Hours pass. Not sure how many or the time. The bar is livelier now. The bartender has swapped with another, and new faces pepper the seats around me. I'm ready for home. There's a moment between paying my bill and staggering to my feet that I forget why I'm here at all.

I walk past a group of corporate-looking women and a table full of kids who must be scraping the bottom of twenty-one. No one gives me a second look.

It takes two attempts at tugging on the door before I notice it says *push*. Judging by my shaking hands and trembling knees, I shouldn't drive. But I can get in my car. Recline the seat. Sleep it off for a few hours. That's where I'm going, heels clacking over black pavement lit only by the light seeping from the bar windows.

My phone is full of texts from Emma. She's worried about me. I breathe in the black night air and glance up at the vast, empty sky, and I think of Mom. Her sobs. The agony on her face.

My car is at the back of the lot, and I'm under a streetlight, but it must be broken because it is the only one in the lot that isn't on. Across the street there's a bustling restaurant and people. But here, outside this bar, under this expanse of sky, it feels like I'm the only person in the world.

I want my sister.

My keys hit the ground, and I brace myself on the driver's-side door to pick them up. That's when I feel the hand on my waist. I jerk upright and sway on my feet. The world is spinning, and it isn't just because of the physical touch. I hadn't heard anyone approach. Hadn't heard a single footstep. Fingers dig into my side.

"Where are you going so early, sweetie?"

I face him.

*Them.*

Three men. I remember them vaguely from the bar. They'd been near the door at a table when I exited. One is still touching me. One is several paces back, glancing from me to the door and back. He looks younger than the others and nervous. And the other is to my left. All of them are average size and build. White. Average. My vision blurs.

"Why don't you hang out with us a little longer?"

"Get away from me." The words are slurred and slow even to my own ears.

He chuckles real close. Too close. His grip on me tightens. "You're feisty. I like that."

Everything about this feels wrong. I try and jerk back but hit my car, and he just moves closer. My body won't cooperate, like it's operating one step behind and can't catch up.

He grabs the handle to my car, and that's when the panic rolls in, white-hot.

"There you are." A familiar voice. A face blurring in and out. "You wandered off." The man lets go of me and takes a step back.

There's another touch to my hand.

A warmth beside me and a firm voice. "Thanks for finding my friend."

"Your friend?" The man takes another step back and another. "Hey, there's room for both of you."

"And there's room for all three of you in my freezer. But first we'll cut your balls off and make you eat them. Now back up."

My stomach swims, and I hold a hand over it. The man says something I don't catch. Something about "crazy bitches," and they walk away, muttering to each other.

I flop to my side, still leaning against the car. The face next to me comes into focus.

Olivia.

She stares in the direction the men wandered to and then finally looks at me. "I actually don't know much about storing bodies in freezers or chopping off balls. But they say if you say something with enough confidence, people go with it."

The world sways again. "It's you. What are you doing here?"

"Whoa." Her hand goes under my arm. "Steady. I didn't know if you wanted to go with them or not. I saw you. It looked like, well, it looked like you weren't giving consent. That's why I came over here."

"I was just trying to get in my car."

"You're going to drive like that?"

"No. I just needed to sit down. To sleep this off."

"I'll drive you."

I hand her the keys because I don't have the strength or energy to argue, and keep a hand on my car for balance as I walk around. Soon enough we're on the road, and my buzz is wearing off just enough for the shame to creep in. The embarrassment. I sit forward and hold my head in my hands without looking at Olivia. It takes everything to keep the contents of my stomach inside.

"This is inappropriate. You shouldn't be seeing me like this."

Olivia's hands tighten on the wheel, and when she looks at me there isn't any judgment. Only concern. It makes my cheeks heat. I should be the one saving drunken teenagers. It shouldn't be happening like this, especially with Olivia.

"It's OK. My mom drinks a lot. I get phone calls to pick her up."

"Just because other adults in your life have failed you doesn't mean I need to be one of them." I flop back in the seat. "Shit. *Shoot*, I mean. Sorry. I shouldn't have said that. I'm just sorry.

Sorry you have to see me like this. And those men—" I shudder as shame shifts to anger. Fear. "There were three of them. What was your plan back there?"

"No plan," she says with a shrug, like her stepping in between me and three full-grown men was an everyday occurrence. "I just saw you and reacted. I don't really know where I'm going, by the way."

"Just keep going straight. I'll tell you where to turn. What were you doing on this side of town so late?"

She shoves her thick blond ponytail over one shoulder. "I work at the diner across the street from that bar. I wasn't working tonight. I just go there sometimes when I'm bored to chill with my co-workers when I don't want to be alone. I saw you through the window. Saw the men come behind you. It looked like you didn't know they were there, and like I said, I reacted."

There's so much to take in from her statement. A teen girl so lonely she goes to her work to spend her free time. Used to driving drunk adults around because her parents are garbage. One brave enough to storm across a busy street on a dark night just because her adult teacher might be in trouble. I look at her. Really look at her, and she still looks like a kid.

That scares me.

Infuriates me.

Is it what Bryson saw?

Henry?

And how can I associate this child with strength and my own self as a child with weakness?

I lead Olivia to my house, and we sit in the dark of the car when she parks.

"Look," I say hesitantly. "If something like this ever happens again, if you see something, don't try to be the hero. Call the cops or something instead."

"I wasn't trying to be a hero," she mumbles, avoiding my eyes. "You're my friend, Ren. You looked sick. Truthfully, I wasn't thinking at all. Like I said, it was mostly a reaction."

"You could have gotten hurt, and you have enough going on right now without worrying about my stuff."

It's too dark to make out her features, but I hear her sigh. "They don't believe me. They still don't believe me. Is that normal? Is it normal to assume an honor roll student who has never gotten in trouble once in her life is making something like this up?"

I turn to face her in the seat. My body feels so heavy, but I force my limbs to move and urge my stomach to stop turning. "It shouldn't be normal. But it is. This is the world we live in." I think of the way Smart wrote me off. The way I wrote myself off as a teenager. We have a habit of not trusting girls and not believing women even when we are one.

"What's going to happen to him, Ren?"

By now, my eyes have adjusted, and I almost wish they hadn't. Then I wouldn't have to look at this scared kid in front of me and feel the pressure that's haunted me for fourteen years. Another teen girl looking to me. Expecting something from me. Answers? Assurance? I don't know, but I don't feel qualified for it, for any of it. Not after Margo.

"Justice," I say. "He'll have to deal with justice. It's going to come out. The truth. All of it."

"I feel like the only one I can talk to is my grandmother…and you. Everyone else is angry."

"I'm glad you have her." I don't mention myself because I don't count. I'm no help. I'm no hero to anyone. I'm just a liar.

"Who do you have?" And Olivia is still the scared kid, bony elbows and frizzy hair, but she's also something else. Wiser. Better. I think if I had been more like Olivia, maybe Margo would still be here, and everything would be different.

"I have my students. My job."

"Huh," she breathes out. "I know about your sister. Everyone does. They talk about it a lot. The rumors."

"I've heard them."

"Me too, but I understand how rumors work." Her voice catches, and once again, she sounds way older than her sixteen years. "It isn't fair what they say about you."

"No." I shake my head. "It is. It isn't fair what they say about you. It's only not fair when the rumors aren't true."

"I don't understand."

I stare forward at my tired, dark house. "It was my fault, Olivia. The night Margo died, I could have stopped it, but I didn't."

And in the quiet, too warm interior of my car, I tell her the whole story.

# 31

They say that teenagers don't know what real love is. That they're all raging hormones and angst. But I know real. I've seen it. Seen the way he watches me when he thinks no one is looking.

The lingering looks down crowded hallways.

I love history. That's how it started, when Mr. Henry and I developed an inside joke about Christopher Columbus. Bonded over the movie *Stepbrothers*. Soon, I was spending lunch hours in his class. Getting to class early just to tell him something anecdotal and quirky.

And I felt like unspooling yarn.

At first, I thought I was imagining it, but then I started paying attention. Catching glimpses of his eyes focused solely on me.

The other boys at school don't watch me like that. They don't look twice. I'm too skinny and flat. My arms are hairy. My hair is wavy in some parts and frizzy in others. It doesn't matter what I do, I'm the summation of these things.

Plus, my sister is Margo.

And I see the way the boys watch her. With ruddy cheeks and smirks that will get them nowhere. The girls aren't any better. They watch her with mixtures of envy or disdain. And it's stupid but true that none of them actually see Margo either.

They see a pretty blond who is both kind and smart. She's outgoing. A cheerleader who, according to most misfits, isn't like the other cheerleaders. She's careful with her words. Not easily angered. She's the one who partners with the quiet kid in science class who no one else wants to be with even though people are lining up to partner with her.

I've watched her since I was young. Wished to emulate her sweetness and the ease with which she interacts with others. I've always fallen a step short. Stumbled beneath the weight of her shadow, not quite catching up. Teachers expect Margo 2.0 when I enter their classes, but I'm not quite as pretty or gentle or discerning. Margo will spend hours nailing a project, making it beautiful, making it colorful. Going above and beyond the rubric. I follow the rubric to a T, doing just enough to get the grade I want and not going a step over.

Minimal. That's me.

But Margo is something else entirely, and I never measured up.

Until Mr. Henry. He laughs at my jokes. Loves to spend time with me. Watches me like he's constantly holding himself back.

I'd only been in his class a couple weeks when I first realized I was enamored by him. It was almost embarrassing. Sometimes my thoughts would wander, and my cheeks would burn red. I could only be thankful no one knew what I was thinking.

Like tonight, I should be hurt and sad. Usually I would be. Mom made spaghetti, Margo's favorite, to celebrate her being voted as cheer captain. No one mentioned my own promotion to stage manager for this year's winter play. But I was so consumed with thoughts of Henry—the jokes I couldn't wait to tell him, a meme I saw that he'd love—that none of that mattered. I'm completely checked out of the conversation until Margo mentions his name.

"Mr. Henry says he thinks I can get into college anywhere. He says he'll help me fill out applications, but he thinks I can go somewhere Ivy League." She says that last part nervously, glancing at our parents as if needing validation. Only people as perfect as Margo don't see that perfection in themselves.

Dad harrumphs. "Course you can."

"Who's Mr. Henry?" Mom asks.

"My old history teacher," Margo says.

"Old?"

"Yeah, I don't have him anymore. Ren does. Hey, we should also be celebrating Ren today. Stage manager." She smiles, and there isn't a drop of red sauce on her face or teeth. I swipe a napkin self-consciously over my mouth, and it comes back stained red.

"You're going to do great back there," Margo says.

"Stage manager?" Mom asks, fork halfway to her mouth.

"Drama club. I was working the lights, but Mrs. Biles says that I have a knack for organization. I get to wear a headset and everything."

"That's great honey." Mom turns to Margo. "Oh, Margo, don't forget to add *captain* to your applications."

Margo nods and catches my eyes, rolling hers playfully, like Mom is annoying her. But I can only look away and wish Mom was annoying me.

Later that night when we were at our double sink in the bathroom, and she was working floss through her teeth, I asked her about him. "So when did you talk to Mr. Henry? You know, since you don't have him anymore."

"Oh, yeah." She ducks down to spit and turns away, tossing the floss into the trash. I can't see her face, but something about her voice is distant. "I drop in sometimes for advice. He adores you, by the way. I told you he would." Her words warm me immediately. *Adores me.*

In my mind I see fireworks. An explosion that would rival the most festive Fourth of July celebration.

Adores me.

He adores *me*?

I'd been fighting my feelings so hard, but what if...what if I didn't have to? What if he felt them too?

She moves through her bedroom with the grace of a ballet dancer and takes off her shirt to slip on her favorite sleep T, a faded gray Georgia Bulldog shirt that used to be Dad's. She grabs the remote and flops on her bed. "What do you want to watch?"

I shake thoughts of Mr. Henry away, but there's nothing I can do about my sweaty palms and pounding heart. "Oh, you're letting me choose?"

She whacks me with a pillow, and I forget about my teacher. Almost.

Margo's words linger like a blanket covering me. I'm warm the rest of the night.

The days pass, and my relationship with him grows. We have this ongoing joke where we add physical traits to a stick person drawn on a note. We'd started doing it one day in his class when someone wrote a note about me. I picked it up, and my face had burned so badly. Tears prickled my eyes, and I tried to wipe them away before anyone saw. I couldn't control my blush, but I refused to let any of them see me get emotional. Not like this.

Before I knew it, Mr. Henry was sliding the note off my desk. He saw it, lips drawing in a tight line. He'd escorted the boy who wrote it from class, and I thought that would be it, but afterward he'd tossed a piece of paper on my desk.

I looked at him in confusion, but he was already walking from the room. It was a stick figure drawing of Mitch Connelly. And I smiled. I smiled for the first time since reading the note Mitch had written: *I would kill myself if I looked like that and my sister was Margo Glass.*

I drew a mustache on him then left it on his desk. The next day Mitch had a top hat. I added pimples. It went on like that for weeks until Mr. Henry started a new drawing.

But nothing with Mr. Henry ever went further.

On days Margo and I walked into school together, rambling about new music or about the latest boy asking her to a dance, I would itch to get to class.

To see him.

Mr. Henry made things better.

But each day as we walked to our morning classes together,

I didn't notice her. Didn't notice every single sign staring me in the face.

Her warm eyes staring straight ahead at the end of the hallway, where a boy was chatting with Mr. Henry. The lightness to her steps. The smirk on her lips, like she had a secret she'll never share.

Because there was always that moment when Mr. Henry glanced up, his gaze gliding to mine, and I couldn't worry about Margo. Couldn't wonder what boy she was thinking of. I've got my own boy to think about, though *boy* doesn't seem to be the right word.

A week before Margo dies, I find her sobbing in her bedroom. Usually, Margo always has time for me. Usually, she'll smile sadly and explain why she was upset and why she shouldn't be. She'll say she's being silly and then we'll eat ice cream. But this time is different. Margo is curled on her side, a pillow tucked against her, and it looks like something painful is happening inside of her. Like something is trying to claw its way out.

I've never heard her cry quite like this before.

"Are you OK?"

She doesn't answer or move for a long minute. "Just go away, Ren. Shut my door."

"What's going on with you? What happened?" It's true Margo and I fight. We're competitive. Neither one of us likes to lose or feel defeated. But when it comes down to it, we aren't mean to one another. We're just not those types of sisters. "Talk to me. I can tell something is wrong."

"I said go away!" She sits up, swollen faced and angry. This is a version of Margo I'm not accustomed to, and I'm too stunned to ask any questions.

It's hours later that I hear the knock on my door. Margo is standing there with eyes that are still red with sadness. "I'm sorry." Her voice breaks, head shakes. "I'm upset, and I shouldn't have taken it out on you when you were just checking on me."

I don't say anything.

She sighs and walks to my bed, sitting down heavily beside me. "What are you doing?"

I gesture to the papers surrounding me. "Getting some last-minute stage details together for the spring play."

"You pretty much make it happen back there, don't you?"

It's been nearly a full school year. I'm thriving as stage manager. I love my classes. And there's Mr. Henry. Somehow over this year, my feelings for him have grown into something I've never felt before. He gave me his phone number a few months ago when I told him I had to walk home because my mother forgot to pick me up. Now we send each other funny history jokes and restaurant recommendations. I have typed out and deleted so many messages to him.

I can't help but think that he's biding his time, waiting until I'm not his student anymore.

And I'm fine with that. I can wait forever for him if I need to.

Besides, I have enough to focus on with the spring musical. They're doing *Thoroughly Modern Millie* this year, and after I did so well in the winter musical as stage manager, Mrs. Biles also promoted me to assistant director. As a freshman, it's a pretty big achievement.

"Yeah, I keep the actors moving. Make sure they're in the right costumes and in place. Have I mentioned the headset?"

"So cool." Margo giggles. "I'm going to the show of course, but I wish I could just watch you the whole time."

I laugh, but the sound is empty. Her words puncture something deep inside. Margo is the only one who would ever want to
watch me. And what a boring show that would be anyway.

Like always, Margo is good at sensing the direction of my
thoughts. She grabs my hand. "Come on. Mom should be home
soon. Maybe she'll let us take the car to Sonic. I'm craving cheese
fries."

I don't ask Margo why she was crying again, even though I
feel like I should. But I'm not used to this version of my sister.
From elated this morning in the hallway to screaming me out of
her room.

I tell myself she'll grow out of it soon. She's graduating in a
couple months, and all she has talked about for years is the senior
trip to Europe she's been planning since freshman year.

She'll be OK.

I think of Mr. Henry. My blood heats.

I guess I'll be OK too.

And there's something thrilling about the thought. Adult
me bringing a man home for Christmas. Sure, my family might
be a bit surprised at first when I bring home my old teacher,
but we will reassure them that we never crossed any lines until I
graduated.

There's an even more delicious feeling to look forward to, too.
Showing Mr. Henry to Margo. Showing her that I was able to get
the most wanted man in school. A man no one else could touch.

That evening we sit around the dinner table like usual. Mom
and Dad talk to Margo about cheer and school. They even seem
curious about theater. Margo is back to her cheerful and bubbly
self. Whatever was bothering her has clearly passed.

And what was it anyway? What could draw that reaction from someone?

But I don't ask her.

And I've wondered every day since if that was my first mistake. Not taking a moment to ask. A moment I could have said or done something that would have changed everything.

My first missed opportunity at saving Margo's life.

# 32

On Margo's last day on earth, she is happy. There's a spring in her step. A chirpiness to her tone and demeanor.

What I remember most that day is being thankful. She was happy. I was finally happy. Things were looking up.

That evening, holed up in my room reading, I hear it. A creak. It's midnight, and everyone in the house should be asleep. I peer quietly outside my door. There's the faintest shadow of someone creeping down the stairs. It must be my dad sneaking out of bed for a handful of mixed nuts or a couple Oreos. But instead of going back to my room, I follow.

There are no lights in the kitchen. No bumbling sounds of my father as he murmurs to himself. I know I saw someone.

Another sound.

The click of the front door.

There's a pinprick of light when I slip outside. A dark figure at the bottom of the porch stairs, staring at a cell phone.

"Margo?"

She whirls around, but it's too dark for me to make out the expression on her face. "Go back to bed."

"Where are you going?"

"Just hanging out with some friends."

"In the middle of the night?"

"Just—keep your voice down, will you? Come here."

I creep down the steps and stop beside her. She's wearing a loose T-shirt and denim shorts. A bikini top peeks out from beneath the shirt.

"Are you going swimming?"

She watches me seriously for a long moment. "You can keep a secret, can't you?"

"Of course."

"You're my best friend. Even more than Mindy. Mindy doesn't even know this. No one does."

"What is it?" There's a curling, nauseous sensation making its way through me like a snake. A chant inside me: *I don't want to know. I don't want to know. I don't want to know.*

"I have a boyfriend."

The sickening feeling gets stronger, more overwhelming. But it makes sense. How happy she's been lately. The way she lost it the other night. Maybe they had a fight and then made up? "You and Brent are back together?"

"No, we haven't dated in months."

My brows furrow as I try and think about the boys at school. It could be anyone. "OK? Why are you being so secretive?"

"You can't tell. You have to promise not to tell." I can't place the severe look on her face. I just know I've never seen her look quite so serious before.

"I promise." The sinking feeling becomes a black hole in my stomach.

"Do you vow?"

This makes me stumble. We haven't made an unbreakable vow in years. "Margo—"

"You have to make the vow." She holds her fingers up. To anyone looking at us, it seems like she's making a peace sign.

I hold my fingers up and press the tip of my index and middle fingers to hers. "I formally vow to never utter the secret identity of your boyfriend to any human."

"OK." Her hands drop to her sides, and she takes a deep breath. "It's Mr. Henry."

Her answer knocks the breath out of me. It's a weird feeling. Destructive. A moment where I realize everything I believed to be true isn't.

"But he has a girlfriend named Pearl. I've seen messages from her." And I haven't been able to stop thinking of those texts since. Even though I'd kind of rationalized in my mind, he was just finding a way to distract himself until I graduated. Until we could finally be together.

"That was his idea. The French version of my name Margot derives from the name Marguerite. Which…means Pearl. It's just a silly nickname."

It all floods back into my mind. Those moments in the hall-way, his eyes on me, his laughs at my jokes. I thought they meant one thing, but now the past is being rewritten. A past where he isn't looking at me. He's looking at my sister beside me. He's not laughing at my jokes because he likes me, and I'm funny. He's doing it because I'm Margo's little sister.

He doesn't love me.

He feels sorry for me.

Then I think back on that conversation with Margo. When she saw his name written on my hand.

*He'll never love you.*

*I just don't want you to get hurt.*

God. It all makes sense.

The pain follows the shock. Blinding and humiliating pain, and Margo sees it. Her face falls as understanding dawns. "Ren, I know you like… I know you had a little crush on him."

"Stop," I whisper, barely getting the word out. I can't. I can't do this.

She's quick to start explaining. "I never wanted you to get hurt. We didn't plan this. It just happened. His first name is Tyler. That's what I call him. And Ren, it's not like what you think. He loves me. Really loves me. He treats me with so much respect. And we're going to get married after I graduate and go to college. He said he'll follow me wherever I want to go. He makes me so happy… Renny?"

I blink and rub my cheeks. I can't tell if it's her secret or the humid night air choking me. The pain lapses into anger. My top lip curls in disgust. "He's, like, forty."

"He's thirty-one." She frowns. "That's only thirteen years older than me. Look, I know you're hurt. I know you liked—"

"You have no idea what I felt for him."

There is venom in my voice. Hatred brewing deep within. And I hate this feeling because I do love my sister. But it's *him.* She could have anyone in the world she wants. Why did she have to choose *him?*

Why was I stupid enough to think he could ever want me when he could have her? I've been Margo's little sister to him this whole time. That's why he's been so nice. That's why he's looked after me. He doesn't like me. He's never wanted me.

It's always been Margo.

"Why are you acting like this?"

"How did you expect me to act?" I bite back. "What did you want me to say? Congrats on screwing our teacher?"

She shakes her head, lips trembling. "I'm sorry, Ren. I shouldn't have said anything to you. I didn't realize you felt so strongly. I don't want to hurt you."

Guilt creeps in. It almost makes me laugh. Like I have any reason to feel guilty for my feelings of betrayal. But that's the Margo effect. She's standing there like Bambi after his mother was shot, and every one of my natural urges is to comfort her.

How could I have been so stupid?

"Ren," she tries again. "I really do love him. And I hope one day you can understand and be happy for me."

I swallow back the pain and fury. Focus on her. The vulnerability. The sincerity in her words and expression. "This isn't right. If anyone were to find out—"

"No one is going to find out. I'm not telling anyone. He isn't. Are you?"

"I found out! You don't think it could happen again? If you feel like you should hide it, and you're sneaking around, then maybe that's your sign that you shouldn't be doing something."

She looks away. "I know. I know how bad it sounds. How much trouble he'd be in. But Ren." She looks at me, eyes full of unshed tears. "It's so real it hurts."

"No one will believe that."

"He won't even have sex with me."

The warmth on my neck and face deepens. "You don't have to tell me all this."

"He says he wants to wait until it isn't illegal. He loves me, and I love him. You don't get to choose who you love or when they come into your life. But he's trying to respect the law as much as he can. Doesn't that mean something?"

Those words. *You don't get to choose who you love.* She has no idea what the words mean to me. How much I understand them. More than she ever could. Because the only thing worse than loving someone at the wrong time is loving someone who will never love you back.

Everything boils over. The hate. The anger. The shock. It's like I can't control myself a moment longer. I am a derailed train. He loves her. He loves her the way I thought he loved me.

"You sound so stupid, Margo."

"I'm sorry for telling you. Clearly it was a mistake," she whisper hisses, and her nostrils flare. "Pretend you didn't see anything, Ren."

"I can't."

"You said you wouldn't tell."

"Margo—"

"No, you promised. You made the vow." She goes to stomp away, but I grab her arm.

"Margo!"

"Let me go!" She jerks her arm away, my nails scraping her skin. She hisses out a breath and looks down at the thin streaks of blood blooming to the surface.

"I'm sorry," I whisper, shifting away from her. I feel so wrong. So out of control.

And she's right. We started making the vow in elementary school. As we got older, the promises we made to one another became more important. It's the one thing we trust implicitly. If one of us made the vow, it couldn't be broken. "I just don't want you to leave."

*I don't want you to go to him.*

*I can't know you're with him.*

Her face softens, and her arms drop to her sides. "Then come with us. Trust me. He won't be mad I told you. He adores you, remember? You're like a sister to him. You'd have to find out eventually."

Fresh pain hits my stomach like raw meat dropped on a hot grill, and I'm burning from the inside out. I've always been Margo's little sister. Now I get to be Mr. Henry's too.

"You're meeting him right now?" I ask thickly.

She nods. "Come on. Please. My secrets are yours."

Another moment to think about.

To agonize over.

This moment could have altered history, and each time I come back to it, all I can think of is her tenth birthday when none of her friends wanted me to play. I went to my room and cried, but Margo, after coming back in the room and realizing I wasn't there, searched for me. She'd asked me what was wrong, and I told her. And I remember she didn't say anything back. She only squeezed my hand with this secret smile on her face. "This is my birthday. You're my sister. You're more important than any of them." And she tugged me to my feet. Her friends weren't happy, but they never said anything, and from that point forward, regardless of their obvious distaste for me, no one ever said anything to Margo's little sister.

It's like accepting fate.

My own.

Hers.

In this moment, I wanted more than anything in the world to be more than that. More than Margo's little sister. I didn't know I was well on my way to sealing it in blood.

I take her hand numbly and follow her into the dark.

The truck is parked at the end of the driveway. The same black truck I've fantasized about being inside. I've wondered how it smells. If it's neat. If he keeps the tank full or waits to fill up until it's completely empty.

I never wondered if Margo was riding in that passenger seat.

The truck is running, but the lights are all off, and it's way too dark for me to see inside it. Something about it here—on our property—makes my heart take off in a sprint. Makes my feet dig into the dirt. Margo must think I tripped. "Careful," she whispers. "There he is. Don't be nervous."

But before we can get in the car, he's stepping out. And if I thought seeing his truck made my heart race, seeing him, standing there like that, makes my whole body tense. It's abnormal. Wrong. I want him. Even now.

He's shadowed in the dark. Different, all at once, from the man standing at the end of a fluorescent lit hallway. In jeans and a dark T-shirt, his hands are in his hair, nervously tugging at the roots. He won't look at me.

"Give us a second," Margo says and lets go of my hand. She

walks ahead to stop just in front of him. I hear his whispers. Hear
Margo's. But I can't make out exactly what he's saying. I just sense
he's angry about something.

Finally, Margo turns and waves me forward. But this isn't like
her birthday party where the girls quietly fell in line, and Margo
never lost her smile. This is different. There's something wrong
with Margo now. A wariness that hadn't been there before. A desperation in her stance as her hand grabs his arm, holds tight like
he's at risk of running away.

They both go silent, and Margo looks back. He follows her
gaze, hooded eyes resting on me. I see my friend. The man who
knows my inside jokes. The one who took up for me when my
classmates were being mean. I see the man who I thought saw me
when no one else did.

Turns out, he'd never seen me.

Not really.

Not once.

"You know Ren," Margo says quietly, forcing a smile. "Ren,
this is…Tyler."

Mr. Henry tenses again, looking more uncomfortable than I'd
ever seen him. "Hey, Ren."

"Mr. Henry." I never call him that. I call him Henry. But I can't
stomach it right now, can't bear to remember how wrong I was.

"I didn't want you to find out like this," he says, and for once
there's a look on his face that doesn't sting. Regret. Clearly, he
doesn't want to hurt me. Or maybe he just doesn't want me to
think badly of him.

"Come on." Margo grabs his hand and pulls him toward the
truck. "Let's talk inside. I don't want my dad to hear us."

I climb into the back of the truck after Margo jumps in the passenger seat. There are a couple of take-out bags tossed behind the passenger seat and several plastic water bottles. He must have thrown everything in the back to make room for Margo. He definitely wasn't expecting anyone to sit back here.

"Sorry." He catches my eye in the rearview. "It's a mess."

And that's it. No more words spoken in the car, and the silence is so thick, I can feel it pulsing against my flesh. Usually, I'd tease him about his messiness. Give him the spiel on how plastic bottles are bad for the environment.

But my heart's not in it.

My heart is no longer beating in my chest at all.

I feel awkward and way too young. And as we drive, sleep tugs at my eyes. This all feels like a weird dream. A mistake. I want to go home. The feeling builds for the next twenty minutes over the drive until the truck finally rolls to a stop.

We're at a lake where there's a boat waiting. Mr. Henry jumps out without saying anything and moves to the boat.

"Margo," I whisper, though I'm not sure why. "I think I want to go home."

She turns around to look at me, and I can't be certain in the darkness, but it appears as if she's been crying. Weeping silently in the front seat while I'd been fighting sleep in the back.

"We can't," she says quickly. "I told him we could handle this. That you could handle it. If you can't, if you make him take you home, he's going to be—"

"He's going to be what?" It wasn't clicking in my head. Why would Mr. Henry care what I did? Surely, he'd be happy to have my sister all to himself.

"He'll be upset. I told him you were mature for your age. That you were cool and could handle this secret. But he's worried because you're in his class. Please be cool about this, Ren."

"I don't know how to feel."

"Be happy for me." She smiles big and tight. "Tyler makes me happy. I'm sorry everything is so tense right now. I shouldn't have sprung you on him like this. He's worried, you know? He cares a lot about his career and has worked so hard to get where he is. He's scared that our love might be viewed as something different to others. That's why he doesn't want to tell anyone until after I've graduated and turned eighteen."

The nauseous feeling in my gut turns sticky somehow. Something about her words feels so wrong. Seventeen. She's seventeen.

Like she can read my mind, she says, "I know you're still stuck on the age gap. But this is different. We're different. I promise. Please give him a chance. Give tonight a chance for me."

"I'm here, aren't I?" Suddenly, I'm annoyed with her. Can't she see that I don't want to be here? That I don't want *her* to be here. But I am. For her. I'm clearly trying to give him a chance.

She winces. "No, I know. Thank you. Thanks for not telling."

Just as suddenly as the annoyance comes, it leaves. I lean forward and grab her hand. Squeeze it.

Her door opens, and Mr. Henry is there. "Why don't you girls wait on the pier while I get the boat in the water?" The way he says it without looking at her, I can tell he's upset.

Margo instantly hops out, and I follow her lead, whispering as we walk to the pier. "Wait, we're getting on this boat? In the middle of the night? Aren't there rules against this?"

"It's OK. We've done it before," Margo tells me. "It's the one place where we feel safe to be ourselves."

We stand huddled together as he connects the truck to the boat trailer and backs it into the water. Then he's hopping on it, cranking it to life, and easing it beside the dock. Margo climbs aboard without a second thought, but I hesitate. That sticky feeling in my gut again. I want to go home. I want Margo to come with me.

And she would.

This is my big sister. She may be disappointed or embarrassed, but she'd come. She'd make me feel better. Mr. Henry and Margo are standing close together now, arms around each other. Both of them seem just a little lighter.

Beneath the light of a nearly full moon, I can see him clearly. Just as handsome as he is standing against his door in the hallway. I can see why Margo is so smitten. She'd landed the most unattainable man in the school. The one whose names her friends scribble all over the margins of their notes.

The one whose name I scribble on my notes. The one I wanted. The one I thought wanted me too.

They look beautiful together.

I should want to run home. To never look at them again. But this is Margo, and just like everyone else, I can't look away. Besides, I don't want her out here alone with him. I glance down at the water. It's practically black.

We shouldn't be here at all.

"Come on, Ren," Margo chirps. "What are you waiting for?"

I step onboard.

# 33

Margo laughs as I sway on my feet. "You'll get used to it."

"What about life jackets?" I say as a panicky feeling sets in once again.

"We don't need them. No one else is out here, and Tyler is a good driver."

"Just relax," Mr. Henry says, sounding for the first time this evening like the man I know. "Have fun."

I nod and sink deeper into the seat.

I try to picture the situation differently. Like Margo is the third wheel, and I'm the one Henry can't take his eyes off of. But the fantasy is more agonizing than reality, so I let it go just as the boat really starts moving.

I've been on a boat before. A little speedboat and a fishing boat. But never one like this. Never in the middle of the night at the tail end of spring. It's cold. I wrap my arms around myself wishing I had a sweatshirt or something. But maybe even that wouldn't help ward off this chill.

Margo walks past and reaches for my hand. "Come on. I like to sit up here."

"What?"

She opens the tiny door to the very front of the boat where there's a ledge big enough for two people. I'm not worried about falling off. Mr. Henry isn't going very fast, and the path is straight enough. But something about seeing the dark, rushing water, knowing it's directly beneath my feet—it makes me queasy.

"Come on." She sits, laughing, patting the spot beside her. "I do this all the time."

So I sit beside my sister. The breeze is nice against my face even with the chill in the air. It's like with every pulsing, bitter moment the wind is cleaning me. Clearing my thoughts when it seems to be the most impossible, and in this freeing quiet moment, I forget Mr. Henry is here at all.

"How did this start?" I ask her, and I don't need to explain. She instantly knows what I'm wondering.

"I don't know. It built up for a long time," she replies, with a giddiness in her voice. "Just, like, the looks we gave each other, you know? As if our souls recognized one another. I don't usually believe in that mushy stuff. But it was just like that. Then one day I stayed behind in class to ask about a project. We started talking. He, uh, made me laugh, and I made him laugh. I remember he was so close, and he smelled so good. We just kissed." She giggles nervously. "It was weird at first. I was so nervous. But he was so gentle. He pulled back and looked at me like no boy had before, Ren. And he told me we shouldn't do this, but then we kissed again right there in his room. The next thing I know, we're writing each other notes and he's taking me out of town for dates." Her eyes connect with mine, a hesitant smile gracing her lips. "I was so excited for you to know about us. I wanted more than anything for you two to be friends. My two favorite people in the world. And now it can finally happen."

I watch her face. The way her eyes light up. A light that I feel will never come into my own eyes again. I think of every boyfriend she's ever had. The way they line up for her, patiently waiting their turn.

Mr. Henry was the only one I've ever wanted for myself. The only person I ever truly thought liked me instead of my sister. It's like that magic act where they rip the tablecloth away and all the dishes remain on the tabletop. Only they don't. Glass flies to the ground and shatters. Every beautiful piece of me breaks apart.

"He's my soul mate." Something about the way she says it seems personal. A dig. A justification for hurting me or breaking rules or doing whatever the hell she wants to do.

"You're only seventeen." And he's mine. He's supposed to be mine. "I'm just finding it difficult to understand how you could say that when Brent was supposedly the love of your life only last summer."

She frowns. "This is different, and age is only a number. When you know, you know."

"That's just it, you can't know." My voice grows harsher with every word. "You're a child, and he's grown man. It's gross, Margo." I can hear myself. How cruel I'm being. But I can't stop. I want her to hurt the way I do. I want her to know what it's like.

She flinches, hands bracing herself as she leans back. "It's not like that. Don't cheapen it."

"You're dating your teacher, and you're asking me not to cheapen it? Do you understand how sick that is?"

"Babe," Mr. Henry calls out as if sensing her unease. Her pain. But I can't stop.

Margo watches with drawn brows and a pinched expression. "I knew you would be shocked, but I thought you'd eventually understand. I mean, you have to know, Renny, he never...he never looked at you like that. The way you looked at him."

"And he'll never have the chance, because you had to have him, didn't you? You have to have everything that I want."

"No, no, I swear. It isn't like that." Her voice thickens with emotion. "I wouldn't hurt you on purpose. I never thought—I'm just so sorry, Renny."

She reaches for me. As she does it, she leans forward, and her toe dips into the water. That's all. Just the very tip of her toe.

One second, she's right there, and the next second she's gone. There's a sickening bump.

And then silence.

Nothing clicks in my head. Nothing is making sense at all. Margo. Where is Margo?

"Margo?" Mr. Henry calls out, distress in his voice. He cuts the engine and runs to the front of the boat. To me. Looks between me and the spot she was sitting and then looks into the water.

Someone is screaming, and I don't get it at first that it's me.

He jerks me up by my arms. Tells me to be quiet. Tells me to shut up. But I scream her name and jump into the freezing cold water because I don't have a choice.

Margo is in here.

I swim down as far as I can, never quite reaching the bottom. My hands tangle with plant life and slime, but it doesn't bother me. I don't even notice. I swim up, gasp for air, sputtering, spitting lake water.

Mr. Henry is on the front of the boat, his hands in his hair. "No, no, no. Oh, God. No."

"Help me," I demand of him, not recognizing my own voice. "We have to get her out before she drowns." I try to calculate in my head how on she'd been under. A minute now? Five?

He doesn't look up. Doesn't stop muttering to himself.

"Help me!" I scream again, and I don't wait to see what he does. I dive back under the water. Feeling around me. Desperately trying grab for her. She has to be here. She has to be right here.

As the minutes tick by and the water moves us further away, inch by inch. I can't keep track of where I searched.

How long has it been? Ten minutes now? It's OK. I saw a show once where someone was under twenty minutes, and they still lived. It's possible. And maybe she got out! Maybe we didn't see her, and she'll be waiting for us on the shore. She's just holding her breath. I'll find her. I'll do CPR, and she'll spit water out like in the movies. Then she'll be OK.

She's here.

She has to be right here.

Above the water, I barely hear the hum of the engine. It's not until I bob to the surface and glance around in a whole other type of panic that I realize that Mr. Henry has left. I'm alone out here.

Everything is shaky. My vision blurs in and out.

"I can't—" I gasp the words, bob under the water then back up. "Help! Help me!" I'm under again. Can't see. Can't think. Can't breathe.

My fingers brush something. Something firm. I hold on.

A hand. Margo's hand.

And that's enough to push me up, up, up. Toward the surface. Smiling through the sobs. Margo is here. Margo is alive. I gasp for a breath and wipe my eyes, pulling Margo closer.

But I am alone in this freezing, glassy lake.

In my hand is a slimy, thin branch.

This is where they find me.

There were people camping at a site near the lake. A man had crawled out of his tent and walked to the shore to pee. He saw me floating in the water and thought I was dead. Within fifteen minutes of Mr. Henry leaving, another boat with flashing lights was circling the water.

I stayed still and quiet, floating in place. I didn't want to swim to them and risk losing the spot where Margo is. She's here somewhere, and if I lose her place then I won't be able to pull her out. Won't be able to do CPR.

But the boat finds me, and a bright light flashes on my face as a voice calls out, "Ma'am, are you OK?"

I stare up at the starless sky. One big moon and nothing else. "She's in the water," I whisper to the man. There's a splash and someone is pulling me toward the boat.

"Ma'am, are you OK? Are you hurt?"

"She's in the water."

"Who? Who is?"

I'm hoisted into a boat, a blanket draped over my shoulders. "My sister."

I hold the blanket tight while I sit on the dock with all the flashing lights behind me. I don't move. Focus on the rough wood beneath me. The bite of cold from my wet hair stuck to my neck.

Footsteps on the dock. "Oh my god, Ren! Ren!" Arms pulling me up. In. Warmth.

Mom.

Dad.

A cop behind them.

Mom holds me at arm's length. "Where's your sister? Where's Margo, Ren? They said—it doesn't matter what they said. They're wrong. You tell me." Her voice cracks. "Tell me where she is."

My mother's panicked eyes scan my face over and over as if she's trying to read me like a book. Get the answers out of me while I'm only thinking them. I open my mouth to speak, but it's dry. There are no words.

Mom shakes me. "Now, Ren, dammit! Where's Margo?"

"Becks, give her a second."

"She's dead," I say dully.

Mom freezes, all expression leaving her face. Her eyes narrow. "That's not funny. This isn't funny, Ren." She lets me go and screams my sister's name. It's loud, but nothing can drown out the screaming in my head.

———

They pull Margo's body from the water five hours later.

And it isn't until that very moment that my mother stops screaming.

———

Tyler Henry is arrested.

I was lying on my side in bed when I heard the news. Listening to my mother's howls and my father's anguish.

The nauseous feeling that has burdened me since stepping into Mr. Henry's truck hasn't gone away but something else burns there with it. An anger so intense I couldn't stamp it down if I wanted to.

Margo's happy face. A splash. A crack. A bottomless lake. And the darkest night.

It plays over and over and over.

And I don't even try to stop it.

It's exactly what I deserve.

But there is one thing, one thing that death can't take from me. I never broke my promise to Margo. I never broke our vow. No one would ever know about her relationship with Tyler Henry.

And I guess I deserve that too.

# 34

I talk, and Olivia listens.

As I speak, I'm very aware of her. Her breaths. The way her chest heaves and then freezes like she's afraid to breathe out.

"He took a plea deal for twelve years and served eight."

Olivia inhales sharply. "He's out of jail? But he killed her. He was driving. He didn't make sure you had life jackets, and he let you both sit on the most dangerous spot of a pontoon boat. Then he left you. You could have died too, Ren."

"That's the way it works sometimes." Sometimes people get twenty years for possession of drugs while sexual predators get probation.

"You know it wasn't your fault," Olivia says softly. "What happened to your sister wasn't your fault."

But it's so much deeper than that. There's so much she doesn't understand. "She was reaching for me. Arguing with me. It's the only reason her foot slipped. Besides, we never should have been there. I could have stopped it from the beginning."

Olivia frowns, shaking her head. "If he was the adult he should have been, then she'd still be alive."

"Both statements can be true."

"There's something else. Another reason you blame yourself."

Her perception should surprise me, but it doesn't. This is Olivia. She notices things and people.

I say the worst part. The part I never tell anyone. "I was angry at her. The moment right before she died, I've never been more angry with her. It was because of him. Mr. Henry."

"Wait," Olivia asks. "The rumors about you and him. They're true?"

I stare at my dark house. No movement. No person waiting inside to turn on the porch light or help me to bed. And it all comes back to that night. That year. The reason I can't love or be loved. "No. But I thought they were. I wanted them to be so badly that I saw things that weren't there. He never wanted me, though. It was always about her."

"You let them think it was you." Realization dawns in her eyes as the narrative slowly makes sense in her head. "You've let them blame you for being on that boat all these years. Everyone thinks it was you in a relationship with the teacher. They think Margo was on the boat for you. And you've let them believe it."

"It was the last promise I made to my sister." And I remember the look in her eye as she pressed her fingertips to mine. The hopefulness there. Then there's the feeling of staring at the rushing water. Knowing I'd never look in her eyes again. I couldn't break the last thing I ever promised her. I told her I wouldn't tell anyone about her and Mr. Henry. So I didn't. I didn't say anything at all. Besides, everyone assumed it was me and Henry in a relationship because of how close we were. I was the one that hung out in his class and spent lunch breaks there. I was the one with an obvious crush. The rumors started flying right after Margo's death.

In them, Margo got on that boat that night to protect me.

And I'll always be the reason she never got off.

Olivia's face pinches into confusion. "But he went along with it?"

"No. He never claimed to have a relationship with either of us. He pled out, and everything was pushed under the rug after that."

"I'm sorry, Ren." Her voice is quiet, withdrawn. But her gaze is deep and bottomless. Like there are a million things she needs to say, but she doesn't know how. "My parents were divorced when I was like three."

"I'm sorry."

Olivia shrugs one shoulder, but the motion is heavy. "My step-dad is a lot older than my mom, and when they got married, he had two sons. One was a seventeen-year-old, Robbie." When she says the name her lips curl, and she winces. "We would play this game, me and him. The game always began with me taking off my clothes."

My throat closes and vomit curdles in my stomach. Olivia takes a deep breath. "I'm sure you can see where this is going. Anyway, I was so young. I never told anyone. It only happened a few times. Then he ended up moving out for college. Getting married. His wife got pregnant when I was twelve, and I remember when my mother told me. I remember going to bed that night. I'd never prayed before, but that night I did. I prayed that the little baby girl would be safe. That same night Robbie was killed in a mall shooting." Olivia wipes a tear away, and then another. "At the funeral, I didn't cry. Even as I looked at his body in that casket. All I felt was relief." She looks out the window then back to me again. "Everyone talked about him like he was a saint or a hero. His wife was an absolute mess. His brother…his brother always protected me. Loved me like a little sister, the way he should. No one could understand why I was so emotionless. And I couldn't keep it in. Not a second longer. The night of his funeral I told my mother what he did to me. She just…" Olivia's mouth trembles. "She told me I was a liar. That all I wanted was attention. She said if that really happened then I would have told her a long time ago."

She sighs and looks away from me, out the window again. But there's nothing to see. My neighbors' houses are dark, and the streetlight in front of my home has been out for a while.

"You know the only person who has ever believed me is my grandmother. Poppi. She's the best." Olivia faces me again with a sad smile. "I stayed at her house the whole summer when I was a kid. My parents couldn't get me to leave. I still stay with her as much as I can."

"I'm so sorry, Olivia."

"I didn't tell you this to get your pity. She's gotten really old. Not quite all there. But even with this…current situation, she's the only one who will listen to me. I can talk to her for hours. She likes when I read to her too. We'll sit on her porch and just listen to her wind chimes. She's got these giant purple butterflies. I've never seen anything as beautiful. It's the only place I feel at peace. Ren." She stops. "When everything…happened, Poppi told me that it wasn't my fault. She said Mr. Lewis was the adult, the person in the power position, and it's his job to keep his students safe. Same with Robbie. The fact I never told anyone wasn't my fault either.

The same goes to you. What happened with the man who hurt your sister, what happened to your sister, that can't be your fault or else this is all my fault too. What happened to me. Me being with Mr. Lewis. Even Robbie's death. Do you understand?"

"Of course, she's right. Of course, none of it is your fault."

"Then say it. Say that Margo's death isn't your fault either."

Olivia is wearing the earrings again. The hoops. I reach out and touch one. As soon as I realize what I'm doing, I pull back. "I'm sorry."

"It's OK."

"You just…you remind me of Margo."

"Ren, your sister died because a selfish, irresponsible man killed her." There is a look on her face. A determination mingled with something else, a kindness I'm not accustomed to.

"Selfish and irresponsible. Describes someone else we know."

"But we don't have to be victims to them or live in their shadows. I'm going to go back to school and hold my head high because I know I didn't do anything wrong, and you're going to do the same. It doesn't matter what your parents or mine think. We know the truth."

I swallow harshly. How is this girl only seventeen? "Thank you."

She smiles. "I'm only returning the favor. Now let's do it. Let's make a promise that we'll always remember."

"A promise?"

She holds her two fingers up just like in my story. Just like Margo. "Vow that we will always remember we're the survivors. Vow to stop blaming ourselves."

My throat closes, chest tightens. I can't say any words, can't even think them. I just hold my two fingers up just like she asks. She presses the tips of her fingers to my own and smiles sadly.

"We're going to be OK," she says, leaning back into the seat.

"Yes," I agree. "I think we will."

———

That night, I make a single phone call. My dad answers on the third ring. "Ren?"

I breathe deeply, heavily. "How's Mom?"

Silence on the other end. Clicking. He's sucking on a peppermint, and I can hear it bouncing against his teeth. "Good, good. Better. They gave her something to calm down, and she got some rest. She's been good the past few hours. Sleeping now."

I picture her. Lying across that hospital bed. The agony on her face. An agony pain meds will never be able to help. "Does Mom hate me?"

The silence is too long. "No. No, Ren. She doesn't hate you."

"Will she ever forgive me?"

"I don't know." There's a creak and shuffling like he's leaving her bedside. I see him. Standing in the hall, leaning against the wall with the phone held to his ear tightly. "I think seeing you just reminds her too much of Margo. Too much of what happened that night."

"What am I supposed to do about that?"

"Nothing," he answers simply. "You're not doing anything wrong."

"But you blame me too."

More silence. The deafening kind. My cheeks are wet, but I don't wipe the tears away. I can't make myself move at all.

"We blame him. Always him."

"But I could have stopped it."

He sighs. "I don't know what you want from me."

"I just want to know how things can go back to the way they were. When things were better. I miss you and Mom. I miss home."

"I know." Another sigh. "I'm sorry."

"Maybe I could come back to the hospital and try again. If I could just talk to her—"

"No. I don't think that's a good idea. I love you. We love you. But it's better for your mother if you stay away for a while. Just for a little while. Let her heal."

I can't remember the words I use to get off the phone, only that I do it quickly. And I stare up at my ceiling, watching the fan blur in and out with my tears. They run sideways down my cheeks, wetting the creases on either side of my neck.

And I think of what I really want.

What I really need.

———

I wake, mouth dry, back aching. The sun beats hot and heavy through my living room window, right on my face. I stretch, forcing myself into a sitting position, and blink blearily around the room. Last night.

It's all a bit fuzzy.

What time is it anyway?

*Shit.*

I snatch my phone up, nearly groaning in relief when I realize it's not even seven. I still have time to shower and get myself together. To try to make sense of everything that happened yesterday and last night.

Before I place my phone back on the coffee table, I notice the notification on my messages icon.

A single text from Michaela. I open it quickly, stomach lurching as soon as I read.

*He's dead.*

She's sent me a link. I click it, numbly.

*Local High School Teacher Accused of Misconduct Found Dead*

The phone falls from my hand.

# 35

I find another sub and use another sick day. There are too many feelings rolling over me and through me. I try calling Olivia several times, but she doesn't answer. Michaela doesn't either. I couldn't tell from Michaela's text how she was feeling, and I can't even guess how it's affecting Olivia.

The man who took advantage of her.

Dead.

It's after ten when there are three firm knocks on the door. I keep the covers pulled up to my chin, not ready to get up. Not ready to see anyone.

But who could it be?

Margo stands beside the window, peeking through the curtain. "You can't just lie here all day."

*Knock, knock, knock.*

The sound is faster this time, harsher.

"Who is it?"

She turns to me with her lips pursed. "You'll only know if you get up."

*Knock, knock, knock.*

I throw the covers off and stumble toward the door. Mostly because I'm afraid it could be Olivia or Michaela, and I desperately want to talk to them. But when I see the figure at the door, I realize I was wrong.

Detective Wu glimpses me through the window and waves.

When I open the door, she says, "I hope I didn't wake you."

"I was up," I reply, clearing the sleep from my voice, wishing it was that simple to clear away everything else.

Detective Wu gives me a once-over. It makes me wonder what I look like. I didn't wash or condition my hair in the shower and know it must be hanging in tangled curls to my shoulders. I'd thrown on the first clothing my fingers touched. Black sweatpants with holes in both knees and an oversized T-shirt.

"I figured you'd be teaching," she says, finally meeting my eyes. "I went by the school, but you weren't there."

"I'm not feeling so well today."

Something flickers in her eyes.

"What can I do for you?"

"Actually, I wanted to know if we could talk."

I step outside onto the porch barefoot, wrapping my arms around myself. "About what? I've told you all I know."

"I think it would be better if you came with me to the station."

I tense, trying to control my immediate reaction. "Am I under arrest for something?"

"I just want to talk."

"If I'm not under arrest, then I'll have to decline the offer. I can give you my lawyer's contact information if you have any more questions for me."

"All right. Fair enough." She takes a step back. "By the way, in case you wanted to know, Casey Ballard's wife found out he was in three other relationships with three women from separate cities he has to travel to for work. One of the women is pregnant, and none of them knew about each other."

I don't say anything.

"You didn't mean to kill Casey, did you?"

Not a word or reaction comes from me.

"You know what I think, Ren? I think you're a spider, and you've been catching flies since your sister died. I think you find these men, these cheating scumbag men, and you punish them. Take photos of them. Reveal their secrets to their wives and colleagues. But I think Casey reacted more violently than you expected. He followed you out after you texted his wife."

I lick my dry lips and chuckle low in my throat. "Good thing it's not about what you *think*." I step back over my threshold, place a hand over my door handle. "Is that all?"

Her expression is one I don't expect. Almost a blatant curiosity. A vibrant flash of humanity in her eyes. "That teacher from the news. The one who was arrested and now killed. He taught at the same school as you, didn't he? I'm not working that case. Not in my jurisdiction. But it's funny, isn't it? That men can't seem to stay alive around you."

"Goodbye, Detective. I think next time you wish to come by, you can go through my lawyer."

I close the door, leaning against it heavily. The walls feel closer,

like I'm lying in a casket. Like I'm being buried by this insur-
mountable guilt.

"She's right, you know." Margo stands at the end of the hallway watching as I press two fingers to my temple. As the world
around me begins to unravel. "You didn't mean to kill Casey. But
that doesn't mean you didn't want to."

# 36

Casey Ballard wasn't supposed to die. But he was meant to be humiliated.

It began right after high school. An accident, really. I'd walked into a bar that didn't card and sat on a stool. A man approached me. He'd talked to me. Laughed with me. Made me feel something when all I'd felt for years was numb. It was like being outside in below freezing weather, and suddenly someone starts blowing a hair dryer on your hands. I felt tingly and too hot and *good*. When he asked if I wanted to come out to his car, I obliged.

I've never been the kind of girl to go off with random men, or any men, really. At eighteen I was a virgin. But that night, it was like something awakened inside me, and I didn't care about anything except feeling.

He drove me somewhere secluded, and we'd crawled into the back seat. And for the first time since Margo died, I was distracted. Even if it hurt and he smelled like urine and corn chips. Even if he made a sarcastic comment about the blood on his seats. All of it was better than feeling nothing at all.

When it was over and he was breathing heavy beside me, that's when everything shifted. I'd sat glassy eyed in his passenger seat the whole drive. When we made it back to the bar, he'd leaned over and opened my door. I asked him when I could see him again, and he laughed.

He'd laughed so hard his face turned red. Then he'd fixed a patronizing gaze on my face. "Listen, baby, I'm only in town for one night."

I'd tried to argue, but he'd only laughed more. This time it came out sad, like he felt sorry for me. "I'm married, sweetheart. This meant nothing. Get me?"

"Right." I'd slid out of the car without a word. But he didn't know his phone had been on the seat. He didn't know I took it. He really didn't know I watched him put the password in before we'd even left the bar.

Whose password is 1-2-3-4?

People who want to be messed with.

When his taillights turned to pinpricks, I opened the phone and scrolled to recent phone calls. Addie was the most recent. The woman answered on the first ring.

"I've been trying to get ahold of you," she'd said instantly. "I need to know when your plane comes in. Mark?"

I cleared my throat. "Hi, I'm sorry, but Mark left his cell phone with me. I was trying to figure out how to get it back to him. Who is this?"

"His wife." Her voice was sharp as a blade. "Who is this?"

"Just tell him if he wants his phone, he can find it at the bar where he picked me up." I hung up, ignoring the fact it immediately started ringing again, and tossed the phone on the ground.

That night I went home and cried—curled up in my shower, head in my hands, body shaking sobs.

More than sad, I was angry. Mind numbingly angry. I put my hand between my legs, and they came back covered in blood. I looked away, choking on my own breath, and I didn't look back down. Not as I cleaned the blood and semen from inside me. Not as I felt the slick on my fingers, on my thighs. I scrubbed until I had to be red and raw.

And when I went to the drugstore well after 11:00 p.m. to purchase the Plan B pill, there, beneath harsh fluorescent lights and the dead stare of the cashier, was a single pair of black gloves on display by the counter. And I didn't want to see my hands anymore. The hands that had touched that man.

Hands that cleaned up the mess I'd let that man make. All the messes that men make.

But I tried to move past that night. I went to college. Met Allen. He seemed to fill a void inside me, at least temporarily. He showed me the attention and love I'd lacked since Margo.

But I couldn't fully escape from the back of that car with that greasy, disgusting man. And the moment that I'd always get stuck on was the feeling that struck as I spoke to his wife. As I realized I was helping her. I was making the world just a little better.

That's why, the first night after Allen asked for a divorce and went to stay with his mother, I ended up at a bar. This time I knew exactly what I wanted. I didn't want love or a man or sex. I wanted something else. Something darker. I wanted that feeling again. I wanted a man to pay.

A woman to finally see the truth about the man in her life.

I learned how to spot the men with the lines on their fingers from missing wedding bands. I learned the way they averted their phone screens from me so I couldn't see their family photos on the lock screen. I learned that they liked their women sexy and docile. I learned the best way to position my body, the best way to talk, the best way to order a drink to get them to approach me. To make them think being with me was their choice.

I did it so many times. And my system worked.

But I always became someone else first. Lipstick. My gloves. A nice dress. I became their dream, and it was almost too easy. They thought I was kinky and desperate. At some point during my time with any of these faceless men, I would end up with their phone.

Sometimes I'd send a text. Sometimes a phone call made to seem like a butt dial. Once I'd even sent a photo to his entire contact list. It didn't matter what my checkmate was, only that I made one. Every time. And when I was done, I'd say I was going to the bathroom or checking on something in the hall, and I wouldn't come back. I would be gone before they even realized what I did.

Until Casey.

It was my own fault. I was distracted by my move home, by everything happening with Bryson. I wasn't thinking clearly. I wasn't thinking at all.

Everything started out exactly the same. I spotted him as soon as I walked in, and he spotted me too. A few peeks in his direction, concentrated hair flips, and sips of a fruity cocktail, and he was beside me. His body heat melding into my own, smelling like spice and leather.

Except his breath. That was pure whiskey. He leaned down to

talk to me. Made a comment about it being too hot out for gloves. I told him I liked to be hot.

He made a crude joke that I laughed way too hard at. Made him feel heard. Manly. Appreciated. I'm the "waiting for you by the door with a pot roast on the table" woman. A "put your feet up and I'll handle it" woman. All the while, I tried not to recoil when his hand went around my shoulder and dipped a little too low over my breast.

Who was his wife?

Was she loyal?

Did she know?

He mistook the hair raised on my arms and my shallow breathing as a good sign. He must have thought I was panting for him because he leaned in. Told me he'd like to talk to me somewhere more private.

The thing about men like Casey Ballard is, they need to think they're calling the shots. Making the rules. He needed to be the one to invite me. I accepted. We ended up in a hotel room I watched him rent on the spot. We only needed it for a couple hours.

I always get naked first, and that night was no different. This step is important. It keeps the men comfortable. Reminds them that I'm their toy. Then I slowly inched his clothing down, teasing him along the way. By the time Casey was nude and spread on the bed, his eyes were hooded and half-closed, and I spotted his phone on the bedside table.

I was just reaching for it when it rang.

His wife.

He smirked at me, winked, picked it up and talked to her, all while holding a finger up at me. I waited, frozen in place, wondering what I should do, as he convinced his wife he was at work.

Finally, he hung up, and, with a sleazy grin, reached for me.

My knee jerk reaction was to shove him away. I couldn't even pretend he didn't disgust me at this point. Couldn't make myself fake it anymore. Casey had tried to convince me it was OK. His wife was a nag. She didn't matter. But I said no, got up, and started dressing. This was ridiculous anyway. I told myself I wouldn't do this anymore—no matter how much these men deserved it.

"You cockteasing little bitch," he'd said from the bed, still naked. "You better give me the ninety-four dollars I just paid for this room. You hear me? Get on your knees or get out your wallet."

I was going to leave. He was already seething, after all, but something in his tone stopped me. I'd looked at him, gave him my best flirty smile. "You want me on my knees?" I'd asked as I slowly crawled up his body.

He was clearly a bit shocked by my sudden change in demeanor. Too shocked to say anything.

"Close your eyes," I whispered in his ear, biting his earlobe, and he groaned, eyes fluttering shut.

Still nibbling and kissing on his neck, I reached for his phone. Sent his location to his wife one-handed. I was about to snap a picture of him too when his eyes flashed open.

He cursed. "What did you do? Is that—what in the hell did you just do?"

Then I was up, already half-dressed. I slipped on my shirt, my shoes, and ran out the door.

What I didn't expect was for Casey to follow me.

I didn't expect him to chase me. To catch me in an empty parking lot, to snarl and slam my hand in my car's door.

But he didn't expect me either. The headbutt. The kick to his groin. Then I was in my car, vision swirling from the pain in my hand, hot blood gushing from the gash, too scared to even scream, and he was right there, standing in front of my vehicle, blocking my exit, spitting, cursing, threatening.

I did the only thing I could do at the time. The only thing that felt safe.

I hit the gas.

His body hit the hood of my car and then bounced off onto the pavement. He was still.

I waited for movement. The rise of his chest.

Nothing.

But maybe knowing just how selfish he was, just how bad of a man he was—maybe this was better anyway. Better than sending him home to an angry wife who'd probably get talked into forgiving him. Maybe they'd attend a couple sessions of therapy, she'd deem him fixed, and they'd go back to their sham of a marriage. Maybe this was the best-case scenario. Men like him, selfish ones, they suck and suck the autonomy from women, their voices from their throats. But I fixed it. I made it better.

And it wasn't on purpose.

"If you hadn't done what you did that night, he'd still be alive," Margo says, bringing me back to the moment.

"Still hitting on women at bars with a wife at home," I say.

"He has kids, Ren."

I turn my back to her. "He attacked me."

Margo is quiet for a long time, and I can almost feel it, the brush of her finger down my spine. Her laugh tickles the short hairs at the back of my neck. "Just like you wanted."

————

I lie in bed the whole day, constantly refreshing my phone for updates about Bryson. It's after 7:00 p.m. when I finally get one. An article published only minutes ago.

### Suspect in Custody for Teacher's Death

*Fallon Drexler, 32, has been arrested for the murder of Bryson Lewis. Drexler is the brother of Tina Drexler, the Rosemary Academy teen whose body was recovered from Locklear Road. Detectives took Drexler into custody at approximately 3:00 p.m. this evening where a formal arrest was made. Bryson Lewis was previously accused of misconduct with more than one minor and was serving a suspension from the school at the time of his death.*

My phone vibrates in my hand, and I answer, pressing it to my ear without looking. "Hello?"

"It's Michaela."

This has me sitting up in bed and swinging my legs over the side. "I've tried reaching you all day."

"Is it real? Is he really dead?" she asks, her voice breathless and low. I can hear other people in the background.

"Yes."

"There's something you need to see. It's so messed up."

"Is everything OK? Are you OK?"

"It's about him. Coach Lewis."

My breath catches in my throat. "What do you mean?"

"It'll be better to show you. Want to meet at the same place again?"

"Yes," I reply. "I can be there in half an hour."

———

There are too many emotions going through me to process. Bryson's death. Fallon's arrest.

Michaela's words.

*There's something you need to see.* I approach the parking lot in front of the park, and I spot Michaela right off. I walk toward her hurriedly, tucking my cardigan tighter around me. I hadn't changed, and judging by Michaela's expression, I should have taken thirty seconds to do so.

She puts her phone away just as I'm approaching. "Hey, that was fast."

"I took a sick day today. I was itching for a reason to get out of the house."

"I'm sorry." Michaela looks tired, but I'm beginning to learn that's a constant state of being for her. "I shouldn't have bothered you."

"Please." I lay a hand on her arm, sitting next to her. "Talk to me. What do you have to show me?"

That's when I notice the item clenched in her palms. A worn pink leather-bound journal. She holds it tightly, staring down at it like she's waiting for it to speak. "It was too much to say over the phone."

"What is this?"

"Alejandra's journal."

My breath comes out shakily. "How did you get this?"

"I go and visit her parents sometimes, Gabby and Israel. They've always been so nice to me, and since Alejandra died, I can tell they like seeing me. I think I'm a connection to their daughter. A reminder of her. Anyway, Gabby told me there was some stuff in Alejandra's room that she wanted to donate. She asked me if I wanted to go up there first. Said I could take whatever of her clothes I wanted." Her voice quivers. "I'd been in that room a million times. I practically lived there. I know that room like the back of my hand, and I couldn't believe it took me this long to think of it."

"Think of what?"

"Our hiding place."

My stomach drops. "What hiding place?"

"There's a loose floorboard right beneath her window. We'd pried it up and it lifts just enough to stick your hand in. It's where Jondra kept anything that she wanted to be private."

"Like what?"

She shifts on the bench uncomfortably.

"I'm not interested in lecturing you on whatever teenage contraband you girls were hiding." I nudge her with my shoulder. "I was young once too."

"We'd keep weed in there. Alejandra was pretty serious about volleyball and never smoked during the season. But in the offseason... Neither one of us drank, so it seemed like a safer alternative. Plus it was easy to hide, and we'd climb out her window and smoke it on her roof while her parents were asleep. I guess I wasn't thinking about it because it was volleyball season, and it had been a while since me or Jondra had smoked."

"But you checked it? While you were at her parents' house. That's where you found the journal?"

She nods slowly. "I wasn't going to read it, but a part of me was hoping there'd be some kind of note. A reason that would explain everything." She looks at me, her lips curling up in anger. "But there was something else. Here. Start on this page."

She hands it to me, and there on a park bench, I begin to read.

# 37

*August 3*

*Butterflies. They've taken over. I finally know what it means to have a real crush. This is nothing like how I felt about any guy ever. Even Ahmed. He never made me feel this giddy. Anytime this guy looks at me, it's like my heart gets in an elevator.*

*But apparently every other girl on the team thinks so too. Our new coach is FIRE. Like 10/10 HOT. Bryson Lewis. Alejandra Lewis!!! Has a nice RING to it doesn't it?*

*I don't know where he came from, but I don't ever want him to leave. Not in a weird way, he's just nice to look at. Better than Coach Jenny at least. I love Jen-Jen, don't get me wrong. But it's nice to have him there. It makes me want to play harder and better. There's a good chance I could be captain next year!*

———

"Michaela?"

"Just keep going."

I skip to the next entry.

———

*August 15*

*I don't know how any of us concentrated on practice today with him around. Kourtney was SO obvious with flirting with him, and I think it was making him uncomfortable. I made a comment to her under my breath how sus she was being, and I think Coach Lewis heard me. He chuckled loudly and covered it with a cough. When my cheeks finally stopped burning and I had the courage to look at him, he winked at me.*

*My heart is still recovering!*

*August 29*

*So. Something strange happened today. Like strange good, I think? After practice the girls all started running to their cars. Mine's still in the shop (THANKS, MOM). I guess it was my fault I ran over that curb, but she could at least pretend helping me get the car back is a priority. I think she likes it when I don't have a ride and need to rely on her.*

*Anyway, I've been taking the bus to school and catching a ride home from practice with Con or Mich. I forgot Michaela had a dentist appointment and skipped out early. I meant to* text Connie and tell her I needed to ride with her, but I forgot. By the time I got outside, she was gone. Knowing how pissed Mom would be if I called her last minute, I decided to just walk. It isn't like I live far, and Michaela and I did it all the time our freshmen year.

But it was raining.

Okay, this is where it gets good. Coach Lewis (no cap!) pulls up beside me. He offers me a ride. Yadda, yadda. Whatever. But get this, while we're driving, we're like talking about music and stuff, and we have SO much in common. (Also his car smells insanely good.)

When he got to my house, we sat and talked for at least FIVE MORE MINUTES before I went inside. He's just so cool, ya know? I know all the girls think he's hot (he is), but I'm beginning to see there is soooooooo much more to him.

I've had butterflies all night!!! Am I crazy or am I crazy? Wait, don't answer that.

———

September 10

I swear this is going to sound ridiculous! But I cannot stop thinking about him. Bryson Lewis. During practice, I'm constantly screwing up because I can't keep my eyes off him. This is bad, this is so bad. I've never felt this way before. I've never wanted anyone like this. And he's thirteen years older than me. THIRTEEN. Mama would freak out. Everyone would.

What's wrong with me?

Why can't I get over him?

*I think it's because there's a part of me that thinks he feels the same. Okay, hear me out! There's this look in his eye when he sees me. He's always Snapping me back, and I know he Snaps everybody and the Snaps are completely innocent, but there's something special about ours.*

*I don't know.*

*I can just feel it.*

*What do I do with this?*

September 12

*It's getting to be too much.*

*These feelings.*

*It hurts so bad.*

*Yesterday he laughed so hard at something Coach Jenny said and tugged her ponytail. It almost broke my heart. It made me question our whole relationship. Which is stupid. What relationship?*

*It's just...I thought he might like me too. Sometimes I catch him looking at me. He always laughs at my jokes more than anyone else's.*

*But then sometimes it's like I don't exist to him.*

*It's driving me crazy.*

*Why can't I just get over him?*

*Tina thinks I'm being ridiculous, but she doesn't get it. No one understands how real these feelings are.*

———

October 11

*Haven't written in a while. Figured I would on the bus ride. We're on our way to Atlanta for the freaking championship!! Mama and Papa are going to meet us up here for the final tournament in a few days with Abuela! Coach Lewis and Coach Jenny have been SO serious lately. It's been weird. But yesterday, after practice, Coach Lewis caught me after everyone else had left the gym and told me he was really looking forward to the trip. Just when I thought it was all one-sided, he said that.*

*These feelings have been building between us for so long, and in that moment, I just felt this, like, fire.*

*It sucks because I've never felt like that from a boy before, and every day when I'm sitting in class next to the obnoxious assholes I go to school with, I just keep going back to Coach Lewis. How mature he is. And funny. And sweet. And so, so, so hot! I really hope we get some alone time together on this trip. I really want to talk to him.*

*I want to tell him how I feel.*

*I want to finally hear him say that he feels the same way.*

———

The next entry is jarring. The handwriting. The saturation of the ink on the page. There is no date. No warning. Alejandra jumps right in. There are drops on the page smearing the ink that have dried. Like she was crying as she wrote.

———

*I HATE HIM.*

*I HATE HIM.*

*I HATE HIM.*

*I thought he felt the same. I thought he'd want us. I came to his room… God, I can't even write this. I waited for Coach in his room just like we talked about. She said I needed to show him I was an adult. I thought tonight would be the perfect night to do it. The day went so well. We won our first tournament. Everyone was so happy! We went to this diner and literally took up every booth. Coach Lewis sat next to me, and his thigh kept touching mine all through the meal. I had all the signs! It doesn't help that earlier he'd left something in his room (an equipment bag). He sent me and Mich upstairs to get it. I still had his key. He didn't ask for it back, and it burned a hole in my pocket the whole day. I thought for sure it was all on purpose.*

*So. I followed the plan. I took my clothes off and lay on his bed and could hardly think straight I was so excited to see him. But I was nervous too. I've never done this before. I've never put myself out there like this. He came into the room (I'd left the door slightly open), and he called out my name. Like he knew it was me waiting, and he'd felt me somehow. I know I look good. I've had so many boys tell me. I've always been confident, but with him it was different. The look on his face when he saw me is something I'll never forget. My heart was beating out of my chest, and he was just looking at me.*

*Then he asked what I was doing. But he didn't move or tell me to leave. I told him the truth. I told him I wanted him, and I knew he wanted me too. He locked the door, and he walked over to me. It's like the whole world faded away. It was just us. He seemed just as nervous as me, and he told me we can't do this. It's not right. But he still didn't move away. So I sat up and grabbed his hand. I put it over my heart. I told him it was okay. I wouldn't tell anyone.*

*Then he kissed me.*

*For a second everything felt perfect.*

*It wasn't exactly how I pictured it. He was rougher than I imagined he'd be. Especially his hands as they squeezed and tugged at my skin. But in the moment, I didn't even care. It just showed he wanted me as much as I wanted him.*

*But then it started moving fast. Faster than I think I wanted. I pulled away and asked him to stop. He kept kissing me. My neck and shoulders. It's what I came here for, I know that, but suddenly it felt like too much. I yelled at him to stop.*

*Then he just froze.*

*I can't explain it. One second, we're fused together and the next he's against the wall looking more angry than I've ever seen him. I tried to explain that I thought I was ready to keep going, but I'm nervous. I asked him if we could just talk and hang out.*

*He was quiet for so long I thought he'd never speak. Then he just told me to get dressed and get out. He said I shouldn't have been in the room. I should never have come here. He told me it was a mistake, and it could never happen again. I tried to plead with him, tell him how perfect we were together. But he wouldn't hear it. He just wanted me to leave.*

*Then I got so angry. I just wanted to hurt him. I told him that I would tell. I would tell everyone what just happened and how he touched me. I didn't mean it of course. I would never do that to him. I love him, and I was still hoping he would change his mind. But as soon as I said it, it's like something changed in him again.*

*He grabbed me by my arms hard and dragged me to the door. I told him to let go. It was hurting me. His voice was quiet, but I swear I've never heard anyone sound more mean. He told me if I told anyone about this, he would deny it. He would never admit to it. And he would make sure everyone in the school knew what a liar I was and that I was just a silly little girl. He told me to leave and to never come back or speak of this again.*

*So I listened.*

*I couldn't see past my tears as I ran for my hotel room.*

*I think my shirt was on backward and my shoes were on the wrong feet, and I was crying too hard to see it or care. I just had to get away from him.*

*I am so stupid.*

*I shouldn't have listened to her.*

*I just want to die.*

———

The writing ends as abruptly as it started, and an awareness settles on me. I read the page once more, trying to make sense of it. Everything about her stream of consciousness reminds me of my own at her age.

And who is she talking about in this entry? *She*? Tina?

"Would she lie?" I ask Michaela. "Would she have any reason to write an entry that's not true?"

"Not in her journal. I don't think so at least." Michaela's nose scrunches in confusion. "Just keep reading. There's one more."

I eagerly turn the page.

The last entry.

Dated the day Alejandra died.

———

*October 15*

*I think I messed up again.*

*It wasn't my idea, and I regretted it as soon as I woke up, but now—the guilt is eating me alive. This was huge. This was really, really bad.*

*What would he say if he knew what I did after leaving his room?*

*I'm not trying to make an excuse, but I was just so sad and angry. It wasn't fair. None of this was fair. He led me on. He made me think he actually cared about me when he clearly didn't. He kissed me and turned on me and told me he would tell everyone I was a liar.*

*I thought it was the right thing to do.*

*I feel so guilty now though, and I've tried to make it right. I told her I wanted to delete it. Told her to get rid of it, and that I want to pretend nothing about that night ever happened. She wouldn't listen. She just got angry, and I said some things I shouldn't have.*

*Is it me? Am I the problem?*

*Everything feels so ruined.*

*I feel like I'm bursting. Like I can't keep these things*

*inside any longer. I want to tell my mom everything. I want to tell someone who will understand and believe me.*

*Okay. MAYDAY MAYDAY!*

*I know I'm writing TWICE IN ONE DAY but Coach Lewis literally just texted me and asked me to meet him.*

*What?????*

*What could it be about? Does he know something? Is it about what I did? Is he giving me a courtesy call before he tells my parents or Coach Jenny?*

*Or has he thought about me?*

*Did he change his mind about that night? About us?*

*I hate myself for having hope, but I can't help but want him to be sorry. I keep picturing us meeting again. Him telling me he does love me. I would forgive him. Of course I would! He was in shock. He was surprised. He just needed time.*

*Maybe it's the fact I'm a student or I'm so young. I don't know. But I do have clarity now. I'm going to meet him. I want to be honest with him about everything. I won't hold anything over my head. It's time I make things right. Will update later. WISH ME LUCK!!!*

# 38

There are no more entries. I flip to the last page just to be sure then go back to check the date.

"This last entry. This was the day she died."

"Yes."

I look at Michaela. "She was going to meet him."

Michaela nods.

"She kissed Bryson." The words slip out slowly, burning my mouth on the way out. "And she did something else that night that she regretted."

"I think it was the photo." Michaela looks at her lap and then back to me, her jaw tightening. "I think she took that picture somehow without him knowing. Think about it. He looked like he was asleep when the picture was taken. He told her people would think she was a liar. Maybe she felt like she needed proof."

"What about the other person she mentioned? Someone who helped her."

The tears spill over Michaela's eyes now. "I don't know. I don't know. She had so many secrets, Ren. She had so many secrets, and I had no idea."

"Have you shown this to her mother?" I ask gently, placing a hand over Michaela's.

"No, I just took it. I didn't know what to do. That's why I called you," Michaela says. "She was going to meet him the day she died. We know that now. But does it change anything? He's dead now, and so is she. I don't want people to read this. I don't want people to think badly of her." Michaela is full-on crying now. She can barely get the words out.

I place a hand over her trembling shoulder. "I understand why you feel that way. You know firsthand how messed up other people can be, how mean. But this is her truth, Michaela." *When girls die, when they can't speak their truths anymore, all we have left are their whispers.* I hold up the journal, feel the smoothness of it in my hands. "This is all we have left. It's time people hear her."

I pass the journal back. "Alejandra's mom needs to see this. And the police." Michaela holds it to her chest tightly and nods, silent tears gliding down her cheeks.

"Do you think he killed her?" Michaela's voice is shaking. "Is that what happened to her? To Tina?"

I take a breath. Think about those girls. About Bryson. He met her in the woods that day. He's the link between all of them. He always has been. "Yeah, I think so."

But we still don't know how. We still don't know why. What happened in those woods? And why did Tina have to die too?

A million thoughts race through my mind, and I can't put a single one together. "You told me that this is where her body was found."

"Through the woods."

"Can you show me where?"

Michaela's body jolts like I'd touched her with live wire. "No. No, I'm not going in there. I can tell you though. I can tell you how to get to the spot."

And she does.

I told Michaela to take that journal straight back to Alejandra's mother and tell her everything. Then I followed her specific instructions to the creek where Alejandra was found. It wasn't hard getting here. You veer easily off a marked trail, but by then you can hear the water running.

Staring at the trickling water, I try to picture what in the hell happened out here. What her entries meant. Why she'd be out here at all. Is this where Bryson wanted to meet her? Why all the way out here?

So many scenarios flash through my head. So many questions.

What did Alejandra and Tina do that night? Did Bryson find out and get mad? Did he just want to shut them up?

"You're too close," Margo says. She's been silent through my whole conversation with Michaela, and I'm almost surprised she's speaking now.

"Too close to what?" I turn to look at her. She's holding an oversized jean jacket tight around her and looking nervous.

"To this girl. To Michaela. To Olivia. You're wrapped up in this."

"Someone has to be." I step forward, closer to the water, still unsure of what I'm looking for. It's like I think Alejandra will have left her shadow here. A bread crumb trail to what happened. Even after all this time.

"They're not me, Ren."

"You think I don't know that?" I swirl around to face her. "You think I don't spend every single day knowing that you're dead? That you're gone forever?"

"Then why are you doing this? Why are you getting so obsessed with these girls?"

"If I don't, who will? And if someone had done this with you, maybe things would be different."

"Me?" Margo scoffs and rolls her eyes. "You're the one who got on that boat with me. You're the one who was so angry you wanted me to die."

My chest caves in at the words I don't allow myself to think. "No."

"You remember that moment, don't you?" She takes a step closer. Then another. "You remember the way you looked at me in disgust. The hatred you felt when I reached for you. The moment my toe brushed that water. The surprise in my eyes as I felt the fingers of that lake wrap around my ankle."

"Of course." I'm hoarse now. Barely squeezing out the words. "Of course, I remember."

"Then you remember that very first second. That one quick second when the lake swallowed me whole, and you thought I was getting what I deserved."

"No." I shake my head, stumble back. My heel sinks into muddy waters. I barely notice as the cold envelops my foot. The memory is there, pulling, kneading at my brain. The rush of wind against my face. The anger packed into my body like blood. How stupid I was. He never wanted me. It was her. It's always been her. Then there's Henry's voice. Margo's movement. There and gone. A magic trick. "Not that. Not death. I thought you were just falling in. Just getting wet. Not dying."

"You let me fall."

"It happened so quickly. I couldn't do anything. And I looked for you. I looked for you for so long."

"You're still looking. You're looking everywhere except the bottom of that lake." Margo smiles sadly. "Those girls aren't me, Ren."

———

I don't know how long I'm out there. But I can feel the exact moment Margo leaves me alone with my guilt. She's right, these girls aren't her. I'll never get a do-over with my sister. But I can do everything in my power to make up for it. I can do things differently now. I need to.

But for who?

Alejandra and Tina are gone.

Just like that night on the lake, there is a heady feeling of abandonment. Eventually it starts getting dark, and I know I have to make my way back. It was simple enough getting here, but things change in the dark. They get twisted. Become hard to differentiate. My life has been dark since the night Margo died, and it finally feels like the darkness is starting to win.

Bryson is dead, and with him his secrets.

I trace my steps out of the forest, and it's like exiting one world and entering another. The silence of the trees, the trickle of the creek, make way to civilization, streetlights, and cars. People cruising by with their windows down. Oblivious to what's happened in these woods.

In a neighboring house, a woman leans on the posts of her porch on the phone while a small child plays in a driveway. In another home every light seems to be on with several cars lining the street. A party. Someone is having a party today. I turn in a circle. There's a dark house and otherwise empty porch. I stop. Listen. The twinkling of wind chimes. It all seems so normal.

Yet something is tugging at my brain.

How could a girl have died in the woods only a few miles away from this picture-perfect scenario?

On the way back to my car, something stops me. I can't explain it. The prickle of feeling that shoots down my body like someone stuck a needle into a nerve. My gaze reverts back to the houses. The mother ushering her child inside now. A couple leaving from the second house, giggling under their breaths. But the third house is still unchanged. Quiet and dark except for those wind chimes. A flash of purple in an otherwise colorless night.

"It's peaceful," Margo says, "looking at them. The juxtaposition of those bustling houses and that quiet one. Just because it's quiet doesn't mean it's not a threat. It could be brimming with secrets. Just like you, Ren."

I think of secrets. How they take root in us and grow, curving around our bodies, blocking us—the real us—from the view of others. Until, to those who see us, we become someone else entirely. That's what happened to Margo. Alejandra. Tina. Their secrets plunged into them, intertwining with their very chemical makeup. Maybe they didn't know to scream until it was too late.

If Bryson killed Alejandra and Tina, then what else was he capable of before he died?

The thought hits me like a kick in the stomach.

Olivia.

How long has it been since I spoke to her? Did she go to school today? Is she OK?

The only thing I do know is from the moment she spoke her truth about Bryson, she hasn't been safe.

The need to see her, to get eyes on her, is overwhelming.

She's the last girl that needs to be saved from her secrets. My last chance. And something tells me I'm running out of time.

# 39

Storm clouds that are heavy with rain not yet fallen gather in the sky, and there's an electricity in the air. A tangible difference in the atmosphere.

My spine is straight and my foot's too heavy on the gas as I make the drive home. I try calling Olivia three times. No answer. I'm unfamiliar with these curves, with this motion. It makes me take the turns too wide or too short, nearly running off the road twice. But I keep going, keep plowing forward until I make it home. I barely shift my car to park before I'm out, running inside, straight for my laptop.

The seconds it takes to boot up feel like hours. I log into INOW and search Olivia's name. Pull up her address and type it into the GPS of my phone. Then I'm back on the road, hands clenched as hard as my teeth.

I eventually turn down a long bumpy dirt road, peppered with mobile homes, some abandoned, some clearly lived in. I pass old vehicles with political stickers and ratty, dirty Confederate flags.

Then, nothing but trees for a couple miles until I get there.

Olivia's house is small and sits by itself on a hill on the edge of Benton. Surrounded by farmland, she has no immediate neighbors. Charcoal gray and covered in large windows and a wraparound porch, it looks newly built.

There are no cars in the driveway. All the lights are off.

No one is home.

What had Olivia said the last time I saw her? She doesn't like to be alone.

Hopping on the interstate, my foot is lead on the gas as I head toward the neighboring town where I know she works. The restaurant across from the bar where she saved me, the night we both told each other our secrets.

The night we both held some back.

There's only one restaurant. The diner across from the bar. This has to be where she works. I don't immediately see her car in the parking lot, but I park and hop out anyway. Pushing through the double doors, I'm assaulted by the smell of fried eggs and syrup. My feet instantly stick to the greasy tiled floor. The place is busy, and no one gives me a second look as I scan behind the counter and the tables.

She's not here.

"Need help?" The voice belongs to an older woman with a deep voice and long gray hair pinned back with a clip. She's looking at me, menu in hand, with a bored expression on her face. "You can just sit anywhere."

"Actually," I say. "I'm looking for someone. A waitress. Olivia Green. Is she on the schedule tonight?"

The woman's brows come down in confusion. "Who?"

"Olivia Green. Young. Blond."

"I don't know, honey." The woman glances over her shoulder and sighs before looking back at me. "You eating or what?"

"I just need to talk to my friend."

"Look, I've got no clue who you're talking about. Far as I know, no one here works here with that name or description."

"Oh." I back up, a weird feeling fluttering inside me. "Maybe she just works a different shift."

The woman snorts. "Baby, I work all the shifts. Listen I've gotta get this man his coffee. If you want to sit, go for it." She saunters away from me, waving at a man on her way to the counter to grab a pot of thick-looking coffee.

The noises around me fade in and out.

She must be mistaken. Or maybe I misheard Olivia. Maybe she works at one of the other places on the strip? The bank is closed, but I check the gym next. No one there knows Olivia either.

I walk back to my car in silence, sit down, and pull out my phone, trying Olivia's number again. It goes straight to voicemail, and I can physically feel my blood pressure rise. The fear in my body gets colder and colder.

Maybe I could look up some addresses of other students? Maybe she's staying with someone else? I just need to get back on my laptop. I'll find her. I have to find her. I ease back onto the road, trying to fight the painful thoughts. Trying to battle the even more agonizing silence.

What am I missing?

The tugging on my brain persists.

Within twenty minutes, I'm back in Benton. By now it's full-on pouring rain—a windshield-wipers-don't-work kind of rain. Somewhere in the distance I hear the first grumbles of thunder.

The road is empty as I roll to a stop at the only traffic light in town and bite back a groan; of course it's red. Of course. Just ahead, the high school sits, abandoned and drenched in darkness, drenched in the torrential downpour. It looks frightening. Ominous. There must be no after-school activities. No sports. They probably cleared the place out because of the storm.

I'm scanning the student lot and the side of the building when I see a glint of silver. A truck. The back of it peeking from around the corner of the gym like they'd parked as close as possible. Like they didn't want to be seen. I blink, trying to grasp just what I'm looking at.

Billy's truck.

What's he doing at the building? Maybe there was some kind of leak and they called him in for maintenance? Maybe he forgot something?

The light turns green, and I tap the gas, but then I see something else. Something that makes my breath stall and blood run cold. Just ahead, beneath the cover of a tree and nearly out of sight is Olivia's car.

# 40

I make a sudden turn, and Margo braces herself on the dash. "You still think she needs you to protect her?"

The car skids over the rain-soaked pavement, screeching as I throw it into park. A shot of lightning bursts in the sky.

Olivia.

I need to find her.

I ignore Margo and step into the downpour. It's hard to think in the cold night, victim to the icy rain and wind. The first door I try is locked. I walk around to the gym and nearly groan in relief when it opens the first try. I step inside, feeling a violent shiver rack through me as water drips off, forming a puddle around my feet. I try to wipe my shoes as best I can and then creep forward into the hallway. There are no lights on. No noise.

"Isn't it true that nothing goes together quite like silence and darkness?" Margo whispers from somewhere behind me.

I don't know what leads me to the stairs, but it's like my body is operating entirely on its own, until I'm at the end of the hallway, staring at a tiny ray of light at the end. There's something hard and heavy lodged in my throat. A sick feeling in my gut. For a split second I think the light is coming from my classroom before I realize it's coming from Bryson's.

I move swiftly and quietly on the balls of my feet as to not make a sound. The door is closed snugly, and there is no window. I press my ear against the wood. Nothing.

Carefully, I inch it open.

The room is empty.

I walk inside, glancing around, and my whole body tightens and sways when I see it.

The smear of red on the ground. I walk slowly forward and kneel. Touch my finger to the red splotch.

Wet.

I'm in a panic now as my gaze travels sideways. Only one word on my mind as I look toward Bryson's desk.

*Olivia.*

I see the shoes first, connected to a body I recognize. I fight the urge to be sick as I lurch forward, kneeling at his side. Billy's breathing is raspy, his eyes nearly unseeing as blood pours from his chest. There's something thin and silver still sticking out of his chest. A letter opener.

"Dammit," I say, falling down beside him. I don't know how long he's been bleeding like this, but even if it's only been a few minutes, it's been too long. Using my body weight, I lean over him, putting pressure on the gaping wound.

He watches me weakly.

"It's OK," I murmur. "It's going to be OK." An ambulance.

I need to call 911. My hands are slick with his blood as I pat my pockets, try to pull my phone out but can't really get a firm grasp on it.

Billy makes a noise, and I look to him. See his hand at his side clenched around something. A cell phone. The screen is lit, and there's a picture on the screen that doesn't make sense.

A picture that makes my brain short circuit.

Olivia and Alejandra with their arms thrown around one another.

"It was an accident," Olivia says from behind me.

# 41

The first thing I should feel when I see her, clearly alive and well, is relief. But there's something wrong here. "I'm calling the police," I say to her. "He needs an ambulance." I rip my gaze from her and wipe my hands on my shirt as best I can. Try to clean my thumb enough to unlock my phone.

The screen is stained red, and nothing is working.

Billy coughs and chokes up blood. I try to tap emergency call—once, twice, three times—. But my fingers are too wet.

"I wouldn't do that," Olivia says quickly. "Please, Ren. He's just going to hurt me again."

I look up. First at Billy. His eyes are closed, and his breathing is shallow. Then Olivia. "What do you mean? He's going to die, Olivia."

"I stabbed him." Her voice breaks. "Oh, God. It's my fault. All of it is my fault. He threatened me first. I did what I had to do. I don't know, Ren. It all went so fast." Olivia is crying now, but there's something about her words that ring oddly.

"We have to call the police. They'll sort everything."

"No." Olivia glances to me, her face going blank. "No, I don't think that's a good idea."

"You won't get in trouble if it was self-defense." It feels like fingers are curling painfully into my intestines, beckoning me closer to witness something I don't want to.

"But I don't want to call the police. I don't want him to be saved." She gets closer until she's standing right over me.

"We can't just leave him here. Right now, this is self-defense. It isn't your fault. But if we let him die, there's no going back from that."

She snatches the phone from my hand. I'm stunned for only a second before I react. I grab Billy's cell phone, knowing we only have minutes to spare before he dies.

"Wait, Ren."

I click out of his photos to the home screen, searching for the keypad, and abruptly stop. I pull my eyes from the home screen on Billy's phone to look at Olivia. It's like we're both suspended somewhere else. In another realm. Somewhere where time doesn't exist. Oxygen doesn't exist.

Reason doesn't exist.

"Why are you his home screen?" Not just Olivia. Billy, Olivia, Olivia's mother, and, presumably, Olivia's stepfather, along with another girl of about five. "This is a family photo."

"Billy is my stepbrother." Olivia looks down at him and covers her mouth. "This is bad. It's so bad. Ren, you have to believe me."

"Your stepbrother." I test the words out. I might as well be saying a kids nursery rhyme or a tongue twister the words are so nonsensical. "Like Robbie?"

She nods. "Yes. He's Robbie's brother."

The final tectonic plate shifts from beneath my feet. And I remember a few conversations. Him mentioning a sister. Her talking about two brothers. One who hurt her and one who protected her.

"Why did he have a picture of you and Alejandra pulled up on his phone?" Olivia had said he was trying to hurt her when she stabbed him. How would he do that with a phone in his hand?

And why that photo?

Suddenly Olivia jerks his phone out of my hand and moves several steps away. "Just listen for a minute. Just listen to me."

"We have to call him an ambulance." The words die on my lips. There's no life in them. I get to my feet, bracing myself on Bryson's desk when the room feels wobbly. "Olivia, he will *die*. Look at him."

"You don't believe me."

"Who would believe you right now? You're acting suspicious as hell. Let's call the police, and then we can talk. I promise I'll hear you out."

"You were supposed to be my friend, Ren. You and Poppi are all I have. You *know* that."

Another puzzle shifts into place. There's almost a whole picture. "You told me something once. About wind chimes. Purple butterflies on your grandmother's front porch," I say numbly, remembering the sound outside those woods. The slash of purple against an otherwise dark night. "That's your grandmother's house, isn't it? At the park between Benton and Rosemary Academy high school. The yellow house directly in front of the woods. That's where you met Alejandra."

"I don't know what you're talking about."

"The picture on Billy's phone. You and Alejandra." Margo is at my side, her hand on my shoulder. A hand I can't feel. Warmth I can only imagine. I want to lean into her touch, to disappear into her. To get far away from here. "It's you, not Bryson. You're the piece that connects everything."

"Easy, Ren," Margo whispers. "I need you to make it out of here. You have to make it out of here."

"Was any of it true?" The words fall off my tongue on a single breath, like I can't muster the energy to say or explain more. "Bryson? Robbie? Any of it?"

Olivia's eyes widen just slightly, her mouth parted on a breath. Then all at once her expression changes. Her tears dry. Her face relaxes into something I don't know, someone I don't recognize. "Everyone hates me. You don't know what that's like."

All evidence of the girl I've come to know is gone, and I squint at her. Try to find Olivia in her face. But she's not there.

"What happened, Olivia? How did we get here?"

She stops, bites the inside of her cheek and glances to the door behind me before sighing. "He needed to be punished. He led her on. Broke her heart. Threatened her. The dude got what was coming."

"You were the friend Alejandra mentioned in her journal. You came up with a plan to punish Bryson. How did you do it?"

"I think you already know." There's amusement in her eyes now. "We took that photo. Though I guess it wouldn't have been a big deal, if I didn't send it to everyone and ruin his life. I don't even think he knew about the photo before that. We had to drug him that night. Didn't take much. My mom always keeps sleeping pills in the house. I always keep a few of her favorite prescriptions with me. You never know when you might need them."

"What about Billy? Why would you hurt him? You said he protected you."

"That's the problem. He protected me. Him and Fallon protected me a little too much."

My breath catches. "You mean from Bryson? You think they—"

"I didn't ask them to do it. I certainly never thought they would attack him. But they did. Once Alejandra's shoes were found in the school, Fallon just lost it. He assumed Bryson hid them there when the police started looking into him. That's why Billy was driving around looking for me. He was worried about me. I guess like you were. He found me here." She holds up an orange key ring and drops it on a lab table. "Swiped this from my brother. I came here to make some TikToks in Bryson's class-room. No one believes me. They need to see me in here. I need to make them believe that we had a relationship. So I wanted footage of me in here. That's all I was doing. But Billy found me. He started asking all these ridiculous questions. He knows I'm always at Poppi's. He also knows where Jondra was found. He had that stupid picture on his phone. It's the only one that exists of Jondra and I together. I'm not sure where he even got it. He just wouldn't give up. Eventually I had to just tell him the truth. I thought he'd understand. He's supposed to know me. But he just looked at me like I was a monster." Her eyes flit to him and back again, and I swear there's pain in them. Regret. "I couldn't let him leave."

"What truth did you tell him?"

"The real one." She takes a breath. "I didn't mean to kill them."

# 42

It was weird, the day I met Alejandra. She was running around the neighborhood. I'd seen her before. Usually, I just watch, and she doesn't notice me, but one day she did. She'd wave. Then I started walking to the end of the driveway when I knew she'd be coming by. Not in a creepy way. Usually, I'd check the mail for Poppi. Whatever she needed. But then Alejandra started talking. It was just a greeting the first couple times until one day she told me she thought my bumper sticker was funny. She asked where I got it, and then we were talking. The next time she came by, I had a sticker for her. She was so excited, she gave me a hug."

"The bumper sticker," I whisper. A conversation with Michaela plays back in my mind. "It wasn't Tina that picked her up on the fourteenth. It was you."

"I followed the bus after leaving the hotel."

"She was your friend."

"I thought so." A dark expression crosses her face. "Then one day she ran by with Michaela. I was at the end of my driveway waiting on her, but she jogged right past me with barely a wave. And I thought that was it. She was done with me just like everyone else, but she came back that night to smoke—Billy is, like, super into weed. He always made sure we had some if we wanted it." There it is on her face again. Remorse. Gone as quickly as it appeared. "Those nights in Poppi's backyard she acted like nothing was wrong, and I felt like I overreacted and never said anything."

There's a crack of thunder from outside that almost drowns out Billy's shallow breaths. How much time does he have now? I inch closer to Olivia. "So what happened next, Olivia? What else is there?"

"I don't know if I should tell you."

"Do you have a better plan? You're clenching that pencil behind your back pretty hard."

She breathes out a chuckle and drops her hand to her side holding the newly sharpened pencil. "You're observant."

"Are you going to stab me too?"

"Of course not." She twirls the pencil around her fingers. "Believe it or not, I liked Alejandra. She was cool. Popular. I could tell without even being at her school. That's weird, isn't it?" Olivia looks at me with vulnerability again. "It's weird that I latched onto that. I didn't know her well. Not really. But I lived for those moments in my driveway or backyard, just talking to her. But then she changed."

"What do you mean?"

"One night she wasn't alone. She jogged past my house with another friend. She never invited or introduced me. She pretended like she didn't see me at all. Of course I blamed myself. My own mother was embarrassed of me. Of course Jondra would be. I knew I needed something more to offer her. Something more than weed to keep her attention. Then I saw Coach Lewis." Her eyes spark with something as the room glows with a strike of lightning.

I step around the table, keeping my back to the door and my eyes on her. "You met Bryson Lewis?"

"Alejandra was outside with me. She'd always come back for the weed hookup, but we weren't smoking. My brother couldn't get us anything that night. She was clearly bummed. I was talking to her, but she was just distracted, I guess. I could tell she wanted to leave. I'd seen Mr. Lewis a couple of times. Usually on the weekends and early in the morning. He'd loop around the neighborhood and take the trails in the woods. He came by that night, and Alejandra noticed him instantly. She stood up and waved, walked over to him. They talked for a minute, but I just hung back. It was so dark. I don't think he even saw me at all. And when she came back…" There's a far-off look on her face. "She was so happy. She'd mentioned him before as her coach, but I could tell she liked him. That she thought he was hot or whatever. So I told her something that I thought she'd want to hear. I told her I'd help her get with him. I told her I had an older boyfriend. I know how it worked. Know how to keep secrets. I convinced her she could trust me, but she shouldn't tell any of her other friends what we were going to do because we could get in trouble, and so could her coach."

Unease coils tight in my abdomen like a rattlesnake threatening to strike. I can't speak. My mouth is too dry, and I'm too afraid of what Olivia might say. I'd die if she stopped talking, but it feels like with each word she says, I'm dying anyway.

"What happened that night after she left his room?" I ask.

"I convinced her to come to my room. We talked. I eventually calmed her down. Then I told her I had an idea for revenge."

"The picture."

"It wasn't difficult to drug him. Just snuck into his room when he wasn't there. He stormed out after Jondra did. She still had the key, so we knocked, and he didn't answer. We figured he was at the bar blowing off steam. We went inside and crushed sleeping pills into the water by his bed. Then we just waited."

"How did you know he would drink it?"

"Something he told Alejandra and the rest of the team. He drinks a certain amount of water before bed every night."

"If a man did this to a woman, he'd go to prison."

"If she could prove it." She laughs. "Men can't be victims. Not really. Not when they're so innately hardwired to be predators."

"You took the pictures, and then what? What was the plan?"

"We wanted to have them. To hold them over his head in case he ever denied what happened between them."

"You were trying to blackmail him?"

Olivia shrugs. "It was just something to get back at him and leverage in case he ever tried to call Jondra a liar. But Alejandra regretted it almost immediately. She came to my house the night we got back, and she was an absolute wreck. She blamed me. Can you believe that? She said it was my fault everything was ruined. She wanted everything deleted and to pretend it never happened. Clearly she was majorly disturbed. What I didn't know was that she'd already talked to Tina about it."

"Tina Drexler?"

"Who else?" Olivia hops down from the desk, runs her finger across it. "She was at the tournament that weekend. She was always around. Alejandra was stuck so far up her butt. And that night, the night before Alejandra died, she was just sitting in her car, watching while Jondra just, like, lost it on me. Alejandra wouldn't stop screaming. She called me crazy. Told me everything was my fault. I was the reason she even went into his room. Which isn't true. She wanted it. I just convinced her to have some confidence and take what she wanted. But she blamed me for what happened between them and said she never wanted to see me again. You have to understand, Ren, I tried talking sense into her. I begged her to stay, to let me explain. But then she finally told me the truth. She never liked me, and she didn't want anything else to do with me."

"What did you do?"

"I should make excuses. I should try to list reasons. Explanations." Her expression turns severe. "But there aren't any. I was pissed. I just wanted to talk to her, but she had me blocked on everything. I knew she wouldn't meet me, so the next day I messaged her from an app, told her I was Mr. Lewis. Told her to meet me in the woods in the park by Poppi's."

I can't speak or even gasp. A part of me knew this was the direction she was going. A part of me might have known all along.

"She was pissed when she saw it was me. But I had some weed. Convinced her to come deeper into the woods by the creek to talk about everything. She still refused. I told her if she didn't come then I would send the pictures to everyone, and her precious coach would know what we did. So she followed me."

"Olivia."

"I just wanted to talk to her, Ren. But she wouldn't stop. She wouldn't stop talking, saying these awful things. Threatening me."

"You hurt her?"

"I didn't want to hurt her. I tried to leave her there. I turned to walk away, and when I looked back she was ankle deep in the creek with her back to me. I was afraid, Ren. She wanted to tell people what we did. She was using me the whole time. I just—I just felt this flood of anger and I couldn't help it. I pushed her. It took her by surprise, I guess. I knocked her in the water onto her stomach, and I just—I couldn't stop."

My voice is barely above a whisper. "You drowned her?"

"It wasn't easy either. She was strong. Really strong." The way she says it is like she's in class listing the parts of a cell or elements on the periodic table. She's detached. Emotionless. "But she sucked in a lot of water on that first push. She wasn't expecting it. That worked in my favor. Guess her heart condition helped a little too. Didn't even know about that until the autopsy."

The authorities thought she fell in the water and drowned after her heart flared up. It reminded me of a cramp while swimming, and it seemed like the scariest kind of watery death. One where you desperately fight for survival, but your own body is working against you.

The truth is so much worse.

"You took her shoes, and you're the one who put them in the chiller."

"Guess I shouldn't have done that. But they were just sitting there by the creek. I felt like I had to take them. Then I noticed you poking around the chiller. It was the perfect spot to get rid of them. I knew everyone would think Mr. Lewis was somehow responsible."

There's another burst of lightning and the room goes dark. The power is out. I hold my breath. Wait for it to turn on again.

Surely the school has a generator? But nothing happens. The room stays suffocated in shadows. It takes a second for me to blink and for my eyes to adjust. In those few moments Olivia has edged closer to me. On the ground, Billy is still.

"Why did you tell me this?" I ask.

"Because you're the only one who'd really understand."

"I've never known a monster like you before." The disgust crashing through my body is potent as my blood.

"Sure, you have." Another step closer. Another crack of thunder and lightning. Olivia's white teeth glimmer sharply. "Every time you look in the mirror."

"I'm not like you."

"You don't think?" Olivia's mouth tightens into a line. "You know, I think you're being dramatic anyway. It's not like I'm out there trying to *find* people to kill. Alejandra was a mistake. My mistake. It never should have happened again, but Tina came to me. The summer after her graduation. She was really drunk. Really angry. She told me she knew I hurt Alejandra, and she was going to the cops once she had proof. She was going to tell them what me and Alejandra did to Mr. Lewis, and I couldn't have that. I didn't want to hurt Tina. I tried to appeal to her. I convinced her to get in the car with me, and I don't know if it was her own confidence or the alcohol, but she did. I drove somewhere private and told her everything. I told her about meeting Alejandra. Killing Alejandra. I tried to get her to understand that I had overreacted, and I wasn't a bad person. But she started freaking out. I didn't have a choice. I stabbed her." Olivia makes a face. "It was…gross. A lot worse than what happened to Alejandra. A mess too. It took me all night to clean the car. I ended up dropping her body off near the river and setting the inside of my grandma's car on fire. It used to be my grandfather's and she never drove it. She kept it in storage. That's where it is now. She has no idea."

"What about Bryson? Was that real? Your relationship with him?"

"The day you saw me leave his room crying, those were real tears. Well, real fake tears. When he moved to Benton, I was nervous. I mean, Alejandra was talking about telling the dude everything before I did what I did. I couldn't help but wonder if she had mentioned me. I just wanted to create a moment for us to talk so I could find out if he knew anything. I made up some sob story about a boy hurting my feelings, and Mr. Lewis comforted me. Regardless of what he said to Jondra, he really wasn't that bad. Which, you know, sucks for him, I guess. After we talked, I knew he didn't know anything. I was planning on leaving everything in the past...but then...you happened, Ren."

The world narrows and swerves in and out.

"Me?" I ask, barely scraping the word out.

"The sister of the famous dead girl. If anyone knows what it's like to live in the shadow of others, to be invisible, to feel *real* pain, it was you. And the rumors—I don't even think you know the half of them. As soon as I heard about you, I started researching. I learned everything; at least I thought I did. And it was some kind of cosmic sign, what happened to you and Margo. And when you came to me, concerned for me, that day you saw me crying, you clearly cared. I'd never known that. Poppi is there for me in her own way. But it was different with you. You were paying attention. You *cared*. Do you know what that's like? To live in a house where no one cares about you? Where no one asks if you're OK?"

"No." No, because I had Margo. Even when Margo was dead, and I had no one else, I still had Margo.

"But you cared enough to ask. You thought Mr. Lewis was hurting me. You were sure of it. So I told you exactly what I thought you wanted to hear. I let you help me in the ways that girls like us don't get help."

"You lied."

"You wanted me to." Olivia stops directly in front of me, still fidgeting with the pencil. "That's why you came back, isn't it? You wanted a do-over. That's all it was ever supposed to be. I was going to make something up eventually. Tell you I wanted to put all this behind me. But hopefully I could still stay close to you. But then you asked me about Tina. You connected her to Bryson. You were the first person to ever do that, and when her body was found, I panicked. I knew it was only a matter of time before the police did it too. I needed someone to go down for it."

"That's why you sent the photos? To create suspicion with him."

"If you made the connection to Tina, then I knew the cops would too. I never actually wanted to ruin his life, but I guess if you want to not be arrested you shouldn't do illegal shit. I mean, he did kiss Alejandra, right? He's the one who ended things the way he did. He deserved it, Ren."

"Then you get all the attention as the teen victim and the only survivor of Bryson Lewis. That's why you made that TikTok. You wanted to go viral."

"Imagine the good I would do. Imagine how many girls I could help with my experiences. Plus, he needed to go down anyway. If he'd do it with Jondra, who else would he do it with?

It was only a matter of time." Olivia reaches out, grabs my hand. "Do you understand why I'm telling you now? Why it's important for people to believe me? Why we're so alike?"

I pull my trembling hand away, fighting the urge to vomit. "I'm not like you."

I'm not.

Of course I'm not.

"Billy and Fallon didn't kill Bryson, Ren, and we both know it. They did go to his house and confront him. They did rough him up. But he was alive when they left." Another step closer. I can feel the warmth emanating from her.

She says the words aloud that I haven't even been able to think.

"I saw you that night. I *know*, Ren."

# 43

The gloves fit just right, and I wore them for the drive. These were always my favorite part of the costume. The easiest way I could become someone else. Now they served a different purpose too. I parked in another neighborhood and came in through the backyard. It was better this way. Everyone had doorbell cameras now.

Like last time, the TV is flickering in the living room. His figure is hunched over on the couch. His snores slip out of cracked windows. It's a soundtrack. A movie score playing in the background. Music to me.

Unlike last time, he looks different. A bruised jaw and eye. Cut knuckles. An ice pack fallen on the ground.

Margo is here. She's standing behind the couch watching me severely. "Don't do this."

Doesn't she understand this is for her? This is for all the girls like her? Victims of men who consistently get away with it.

"No." She shakes her head. "Don't make this about me. Don't make this about anyone except yourself."

I grab Bryson's phone. Put it in my pocket.

Bryson stirs. His hand twitching in his pants, his eyes fluttering open. He blinks. Once. Twice. His mouth opens, but before he can speak, I lift the knife. The first cut is so quick he clearly doesn't register it at first.

He looks from me to his wrist. The blood seeping out of the vertical cut.

"You have ten minutes," I tell him, taking a step back to avoid the blood. "You'll feel the rush of adrenaline first."

"What did you do?" He murmurs the words in pure confusion. Maybe he still thinks he's asleep, and this is all a dream.

"You're going to get dizzy soon. Uncomfortable."

He takes his good hand and reaches beside him.

I hold up his phone. "I can't let you have this."

"Ren. No. Please." Each word is a grunt, like it takes every last bit of energy just to get the word out.

"It's for them, you know. The girls you hurt."

He looks confused.

"Alejandra." I say her name slowly, and he flinches.

"It wasn't like that. One time. I didn't hurt her."

"But you did, Bryson," I say. "You did hurt her, and I need to make sure you never hurt another girl again."

I don't say anything as the minutes tick. He leans back on the couch, pleading with his eyes, his breathing shallow.

It only takes seven minutes.

After he succumbs, I place his phone on the coffee table in front of him. It isn't until I'm in my car that I throw up.

# 44

The dark classroom flashes with another bolt of lightning. "See, Ren, me and you, we're not all that different. I took the Uber back to my car, then returned to your house. I was there when you left. I followed you. Watched you, and when it was all over, I protected you."

"What do you mean?"

"The things they found in his house. Stuff connecting him to Tina and Alejandra. I did it for you."

The panic sets in, and with it comes a memory. My mother outside the house that day. Talking about the bug infestation in our home. The bugs no one could see but her. I see them now. They crawl beneath my skin. Little lumps moving just below the surface. I'm ruined.

I made another mistake.

I want to throw up again. To stumble back from this room and pretend none of this happened. That I'm not a part of it.

Margo is at my side now, and I swear I can feel her. "Don't think about it right now. Just get out of here. You have to get out of here."

I hold myself together. Stay standing when gravity beckons me to my knees. "Why did you tell me all of this? Did you just expect it to stay between us?"

"It could," Olivia says. "You're good at keeping secrets."

"You know I can't do that. Not with this." I glance back at Billy. His chest is no longer moving. Oh, God. I can't let another innocent person die. "Look we can talk about this more later. For now, we have to help him. He's your brother, Olivia."

She doesn't look in his direction, but I don't miss the emotion that crosses her face.

The energy in the room shifts. It's an electrical current running between us. Because we both know that there are so many things neither of us are saying. I take a step to the door. Olivia takes a step toward me. Neither of us take our eyes off each other.

"I need to get him help," I say.

Olivia lunges.

She is stronger than she looks. Or maybe it just feels that way as she tackles me into the lab table. Somehow, I arch my back and roll, and she's under me. My hands are around her throat, thighs tightening around her waist. There's a sharp pinch on my hip, and I hiss, releasing my hands reflexively.

The tip of a pencil has gone through my leggings and broken skin. I pull it out, and that gives her enough time to shove me. Olivia is all flailing limbs and biting teeth as we collide. Something cuts my cheek. Something rips. My skin probably.

"I don't want to do this." I grunt. "Please, Olivia. Stop."

Another flash of pain on my cheek. I reach behind me, hands feeling along the countertop. I come in contact with a beaker and smash it against her face.

Olivia stumbles back, and blood dribbles from her forehead. She touches the cut and looks at the bright red blood. "Shit," she says.

"Olivia, it doesn't have to end like this. Please, please stop. I'll help you. You're just a kid. You're a kid. Please, we can get each other help."

She smiles a bloody smile, and she's on me again. This time I'm ready for her. We crash to the ground on a pile of glass.

As we roll, shards pierce my back and sides. Blood smears across tile. Drips from her face onto me. "You started this." She grunts, her fingers pressing deep into my neck.

"Stop, Olivia. Please."

Stars explode behind my eyelids, and it's hard to think past the burning in my lower back. The pressure on my neck.

"But just like with Alejandra, I'm forced to finish—"

I grab a shard and stab it into her side, watching the surprise on her face.

She bites her bottom lip so hard, blood dribbles down her chin. "You stabbed me." She rolls off of me and holds her side.

I roll with her, put another shard to her neck, and squeeze the piece of glass so hard my skin cracks open. Warm blood pours down my wrist. "Don't move, Olivia. That's it. It's over. I don't want to hurt you. I don't want to do this."

She keeps her hands on her side, but her eyes remain on me. "Go ahead," she says. "Kill me."

I press the glass deeper into the sensitive flesh.

"No one will even care. Come on. Do it, Ren," Olivia grits out. Tears fall from the corner of her eyes and slip over her cheeks into her ears. For the first time all night, she finally looks like a kid. A lost, broken kid. One who has done so many terrible things. Like Casey or Bryson, would her silence be better than the silences she creates by living? By taking?

Or will her screams just become whispers no one will hear?

"I'm ready. Just do it."

"No." I shake my head. Push the glass tighter. Finally make up my mind. "I'm going to call the police. They'll deal with you."

She laughs and blood sprays my face. "You think they'll believe you? I'll tell them you killed Billy and Mr. Lewis. Tried to kill me."

"They won't believe you."

"Do you want to risk it?" She tilts her head and spits blood. "Billy's dead, Ren. His chest stopped moving several minutes ago. It's not worth it." A drop of blood leaks from the cut on her neck, but I don't move or release the glass.

She arches her back. "You call the police, and you're calling them on yourself too."

Everything I've ever done, good or bad, it all comes down to this moment. This choice I must make.

Margo is beside me now, kneeling, blond hair spilling over her shoulders. Familiar and loving even when I'm at my worst. I look at her, and I see all of those choices. Each one playing out like a movie. "I can't decide." I grunt the words, feeling a sob climbing up my throat. I've chosen so badly in the past. I've hurt people. I've *killed* people.

How can I choose now?

She smiles, wet and watery. "You already have."

Olivia's blue eyes are hurricanes, and I'm staring into them when I make my choice.

# EPILOGUE

What is justice, really?

I'd always thought I wanted it for my sister. The justice system was supposed to have gotten it for her. Henry went away. Served his time. But it never seemed like enough. The thing about justice though is eventually it just leads you in a circle. Is justice good for good? Bad for bad? Tyler Henry did some terrible things, and he'll suffer the consequences for it the rest of his life.

But he still has a life to suffer through.

There is a fraying blue ribbon hanging beside my classroom door. The same color as Billy's work shirt. In remembrance of Billy—everyone's favorite custodian. They'd passed them out at the assembly where the sheriff came and talked to the students about safety. Locking doors. Being aware. Poor Billy was attacked in the school gym after he'd left the doors open. The room was a bloodbath—or so they say. His phone, wallet, car keys, and car were missing. Everyone assumed it was a robbery gone wrong.

There were no other signs of struggle anywhere else in the building. The cameras in the hall have been broken a long time. Everyone knew it. The school was more concerned with looking safe than actually being safe. That's why, at the time of Billy's death, the only working camera was the one at the front entrance of the school. Unfortunately, there was some sort of technical mishap, and the footage from that day was mysteriously erased.

It's been almost a year since his murder, and Benton High has cracked down on security. Better security system. Working cameras. An additional resource officer. But as the days passed after Billy's death, people began to relax once again. It takes one incident to shake up a town. But even the snow globes most dutifully shaken will eventually go back to normal.

Smart made a lot of changes at the start of the new year. Safety precautions, he'd called them. One of which is no teacher being allowed to be alone with a student in a classroom with the door shut. Emma shared a look with me during the faculty meeting, her newborn baby cooing in her arms. She still can't speak of Bryson without distaste. By now, Alejandra's journal has gone public. Everyone knows what transpired between them. Everyone knows he went to meet her the day she died.

No one can say exactly what happened after that, but everyone has their own theories.

The hallways are quiet now. The eerie silence before the storm. The kids will be here soon. The hallways bustling with life. Across the hall, the new physics teacher prepares the classroom.

As if sensing my stare, Ms. Lerman pops her head out. "Hey, Ren, do you happen to have a purple dry erase marker?"

*I'll make you like me one day, Ren.*

I shake my head. "No, I don't."

"Oh, OK. Well, thanks anyway." She turns, her honey-colored hair falling over a shoulder before stopping suddenly. "Can I ask you something?"

"Uh, yeah. Sure."

"The person who used to teach in this class."

A charming smile. A man who went too far with a student. A man who did something terrible. A man who paid the ultimate price. "What about him?"

"Did he ever mention this weird smell? It's like a chemical smell. I didn't know if there was some kind of science experiment gone awry or..." She trails off and sighs. "Never mind. I'll just open a window."

My gaze remains on the doorway after she disappears inside, and I fight the guilt that bubbles in my esophagus as potent as acid. I hear a ghostly chuckle and expect to see Margo. But she isn't there. I haven't seen her since the day Billy died.

A wrenching pain vibrates my entire body. It took weeks of crying and screaming and begging for me to realize Margo isn't coming back.

It's like she died all over again.

Just like last time, I never got to say goodbye.

The first bell rings, and almost instantly the hallways and classrooms fill up. I wait patiently at my desk as students trickle in, greeting me as they take their seats. It's not until a familiar blonde appears in the doorway that I move.

"Good morning, Ms. Taylor." Olivia smiles.

"Morning, Olivia."

She bypasses me to sit with a group of girls who have clearly saved her a seat. After Billy's death, Olivia made a TikTok about Bryson and Billy that went viral. She gained hundreds of thousands of followers and was even asked to go on *The Kelly Clarkson Show* and *Good Morning America*. Overnight she became America's sweetheart. The only survivor of a man accused of killing two students, and the sister of a martyr. Billy being accused of murdering Bryson with Fallon only solidified Olivia's story. Like he'd heard about what happened to his sister and did what any other red-blooded brother would do.

"OK, guys," I say, moving to stand at the front of the class. "I know it's the first day, but we're going to get started."

A hand goes up.

"Yes, Olivia?"

"I have a question for you."

The thing about justice? Sometimes when you take it into your own hands, it becomes something else entirely. Sometimes justice crumbles to dust and you're left sweeping up the ashes. I've stopped hunting monsters. Not because I want to, but because sometimes when you hunt monsters, you actually find them. My justice should have been served by Detective Wu. But Casey Ballard's murder investigation fizzled out. There wasn't enough evidence to arrest me. His case went cold.

But that's OK.

I'm getting exactly what I deserve.

"What's your question?"

"We've been debating all morning. You're a biology teacher. You be our tiebreaker. What do you think—nature versus nurture?"

In my mind, I'll always know Olivia as the crying girl in the hallway. The gentle girl who told me her darkest and deepest secret in the dark of my car. The only true thing she's ever told me. A horrible thing by a horrible person that created something horrible.

Or maybe there's always been something chemically imbalanced inside her. Something lying dormant and waiting for the right ingredient to trigger it.

Pain.

Loss.

Rejection.

Olivia is a lot of things for a lot of reasons. And one day, for my own reasons, I may know Olivia as something else. One day I may have to step up. She will be just another tragic accident. A corpse in the ground. For now, she's the girl in my class. One I'll have to keep an eye on. That's my punishment.

My justice.

"Both," I answer without hesitation. Every monster I know wasn't born that way. Including me. But it doesn't seem simple enough to say they were created, because maybe, for people like Olivia and me, we were just waiting for the right ingredient.

Waiting for that push into the dark.

"You think you're so righteous, don't you, Ren?" a sarcastic voice asks to my right. Bryson sits on the edge of my desk, rolling his eyes. "Like you're some dark vigilante. An antihero. You sound ridiculous. You think anyone is rooting for *you*? You think anyone wants you to win?"

"That's a cop-out of an answer." Olivia laughs, nudging the girl next to her, oblivious to the man in the room with us.

"How would you answer?"

Her eyes flash. "Nature. I was born this way."

"See." Bryson is chuckling now. "Least she owns it."

I ignore the man I killed and the girl I let live and turn to my class.

# Take a look at *When She Was Me*, another taut thriller from Marlee Bush!

## CHAPTER ONE
# CASSIE

There is always trash at the Blacktop and never anyone around to claim it. Today it's two aluminum beer cans. One is crushed, and I picture a teenager chugging it and smashing the can against his skull, careless as he tosses it to the dirt.

The blacktop is the field west of our campsite. It backs into the dirt road that leads to the highway and is the entry point of the forty-five-acre campground. The dirt road itself swerves through hundreds more acres of barren woods. It's a surprise the kids still make trips out here at all.

Wayne said it's called the Blacktop because there used to be a day when this entire ten-acre field was covered in tents and bustling with campers. You'd pull in along the dirt road, and the sea of black tent tops would make it look as if someone had tossed a black sheet over the field in its entirety.

Now there are only beer cans and the occasional trespasser. Teenagers shushing each other as they silently close their car doors.

Balking at the dark forest around them, too afraid to go farther into the woods. Giggly and drunk as they lay a blanket in the wet grass and then don't come up for hours.

The sun is setting behind the trees, and the heat on my face almost makes me forget it's winter. Almost makes me forget the gentle ache of hard, frigid dirt beneath my toes and the uncontrollable pull at my back—a yearning for home.

Lenora will be wondering where I am.

I turn in the direction of our cabin when a glint of plastic catches my eye just beneath the overhang of a large rock—the one I sit on most often…my favorite rock—a vape pen. And something about this abandoned piece of trash irks me. The trespassers can have the Blacktop but not this. This is my spot. This is too close.

Somewhere behind me a car door slams, and I tuck the pen in my pocket, keeping hold of the beer cans. There's always trash to be found on the Blacktop, but sometimes there are treasures too. Lighters, coins, and keys. Once I even found a shot glass. A dribble of cold, piss-colored liquid leaks down my hand, but I don't pay it mind.

Need to get back.

To Lenora.

There is no path through the woods that will lead me home. At least not one I can see. The beech trees battle for dominance with the hickories and oaks. Their branches twisted and writhing beneath a sky they will never reach. In the winter they are as naked as the teenagers who stumble out here in the dark. I lay a hand on the tree nearest to me. An American beech. My fingers move across its smooth, polished skin.

The trees might spring up from the same plot of earth and look the same, but if you got closer, you'd find their thumbprint. Their bark. No two are exactly alike. I might know this forest and all the dead things in it well enough now that a clearly marked trail isn't needed. I might know this whole campground better than anyone. Maybe except Wayne.

But sometimes I still touch the trees, if only to remind myself that even the most identical things have thumbprints.

I'm coming out of the woods when our home appears before me. The three cabins and a bathhouse. The cabins are small and square. They're built with wood so dark, it looks wet, and they're pushed so deeply into the trees, they may as well be a part of them.

If they ventured just a bit deeper, the teenagers would see there aren't ghosts out here at all, just people who live like them.

I notice the man right away. He has his cell phone in the air like he'll magically find service six inches above his head. I stop at the base of the hill and spit on the ground near my bare feet. Recognition sets in. "No service out here," I call out to him.

He looks up, clearly startled. I've seen Wayne's nephew before in passing, a tall and gangly man with weirdly rounded cheeks that look out of place on his thin body.

"I always forget." He clears his throat and inches closer. "Didn't mean to sneak up on you."

I want to tell him he didn't sneak up on me, and he couldn't. Wayne's cabin, or what was previously Wayne's cabin before he went and died, sits at the tip of a triangle at the bottom of a long slope through the woods. We call it Cabin One. Mine and Lenora's cabin—Cabin Two—sits at the top. Across from ours is Cabin Three. That's where the guests stay when we have them.

In the summer, when the trees are thick with foliage, you can't see Cabin One at all. But it's winter. The dirt is ice, the trees are skeletons, and even if I hadn't seen the nephew coming, I still heard his car door slam.

"You don't have shoes," Wayne's nephew says. "It's freezing out here." He blows on his hands as if emphasizing how cold he is. Like only his warm breath will save his precious fingers.

"Guess I forgot." But I didn't. I don't like shoes. Even in the winter. Even when I can't feel my toes. My sister's therapist would most likely hypothesize why. Something to do with past trauma. The need to *feel* something.

I believe in ghosts more than therapy. Not that I'd ever tell Lenora that.

"Been meaning to come by," he says, his eyes trailing to the leaking beer cans in my hand. He doesn't ask, and I don't offer. Instead, he takes another step closer. "Thank you for what you did, by the way. Finding my uncle. If you hadn't checked on him, who knows when we would have found him."

I want to clarify I wasn't checking on Wayne a week ago. I'd walked down the hill in search of the firewood Wayne sold me and never delivered. It wasn't unusual for Wayne to disappear for a few days. He does—*did*—that frequently. Got lost in projects. Lost in his own mind. But this was different. There was silence at his cabin. Not his muttering to himself about the government or his hammering on nails inside. Wayne hadn't answered the door at all. I looked in his window and saw him.

Which wasn't necessary, having smelled him from the porch.

The smell of decomposing flesh isn't something you forget. One day I won't remember the expression Wayne made when he talked about politics or puttered around his garden. But I'll never let slip the smell that seeped through the cracks of his front door. I know this from experience.

After all, Wayne isn't the first person I've known to become a corpse.

"Listen," the nephew says when I don't say anything back. "I'm glad to run into you. I was going to walk up anyway. We have someone who's interested in the campground. We've told them about the situation with you and your sister. They said they'd honor Wayne's contract with you. Said you could keep renting your cabin and finish your lease. She should be here in a couple of days once we get everything ironed out."

"You're selling the property?"

His cheeks redden. "I just live so far away. It seemed easiest." The red spreads to his neck like a viral rash. "Anyway, I should get back to packing. It's going to take me the rest of the day to clear his place."

"OK." I maneuver around him, knowing I'm way later than I said I'd be. Lenora must be frantic.

"Wait—"

I stop and glance over my shoulder. But Wayne's nephew isn't looking at me. He's clearly distracted by something that lies ahead.

I know what he sees without looking.

The same thing the teenagers would see if they ever came this far. Maybe the sight would be enough to force them back. To make them never come here again.

"That your sister?" he asks, his eyes shifting back to me.

"Yes."

"She could scare the hell out of someone standing there like that."

The flash of irritation is instant. Makes me think of the first few years after that night. The night that led my sister and me here. The looks. The rogue comments. Especially toward Lenora.

I turn to face him, attempting to block his view of her. "Did you need something?"

"What? Oh, right." He stutters, another flush creeping up his neck. This one might stay forever. "I was just going to thank you again."

"You've already thanked me. There's no need to do it twice." I'm about to walk away when I force myself to pause once more. "I'm sorry for your loss, by the way. If it's any consolation, Wayne once told me he'd rather be dead than living in this godforsaken snowflake pile of garbage we made of America."

The man nods slowly, clearly taken aback. "Uh, thanks."

I leave him there, with his mouth slightly parted and his eyes wide. I turn toward my cabin and see what he sees. Lenora is at the window. As I knew she would be. Like a Halloween decoration long forgotten.

Lenora's brown hair is longer than mine, nearly waist length. She lets it hang in her eyes while mine barely brushes my shoulders. That's the only visible difference between us. We have the same thin lips and blue eyes set just a smidge too far apart.

People say we're as identical as it gets.

We shared a sac and placenta in utero, my sister and I, not just a womb, and that, according to our mother's doctor, is an important distinction. Our dad told us the doctor warned my mother of the dangers surrounding mono-mono twins. One of us would inevitably steal nutrients from the other and grow stronger as the other grew weaker. We were born six weeks early during the hottest summer Alabama had seen in a decade. Me at seven pounds and Lenora at four. Dad said even as infants, we'd cried when separated. Apparently, Lenora didn't hold it against me for trying to kill her in the womb.

That would become our pattern. She'd always forgive me. I'd always let her.

Especially when I didn't deserve it.

Lenora is all frown lines and suspicion when I open the back door. "You've been gone for seventy minutes, Cassie. I was starting to worry. Who was that?"

"Wayne's nephew," I answer as I look at her. Try to see what the nephew saw. A pale girl with a worried face just staring at him through the window. Had a chill rolled down his spine? Had he taken a step back as the unease slipped around his neck and tightened like a noose?

But that man, just like all the others, doesn't see what I see. The years Lenora spent outside. The summers we slathered our teenage selves in baby oil and tried to tan on the back deck even though the willow always blocked the sun. He doesn't see the girl who falls apart at sad movies and who hates hard candies.

He doesn't understand that I'm the reason she's ruined.

That it's my job to protect her.

"What did he want? Damn it, Cassie, could you at least wipe off your feet? You'll track dirt all through the house."

"I'm sorry." But I'm not apologizing for my dirty feet. I'm apologizing for something else. Something far more significant.

Lenora's gaze moves over me. "Everything OK? He's not evicting us, is he?"

*And what would we do then, my dear sister, if he were?* The question is right there on the tip of my tongue.

Anyway, maybe that would be for the best. An eviction. A reason to leave.

"Came by to tell us he's selling. I wouldn't let us get evicted," I say, scrubbing my bare feet one at a time over the rug, then tossing the cans in our trash. The heat of the cabin is already sending needle pricks to my frozen toes, and the sensation is painful as I walk. It was better when I was outside. When I couldn't feel anything at all.

Our cabin is just as small as it looks: a tiny alcove of a kitchen, a slightly larger living room, two bedrooms, and no bathroom. Hence the bathhouse. I used to take our laundry to a laundromat once every couple of weeks. But when that became too much, I invested in a compact washing machine we had installed. It sits neatly by the counter in the kitchen.

Sometimes, when I feel like the walls are closing in and I can't breathe, I tell myself it's quaint.

And when the urge to run strikes me, I tell myself it's OK as long as I come back.

To Lenora.

"Selling to who? Did he say what's going to happen to us?" she asks, already fidgeting nervously.

"He said the buyer is going to run the place same as Wayne."

"Huh." She breathes out again and turns back to the window, fogging it with her breath. "That was fast."

There isn't snow on the ground in our pocket of Tennessee, only a bitter chill and the eerie sound of the wind. It's four days into December, and the bite in the air teases the first frost. We're days away from keeping our woodburning stove going all day— not just at night.

"It's so sad, isn't it? What happened to Wayne?"

"Yes," I agree.

But I'm only thinking of Lenora. The girl who used to run outside barefoot with me.

Maybe it's all true. Maybe I don't wear shoes because I need to feel. Like some distant part of me has long since been shut off. Maybe being inside this cabin makes it impossible to feel anything except fear and worry, and I need the jagged rocks to cut my feet and the ice to freeze my toes. That's all better than what waits for me here.

The guilt hits me faster than the thought can leave.

Not her fault. None of this is her fault.

I look at my sister—back in place, staring out the window—and think about what Wayne's nephew said. Lenora and I look just alike. Identical, down to the freckle above our lip.

Identical like the trees growing from the cold dirt floor outside at night.

He'd have to look closer to find our thumbprints.

On that night fifteen years ago, Lenora and I walked down a hallway together. But when the door opened, the scene unfolded like a sick feature film.

Lenora closed her eyes.

I only know because mine were open.

# READING GROUP GUIDE

1. Describe Margo and Ren. How would you define their relationship?

2. Why exactly does Ren find Bryson suspicious in the first place?

3. By all accounts, Ren's hometown makes her miserable. Why do you think she returned?

4. The other teachers seem unable to understand Ren's suspicion. Is their disbelief warranted? Why does no one listen to Ren's concerns?

5. While Bryson is not guilty of murdering anyone, he does cross a line with his students. Would you consider him a good person?

6. How do you feel about what happened to Casey?

7. Despite being dead, Margo is still very present in Ren's life. How close to the "real" Margo is the one in Ren's head?

8. What do you make of Margo's relationship with Henry? Do you think any part of it was love?

9. After everything, what do you think will happen with Olivia and Ren?

# A CONVERSATION
# WITH THE AUTHOR

**In some ways, this is a ghost story. What inspired you to keep Margo on the page—even after her death?**

I love having Margo around. I love getting a glimpse of their sisterly bond and the push and pull it gives the narrative. At the same time, it might read like a ghost story, but it isn't one. Margo isn't real. But Ren is very much haunted. I think being haunted is a very human experience. Though it doesn't always manifest quite like this, I found in presenting the story, having Margo there as insight into Ren's subconscious was quite useful.

**Ren loses herself in memories of the past, often to the detriment of the present. Can you talk about how you went about balancing those narratives?**

The past is so vital to the story. It was a difficult balance at times, but my editor, Jenna, kept me on track as to ensure the slips into the past didn't get confusing. We wanted the moments to bleed into each other as Ren's innermost secrets and thoughts were slowly revealed. The connection between her past and her present had to be clear.

**Ren is a woman with many, many, secrets. Did you always intend for her to be so morally ambiguous?**

To be honest, in earlier drafts, Ren wasn't quite so ambiguous. She was more…let's just say, black and white in her actions and thinking. But through the editing process and through the other extremely talented minds that contributed to this story, we found Ren to be more appealing in that ambiguous gray area.

**Similarly, one could argue that everyone in *Whispers of Dead Girls* is deeply flawed. Was that difficult to navigate as a writer?**

No way. Writing about flawed people is the best. Our flaws make for the best stories, and that's especially true for fictional people.

**In this book, you explore which victims are remembered and how. Can you talk a little about that?**

This idea is explored in several ways in this book. One in particular is the way we choose, as a society, to remember victims. Which ones are remembered most and why. Socioeconomic status, race, and gender all play a role. It's just one of the many ways we consume victims after they're gone. A revictimization in a way.

**How do you think rumors influence Ren's story?**

Ren is both a victim to rumors while at the same time a person who uses them to her advantage. In Ren's eyes, somewhere within the chemical makeup of a rumor, there is always a thread of truth—and that belief drives her actions in many ways.

**This is your second novel. Was it more difficult writing your debut, *When She Was Me* or this one?**

*When She Was Me* was definitely harder, only because that's the book that landed me an agent. And my agent, in my unbiased opinion, one of the best in this wild world of publishing, is extremely editorial. She signed me on an outline, and then we wrote and rewrote it together. Then came the editing process with my wonderful editor. Let's just say, by the end, I was absolutely sick of that book. With this book, I think I was more prepared for the process, so it didn't seem so overwhelming. Plus, the edits weren't as extensive.

**At the end of the day, how do you hope readers feel about Ren?**

I don't hope they feel anything specific toward her. But I do hope they feel *something*, and whatever it is, whatever emotion they end this story with, I hope it grounds them, in some way, in our shared human experience.

# ABOUT THE AUTHOR

© Brooke Ledbetter

Marlee Bush loves to write the kind of stories that make you double check the lock on your door at night. She makes a home in Alabama with her husband and two children. *Whispers of Dead Girls* is her second novel.